MW00364751

A CASE OF
MURDRUM

In Which the Ploughman Miles
Must Find a Killer

ROBERT BROOMALL

A Bluestone Media Publication

ISBN 978-1-7326275-8-1

Cover design by bespokebookcovers.com

Books by Robert Broomall

California Kingdoms
Texas Kingdoms
The Lawmen
The Bank Robber
Dead Man's Crossing (Jake Moran 1)
Dead Man's Town (Jake Moran 2)
Dead Man's Canyon (Jake Moran 3)
Death's Head, A Soldier with Richard the Lionheart
The Red King, A Soldier with Richard the Lionheart, II
Death and Glory, A Soldier with Richard the Lionheart, III
K Company (K Company 1)
Conroy's First Command (K Company 2)
The Dispatch Rider (K Company 3)
Murder in the Seventh Cavalry
Scalp Hunters (Cole Taggart 1)
Paradise Mountain (Cole Taggart 2)
Wild Bill and the Dinosaur Hunters

For James, Heather, Diane,

Claire and David

1

Trentshire, England, 1106 A.D.

"MILES! Miles! Come quick!"

Wat, the swineherd's boy, ran along the headlands of the fallow West Field, his legs pumping for all they were worth. Men and women looked up from their work. It was a warm, sunny afternoon in June, just past St. John's Day. Haymaking was done; the sheep were sheared. The bell at St. Wendreda's church had tolled nones not long before.

Miles Edwulfson was ploughing his strips in the West Field. It had rained the night before, and the furrows were muddy and dotted with puddles, the cool mud caking on Miles's bare feet and between his toes. Miles braked his plough. With a touch of his long goad, Miles's partner, Peter, halted the plough's four oxen, who stood patiently, tails switching the flies off their backs. Behind Miles's plough walked two cottars, day laborers, using wooden mauls to break the clods of earth turned up by the plough. They, too, halted gratefully.

Wat came nearer. "Miles!" he cried. "The earl of Trent is dead!"

Miles was jolted. A profound sadness washed over him. He felt a hard grip on his arm and heard words echoing down the years: *"Stay here, son."*

Where had the time gone? Miles had always imagined that he would see Earl Thibault again, but that was not to be.

Sometimes you're so busy living that you forget what's important . . .

Miles stepped from the worn leather plough straps, wiping his sweaty brow on his forearm. He had a broad, ruddy face and shoulders so muscular they seemed to be humped. His short beard and blond hair were laced with grey. In the heat he had stripped to his knee-length linen shirt and braies, and his mud-splashed legs were bare.

He had known that the earl and members of his family were in Trentshire. They had come to St. Mary's Lodge to hunt. The earl had never been to Miles's village of Ravenswell, but he had sent Miles greetings and a yoke of oxen four years back, when his youngest son Geoffrey had been installed as Ravenswell's lord. Maybe this time they would have met . . .

Wat drew up, chest heaving. The boy was dirty, with lank hair and patched garments. There was a big wart on the tip of his nose, which everyone said came from living with pigs.

Miles placed a large hand on Wat's shoulder. "Calm yourself, lad. What has the earl's death to do with me?"

"He was killed in St. Mary's Wood," Wat gasped. "In the Beeches. They say he was shot by a poacher."

Miles frowned. "How do they know it was a poacher?"

"The arrow—there's no markings. A poacher's arrow, certain, that's what the foresters say."

A poacher.

A poacher's name loomed large in Miles's mind. *No, it couldn't be him.*

"Have the French caught the man who did it?"

“Not yet. Me and Dad, we was in the wood looking for strayed pigs, and the foresters suspected us at first. A rough time of it they gave us, too.”

Other men and women collected around Miles and Wat, stepping over the baulks of the new-ploughed field. A spare, grizzled fellow in an old straw hat ambled up beside Miles. This was Osbert the reeve, who supervised the villeins in their manorial duties. Osbert worked a stalk of grass around his long jaw. “Will it be *murdrum*, d'ye think?” he asked Miles.

“Please God it’s not,” Miles said.

Osbert's plump wife, Leticia, who had been helping her husband oversee the ploughing of the lord's strips in the field, crossed herself. “Lord help us if it is. You recall the great fine in our parents' time.”

“I recall it only too well,” Miles said. The French bishop of Badford, an evil man, had been stabbed to death in his garden, and the fine for that deed had nearly ruined the hundred. People had learned from that, and there had been no more killings of Frenchmen.

“If it is *murdrum*, you’ll have to name the killer,” Osbert told Miles.

“That’s why I’m hoping the French have caught the fellow. I’ve no wish to find him.”

The younger villagers did not understand their elders' concern. “What's this *murdrum*, then?” asked Martin Above the Brook, Miles's former son-in-law.

“A law made by the Bastard King, William,” Miles explained, “to prevent his French followers from being ambushed and killed. It says that if a Frenchman is slain at unknown hands, the killer is presumed to be English. The hundred where the crime took place has to produce the killer or be subject to a fine."

There were stirrings in the crowd. Men and women who had no money or property with which to pay a fine—or for anything else—swore under their breaths. Miles went on. "The law was much used in the Bastard's time, but it's not been invoked in Trentshire since I was a boy."

Osbert, who was older, said, "It took Ravenswell years to recover from the fine that time."

"There's some'll tell you it ain't recovered yet," Leticia chimed in.

Young Wat said, "That's why Dad sent for you, Miles. You're the hundred pledge, he says you need to come."

"Aye," Miles said. Miles had been elected pledge, or spokesman, by the men of Guildford Hundred, a judicial district that took in the better part of six estates and seven villages—including St. Mary's Wood, where the killing had taken place.

Osbert continued to work the stalk of grass around his jaw. "There's an assize in four days. The French will want the killer by then."

"They will," Miles agreed. On Saturday next, the king's justice in eyre, Lord Tutbury, would be holding a royal assize at Badford, the shire's chief town.

While a tide of excited babble rose around him, Miles's mind raced. What if the foresters didn't catch the killer? There were hundreds of people in Guildford; the killer could be any of them. Miles thought of all with whom he would have to speak, and of how little time he would have to do it. And in the end, all that effort would probably be for naught.

"The killer's probably not from Guildford at all," he sighed. "Like as not he's what the rolls call a 'stranger'—a vagabond, an itinerant laborer, an outlaw—someone not subject to purview of the hundred."

"Or someone from town?" Peter suggested.

"Or someone from town," Miles said.

Osbert said, "And the fact that a poacher's arrow was used in the killing?"

"Probably not significant," Miles said—and hoped. "Plenty of men poach on the side, you know that; plenty more can come up with a poacher's arrow. This was likely not a political killing, but simple robbery. Some bugger came upon the earl alone and saw a chance to make off with a few pieces of silver."

"In that case, a *murdrum* fine's almost certain," Osbert said.

"I'm afraid it is. Osbert, send messengers to the other manors in the hundred, would you? Bid the tithing men take view of their charges." Under the English system of justice, called frankpledge, tithing men were responsible for the criminal behavior of every man in their group of ten, or tithing.

Osbert nodded and looked around for boys to do the job.

Miles beckoned his former son-in-law. "Martin, find Garth and Aelred. Tell them what's happened and where I've gone. Garth is on the assart. I'm not certain about Aelred."

There was a nervous titter from his neighbors at that statement, but Miles ignored it, turning instead to the swineherd's wart-nosed son. "You did well to bring me this news, Wat. Go tell Mistress Mary I said to give you one of her oat cakes."

With a delighted cry, the boy darted for the village to get his reward from Mary, wife of Miles's eldest son, Garth. Miles's young partner, Peter—his father, Leofric, had been Miles's best friend—pushed back his shock of fair hair. "We'll finish this furlong for you, Miles," he indicated the cottars, "me and Talbott and Oswold. We'll see your plough and animals back to your toft."

Miles clapped the younger man's shoulder. "Thanks, Peter."

Miles turned from the others and hurried down his strip of land. Ravenswell's two big fields were divided into blocks, or furlongs, of these strips. The furlongs lay at all angles to one another, to fit the rolling contours of the Trentshire countryside, the way their fathers had hacked them out of the forest centuries before. Each field lay fallow every second year to regenerate the soil, though there was talk of adding a third field from the wasteland to the north. Miles had a total of thirteen and a half strips scattered through the West Field and another twenty strips in the older Mill Field, for a combined thirty-three acres under cultivation, making him the largest landowner in Ravenswell, save for Lord Geoffrey.

At the furlong's end, Miles scraped as much mud off his feet as he could. He pulled on his hose, attached them to his braies, and tied on his ankle-length leather shoes, which had been left next to his marker stone. He looped his knife belt around his waist and set off along the headland, walking with long, even strides.

An hour ago, Miles's mind had had been clouded by nothing more than thoughts of the upcoming harvest. The long summer days had seemed to drift away forever, with more always on the horizon. Now, everything had changed. Earl Thibault, Miles's old friend, was dead, and it might well become Miles's duty to find his killer. It might be his duty to save his neighbors from a disastrous *murdrum* fine.

Behind Miles, the villagers huddled, talking and gesturing. Above him was the wide sky; around him, the smell of turned earth and flowers. Ahead loomed the dark outline of St. Mary's Wood. Distant horns sounded the French distress calls. Forty years had made the sound of French horns familiar, but they were still foreign and always would be.

Miles began walking faster, and as he walked, he remembered . . .

2

Wales, 1086 A.D.

THE knights surged back down the woodland path, which was crowded with footmen who had been hurrying toward the sound of the fighting. "*Sauve qui peut!*" the knights cried, and even those who did not speak French understood their meaning.

The raw November sky brought gusts of rain. The army had been chasing the Welsh king, Gryffd, for months, with no success. That morning, scouts had reported the Welsh drawn up for battle in a valley ahead. In their eagerness to finally be at the enemy, the knights had pushed forward, leaving the rest of the army to catch up as best it could.

Now the knights were retiring just as precipitously as they had advanced, led by two of the army's three commanders—the earls of Chester and Shrewsbury. There was no sign of the third leader, the earl of Trent. Many of the knights had Welsh arrows stuck in their mail hauberks and in their long, triangular shields. Blood streamed from men and horses. Mixed in with the fleeing knights were riderless horses and the few scouts who had not been killed. This force piled into the advancing infantry, creating confusion. Men and animals were jumbled together on the narrow path, which was little more than a track through the forest. Formations dissolved, and the army turned into a mob.

"Sauve qui peut!"

Norman archers, Flemish spearmen, Hollanders, Bretons—all turned and frantically began pushing toward the rear. In their panic to escape, the knights used swords and axes on their own foot soldiers, to get them out of the way. Horses trampled men into the cold mud. There were shouts, yells, screams.

The earl of Trent's company of English axe men was at the column's rear. Though the army as a whole owed its allegiance to the king of England, Trent's axe men were the army's only English unit. They had been double timing forward with the rest of the footmen, but now they stumbled to a halt behind their banner—a white swan on a green field—their progress blocked by the tide of retreating men.

Their captain, Azo, reined his horse around. "Off the road! Let them pass!" Azo was a hard-bitten little Norman knight, chosen for this command because he spoke English. He and the surviving centenar, Eastorwine—the other centenar having died of fever weeks before—led the company into a clearing to the left of the path. "Stay together!" Azo cried with the steady voice of a veteran. "Form line of battle! Quickly, now! When this lot is past, we'll move back onto the road and form a rear guard to cover the retreat."

Twenty-year-old Miles Edwulfson took his place in line beside his best friend, Leofric. The Englishmen unslung their long-handled axes and tied their cloaks around their waists, in preparation for battle.

Near Miles, the vintenar Toki watched the earls of Shrewsbury and Chester plough through the footmen behind their bodyguard of knights. "Look at the Frenchies run," Toki said. He shoved Miles in the back. “Scared, Miles? Shit your braies yet?"

Miles ignored him.

"See who’s runnin’ fastest, don't you?" said Toki’s friend Torold the blacksmith. "The commanders.”

Toki spat contemptuously. "Funny how them that causes the mess always gets out of it the quickest."

"Frenchies don't look so invincible now, do they?” said another of Toki’s friends, Burgred the Black. "How the Devil’d they ever conquer England?"

Leofric turned his boyishly handsome face to Azo. "What happened, Captain? Any idea?”

Azo snorted with the cynicism of an old footman, which he was. "Knights got themselves ambushed. That bunch of Welsh in the valley was a decoy, just like the earl of Trent said they were. The main body was hiding this side of the valley, in the woods, where our knights couldn't deploy their horses. When the knights came up, the Welsh jumped ‘em."

From the trees across the clogged road came wild yells. Arrows fell from unseen bows to land in the midst of the fleeing soldiers.

"The Welsh!" rose a panicked cry. "The Welsh are here!" Men fell wounded. Others stepped on them or rode over them, desperate to get away, to reach any kind of safety, no matter how temporary.

The last of the retreating knights, a rear guard, came down the path from the valley, and riding at their rear, the last man off the battlefield, was Thibault of Monteaux, earl of Trent. Miles recognized the earl by his shield, green with the white swan—he was one of the few who used such shield devices. His young squire, Etienne, rode beside him.

Just then, the earl's horse took an arrow in its left eye. The beast reared, screaming, throwing its rider into the throng of terror-stricken men.

Azo swore and straightened in his saddle. "Stay here, men. I'm going out there to bring him—"

There was a *whump*, and a two-foot-long arrow imbedded itself in Azo's chest, penetrating his mail hauberk and the quilted leather gambeson beneath it as though they weren't there. The little Norman's eyes went wide. His mouth worked, but no sound came forth. Slowly he toppled from his horse, dropping his sword.

"Steady, lads!" cried Eastorwine the centenar.

But it was useless. With Azo's death, the company of axe men disintegrated, succumbing to the panic that had engulfed the rest of the army.

“Run!” cried Toki.

Miles grabbed Leofric's arm. "Let's go!"

The two young men sprinted for the road; they were both good runners. Miles was about to throw away his axe and shield when a strong hand grabbed the sleeve of his leather jack, pulling him back.

"Get back!" ordered a voice in heavily accented English.

The voice belonged to a tall, long-faced knight. The knight’s aventail, his mail face covering, hung in a square on his breast, exposing his dark red beard. His short-sleeved hauberk was splashed with blood. A green and white shield hung from his neck.

It was the earl of Trent. He looked a bit unsteady on his feet, due to his fall, but the intensity of his gaze impelled Miles backward.

With his other hand, the earl had grabbed Leofric. He pushed the two Englishmen around. "Back!" he repeated. "*Allez!*" He moved into the mob of retreating men, grabbing them by their collars, turning them around, kicking them. He confronted Toki, shouting at him in broken English. “Back into line!”

Toki snarled, “You can’t—”

The earl drew his long dagger. “Back, or I’ll gut you.”

Reluctantly, Toki complied, followed by his friends Torold and Burgred.

The earl followed the English footmen, his deep voice rising above the din as he herded them back into formation. "Why do you men run? Where is your captain?"

Eastorwine stepped forward. He was an old soldier who had fought in England and France for King William. "Captain's dead, my lord. I'm the—"

"Get these men into order. They wear my badge, and by Our Savior's bones, they'll act like it."

"Yes, my lord," said Eastorwine, chastened. He and his vintenars—each vintenar was in charge of twenty men—began shoving the men back into their places in line. "You heard his lordship. Form up."

Toki swore as he manhandled his charges, among whom were Miles and Leofric, into line. “Damn Frenchie. What’s it to him if we run?”

Arrows were falling all around the axe men now, and several were wounded, but for the moment they were more afraid of this French nobleman than they were of the Welsh. Though Earl Thibault had recruited and equipped the company, they'd had little contact with him before this. They'd barely seen him, in fact, save for a few glimpses on the march. To have a man of such rank personally issuing them orders bordered on the unthinkable. To have disobeyed those orders—even though he was one of the hated French—would have been equally unthinkable, going against habits ingrained in their blood for centuries.

By this time, most of the retreating army had passed. The earl's squire Etienne rode through the thinning press of soldiers, leading a spare horse that he'd found. Etienne couldn't have been more than seventeen. His blond moustache and beard were wisps. He was plainly scared. "Here, my lord," he said, handing the horse's reins to the earl.

"Thank you, Etienne," the earl said calmly. "Let us rejoin Shrewsbury and the others."

He mounted, and the two men prepared to ride off. Just then came a chorus of yells, and from the woods behind them, a force of Welshmen descended onto the road, attacking what was left of the Norman soldiers there. Some of the defeated mercenaries dropped to their knees, begging for mercy. They were cut down with swords, spears, and axes. Others tried to fight, singly or in small groups, only to suffer the same fate. The remainder kept running, pursued by the Welsh.

Trent reined in his horse. "It appears we are cut off," he told his squire. "We must stay here." He looked around distastefully. “We raised these English, Etienne, now we shall see how they fight. Pray that they fight well."

"I am praying, my lord," the squire replied.

The earl waved his sword toward the hill behind them and raised his voice. “The Welsh will come for us next, *messieurs*. Up the hill."

The company scrambled up the slope, equipment clattering. Miles’s feet caught on bracken; he slipped in the mud. The dryness in his throat was not from thirst alone. In front of him Toki puffed, "Fool’s taking us away from the rest of the army."

Torold the blacksmith said, "He’ll get us all killed."

At that moment, Torold was hit in the back by an arrow. He fell with a strangled cry, rolling part way back down the hill. "He was a better prophet than he ever was a blacksmith," remarked Leofric, skipping over the body.

Toki grabbed Leofric’s arm, teeth bared as he said, “You think everything is funny, don’t you, Little Dick? Well, just for that, you and your friend Miles get to stand in the front line when the Welsh attack.”

On their horses, Earl Thibault and his squire brought up the company's rear, their armored presence momentarily discouraging Welsh pursuit of the retreating English. Atop the hill, the company reformed, out of breath, while the walking wounded and stragglers from other units came in. The path below was littered with bodies and discarded equipment. The Welsh who had not followed the retreating army were pointing up the hill at the English, shouting in their unintelligible tongue. More Welshmen joined them from the woods until a good-sized force was present, double the number of Trent's company and growing, wild-haired men armed with swords and spears and rectangular shields. While their comrades looked on helplessly, the English wounded at the bottom of the hill were butchered, then stripped, along with the dead. Welsh archers advanced, using the trees for cover.

Earl Thibault and his squire dismounted, while one of the soldiers took their horses to the rear. "Lie down!" the earl ordered the men. "There—in that ditch. Cover yourselves. Stop gawking, and do as I say."

Just behind the hilltop was a natural trench, with sides formed by rocks and exposed roots of trees. The men lay in this trench, covering themselves with their heavy limewood shields. As they did, the Welsh showered volleys of arrows into their position. Many of the shafts whistled over the trench or thumped into the dirt and tree trunks. Most of the others stuck harmlessly in the upturned shields. A few struck flesh and bone, followed by oaths or cries of pain.

"He's got us trapped like rats up here," Toki growled.

For once, Miles agreed with Toki. He curled his body, trying to get as much of it as he could under the shield. He stared at the mud in front of his face. He smelled it, wet and peaty. He felt arrows jarring into his shield, and he prayed that one of them didn't hit an exposed part of his body. He thought about his wife and son at home, his wife pregnant, and he wondered if he would ever see them again.

Leofric huddled beside him. "Did I thank you yet for getting me into this?" he asked. "'Come with me to Wales,' you said. 'It'll be fun,' you said."

“You know I had other reasons for joining the army,” Miles told him.

“Won’t do you much good if you’re dead,” Leofric said.

Earl Thibault disdained lying down. His green and white banner had been planted on the brow of the hill and the earl stood beside it, conspicuous with his armor and red beard, arrows whizzing by him or thudding into the soft ground. Young Etienne stood manfully, if nervously, at his side. He pulled the aventail over the earl's mouth, lacing it to the earl's conical helmet with its projecting nose guard. Eastorwine took station beside them, if only to prove he was as brave as any Frenchman. The three of them had their shields raised to ward off the arrows directed at them.

More rain began to fall. Below the hilltop, the Welsh cries rose in volume. The hail of arrows dwindled. Earl Thibault moved down the trench, excitement in his voice. "On your feet, *messieurs*. They are coming."

3

Trentshire, 1106 A.D.

THE forest was magical, filled with the unknown. Anything could happen in the forest. Miles followed the path to the Beeches. A hare crashed through the undergrowth at his passing. A startled wood pigeon exploded into the air. He smelled wildflowers, honeysuckle, leafy mold.

It was cool in the forest depths. As Miles walked, he brushed his shirt and smoothed his matted hair. He must try and look presentable for the French nobles—or Normans, as they called themselves.

Miles was forty. Unlike most men he knew his exact age, having been born the year of King William's usurpation of the English throne. He was an old man as things were reckoned, and a widower. He disliked the office of hundred pledge, but he was elected to it every year. In part this was because no one else wanted the job, which was time consuming and brought no material gain. In part it was because he was the most prosperous freeman in the hundred—he and his family were, in fact, the only freemen in the hundred—and he was the only man who spoke French fluently. In part it was because Miles's grandfather, Wulfstan, had been thegn of Ravenswell, and people still respected his memory.

Wulfstan had been a hero. He had helped to win back Trentshire from the Danes and had killed the Danish lord of

Ravenswell. He had lived in a timber hall where Lord Geoffrey's manor house now stood. His eldest son, Edwulf—Miles's father—had set off down the road to the south forty years earlier, answering King Harald's call. He had never returned. From that time, the family's fortunes had declined, until Miles's life was indistinguishable from that of his neighbors, save in one respect. He was free, and they were what the French called villeins. They were bound to the land, and he was not.

Miles crossed a stream, using a log laid down for that purpose. Ahead of him, the horns grew louder. From the stream, the land leveled, then the path led down a steep hill into a part of the forest where giant beech trees had crowded out all other species. The trunks of these beeches were tall, thick, and almost evenly spaced. Their high branches intertwined, forming a leafy canopy that blocked out the sun and kept the forest floor in perpetual twilight. Only moss and a few hardy ferns grew beneath the trees. The ground was carpeted with the dead leaves of previous years. Right now the glade was being trampled by a large hunting party, whose members were still coming in, guided by the horns.

Miles moved into the shouting, swirling mob, squinting against the dust. Horses pranced and whinnied. He passed nobles and ladies, grooms and postillions. He passed green-capped foresters and huntsmen with horn-shaped tin badges. He passed baying greyhounds and small, yapping brachets, with harried kennelers trying to control them. Three English huntsmen in leather leggings flirted with a party of French maids, neither group understanding the other's language.

Miles looked for Lord Geoffrey but didn't see him. There was brown-robed Abbot Joscelin of Huntley standing at the reins of his white courser, deep in talk with a richly attired young lady, who seemed upset but was trying not to show it. Off to one side was what appeared to be a merchant, dressed like a peacock and sitting his horse awkwardly.

Grimy and mud spattered, with a much-mended shirt, Miles drew stares. He was obviously a tiller of the soil and just as obviously out of place here.

"Did you know that a midden could walk, your grace?" mocked the abbot's female companion. "Or is that a pig sty?"

There was laughter around the glade, nervous because of the circumstances, and Miles felt himself redden. The woman had an oval face, an olive complexion and dark hair. Her brows arched so high, it seemed they might reach up to Heaven. Her blue riding dress was trimmed in gold thread at the neck and sleeves. Her starched linen headdress was held in place by a plain gold circlet.

The abbot replied smoothly, "Either way, I suppose the English consider it an act of ingenuity, Lady Blanche."

More laughter. *Blanche*—Miles realized with a start that this imperious young woman must be Lord Thibault's wife. Her deep, intelligent eyes were still on him, unsettling him, and he kept going.

The tip of a riding crop was suddenly jammed into his chin, tilting it up. "Stop."

He found himself facing a tall man, dressed in the new fashion favored by King Henry, with long red hair and beard, and a long bliaut cut up the front and back for riding. His hawk-like face bore a deep tan that could only have been acquired under the blazing sun of the Holy Land. "Who, or what, are you?" the tall man said.

There was laughter from Lady Blanche. With a forefinger, Miles eased the riding crop from beneath his chin. "I am Miles Edwulfson, of Ravenswell Manor. I am the pledge for Guildford Hundred, and I have come to view Earl Thibault's body."

"You've what!" said the man, looking around in disbelief. "What manner of japery is this! Think you that my father's body is on display here for the amusement of the rustics? Get away, before I have you whipped."

This must be the earl's middle son, Ranulf, home from the crusade. Everyone in the glade was staring at Miles now. He drew himself up. "If the earl's death is ruled *murdrum*, I must name the killer in court. It is my duty to view the body. The arrow that killed Earl Thibault may give evidence to the killer's identity. Lord Geoffrey will vouch for me."

"Geoffrey's with the foresters," Ranulf said, "looking for the killer."

"Lord Etienne, then." Etienne had been the earl's squire in Wales. Now he was the earl's seneschal, or steward.

"Etienne? God's bones, but you make free with the names of your betters. A villein is not permitted such familiarities in Normandy."

"We're not *in* Normandy," Miles reminded him. "And I'm no villein. I'm free."

"Free! You're lying."

"I assure you, I'm not."

Ranulf moved closer and tapped the riding crop against Miles's chest. "You say 'my lord' when you address your betters."

Miles smiled. "When I address my betters, I will."

Ranulf swung the crop at Miles's face. Miles caught it in his hand. Ranulf's eyes widened. He tried to pull the crop back, but couldn't. Instead, Miles yanked it from his grasp. Miles heard Lady Blanche laugh again.

Miles and Ranulf eyed each other, Ranulf breathing hard, Miles still smiling. Then Miles handed the crop back. "Careful with this, *my lord*. Someone might get hurt."

Ranulf tried to regain some of his dignity in front of the crowd. "So, you're a free man, are you? I must say, you don't dress the part. Or is this the condition of free men in England?"

Some of the more foppish nobles laughed along with Ranulf, who went on. "Lord Etienne has returned to the lodge. He was taken ill. Overcome with grief, the old fool."

"Who's in charge, then?"

"I am, for now. Lord Galon remained at the lodge today." Galon was the earl's oldest son. "We've sent for him, but he's not yet arrived. Now be gone, before I call the—"

At that moment, Abbot Joscelin stepped forward, reluctance obvious in his handsome face. "I'll vouch for this fellow, Ranulf. He holds land of me."

Miles bowed. "Thank you, your grace."

The tanned crusader Ranulf stared at the abbot in disbelief. "You mean this villein prattles the truth?"

"Unfortunately, he does."

"But the King's forest laws—"

"Don't apply here. St. Mary's Wood is a hunting preserve of your father's, not the king. Legally, it's part of Guildford Hundred, and since this clearly looks like a case of *murdrum*, what this wretch says is true."

Ranulf let out his breath and shook his head in disgust. Abbot Joscelin was a few years younger than Miles. His robe and cowl were made from the finest Bruges cloth, and he wore soft leather riding boots, not the prescribed sandals of his order. He kept his tonsure as small as possible. On his chest hung a silver crucifix crusted with precious stones. He spoke to Miles in rich, cultured tones.

"I vouch for you, master hundred pledge, but understand this. We want no English here, not now. An Englishman killed Lord Thibault. If you insist on this formality of your 'office,' I cannot prevent you, but for God's sake, have the decency to perform your duty quickly and be gone."

Ranulf said, "It's more than one killer I'm worried about, your grace. What if the English have revolted? Our lives may be in danger. St. Mary's Lodge may be under attack even now. This fellow may be an English spy, come to—"

"Oh, stop making a fool of yourself, Ranulf," said Lady Blanche. "You see treachery everywhere—perhaps because you're involved in so much of it yourself."

Ranulf bristled. "Harsh words, Lady Blanche."

"I could say harsher," Blanche replied in an icy tone. She waved a hand airily. "Let this malodorous greyback be about his business. Giving in to him is the quickest way of getting rid of him."

Ranulf looked from Blanche to Abbot Joscelin. "Galon would never allow this."

"Galon isn't here," Blanche pointed out.

Ranulf hesitated, then stepped aside, "Go ahead," he told Miles.

Miles bowed his thanks to Lady Blanche, who looked none too happy to receive it. He pushed past Ranulf without a look. Reluctantly, the knights and ladies of the hunting party stepped back for him, as well. Miles felt their eyes upon him. He felt their hostility. Dead leaves crackled beneath his feet, releasing an odor of must. A nuthatch trilled overhead.

Thibault of Monteaux, earl of Trent, lay on his back in the clearing, a shaft of sunlight streaming down on him through the leaves. His eyes had been closed with pennies, and his hands were folded across his chest, as though in prayer. The arrow had struck him in the throat, but someone had pulled it out.

Miles was shocked at the change in the earl's appearance. He had somehow expected his old friend to look the way he had looked twenty years ago, when they were in Wales. He appeared frail and tired, where once he had been robust and full of energy. His powerful body seemed to have shrunk. Much of his hair had fallen out, and what remained was no longer red, but a dull grey, along with his beard. His clear skin had become mottled. Behind drawn-back lips, his once-shiny teeth were worn and brown, those that were left.

Miles wondered if he himself had changed that much. For a moment, he felt very old. He shook off those thoughts, stepped closer, and knelt.

Reddish-brown blood clotted the earl's beard and covered the front of his green tunic, but there was little blood on the leaves beneath him. The body was cool, just beginning to stiffen.

Then Miles saw the arrow. It had been placed nearby. "Don't stand there gaping," Ranulf said from behind him. "Do you recognize the arrow?"

Miles recognized the arrow, all right. He should have. He'd watched enough of these arrows being made, on winter's afternoons by the fire. He picked up the arrow and ran trembling fingers along its smooth hazelwood shaft. He touched the meticulously clipped goose feathers. He could describe the fire-hardened tip without looking at it.

The arrow belonged to Miles's youngest son, Aelred.

4

MILES'S gut wrenched itself in knots. His worst fears had been realized.

Aelred was a hothead who hated the French and preached revolt against them. He derided his father for accepting the French and learning their language. Aelred was also the most notorious poacher in the hundred, though he poached more to annoy the French than he did for meat. He had never been caught, and he usually gave the game he killed to the poor.

Though he held proof of the deed in his hands, Miles could not believe that Aelred had killed Earl Thibault. He *would* not believe it. Aelred would never do something so dishonorable, so *evil*. Yet what other explanation was there?

"Do you recognize it?" Ranulf repeated.

Slowly, Miles stood. He prided himself on his honesty, but if he told the truth, he would be condemning Aelred to death. He needed time.

"Say something, oaf."

Miles drew himself up. "My lord, I—"

From the rear of the crowd came a sudden shouting and stamping of horses. Men and animals hastened out of the way, and into the clearing rode a dark, brutish man on a shaggy horse as mean-looking as its master. Behind him was a taller, fair-haired rider, and slung over that man's shoulder was a polished black bow.

“Galon!” cried Ranulf. “Thank God you’re here. The messenger told you what's happened?”

“He did,” replied the brutish-looking one. “The one time I’m not here, and there’s some fun. Just my luck.” His Norman accent was so thick that Miles had trouble understanding what he said at first. Galon of Monteaux was of medium height with a thick, powerful build. His leathery face bore scars of battle. He stood out from the other nobles in the clearing with his faded brown tunic and dark hose held up by cross garters. He was clean shaven, and his hair was cut in the old Norman style, short and high up the back, as if a bowl had been placed on his head and all the hair below it sheared off. A black moustache drooped down his chin.

Ranulf went on. “Did you see signs of rebellion on your way here?”

Galon swung out of his saddle, tossing his reins to his tall companion with the bow. “Rebellion?” he snorted. “From the English? Don’t be ridiculous. The English will never revolt, they're too lazy. All they want to do is lie about and drink ale.”

“Perhaps, but one of them killed our father.”

“A poacher no doubt,” Galon said. “Like as not, Father caught him in the act, and the fellow panicked.” He caught the expression on Lady Blanche’s face. “You don’t agree, my lady—or should I say, ‘Mother’?”

“No, I don’t,” the young woman said. “But I’m only the dead man’s wife, so what difference does it make what I think?

"My sentiments exactly," Galon said. He made a mocking bow to his father's widow, then stood over the earl's body, resting a beefy hand on his sword hilt.

"A bad business," murmured Abbot Joscelin, coming up on Galon's right.

"Oh, I don't know," Galon said. "It's worked out rather well for me. It's the greatest luck I was in England when this happened—haven't been here since I was a child, you know. Now I may claim my inheritance in person." He saw disapproval on the abbot's face and added, "Come, come, your grace, don't expect me to pretend I'm sorry about this. The old goat never cared for me."

Galon knelt beside the body, his burly form outlined against the shaft of sunlight that penetrated the trees. "His purse is still on him, and it's full, so he wasn't killed for money."

"Why, then?" Ranulf said.

"Because he's one of us, most likely." Galon picked up the arrow with a gloved hand and turned to the abbot. "Will it be that what-do-you-call-it law?"

"*Murdrum*?" said Abbot Joscelin. "Presumably. As you said, that is a poacher's arrow."

Galon dropped the arrow and rose, addressing the crowd. "I had no love for my father, but I'll not let the English slay him and go unpunished. We'll catch the killer, my lords, or my *murdrum* fine will turn this hundred into a desert. Which, come to think of it, might be fun."

Miles noticed the richly dressed merchant ease his horse into the background, as though he was trying to make himself scarce, and he suspected the man must be English.

Abbot Joscelin grew testy—he held a valuable manor in Guildford Hundred and did not want to see it ruined. "I might remind you, Lord Galon, that in England, justice is a royal prerogative. Only the sheriff may impose a *murdrum* fine. You may be made earl, like your father, but it is by no means certain that you will inherit your father's post of sheriff, as well. The two offices are rarely combined these days."

"Oh, I'll be sheriff, all right," Galon assured him. "My only competition is that bloated toad, Tutbury."

Lady Blanche was skeptical as well, and her tone made it clear that she bore no love for Galon. "You are King Henry's avowed enemy, Galon. You support the duke of Normandy's claim to the English throne. Why should the king even confirm you as earl, much less make you sheriff?"

Something resembling a smile crossed Galon's face. "Because, dear Mother, I have switched allegiances. There will be a trial of strength between Henry and Duke Robert this autumn. I'm not being modest when I say that, with me on his side, King Henry will win. He knows that, and he's like to prove most generous in return."

"Would you betray the duke so easily?" Blanche said.

"I have to look after my own interests. Besides, you've betrayed your own allegiance often enough, if what I hear is true."

Blanche's lips compressed with anger; her dark eyes flashed. Satisfied that he had cut her down, Galon looked around the clearing, letting his gaze come to rest on Miles. "Who is this, the village idiot?"

Ranulf laughed, teeth white against his deep tan. "He calls himself a 'hundred pledge.' He claims that *he* is supposed to find our father's killer."

Galon looked Miles up and down. "You can't be serious. Even in a misbegotten land like England, a peasant would not be given such responsibility."

Miles explained. "If the *murdrum* law is invoked, Guildford Hundred must produce the killer, my lord. I am the one who must name the man in court."

Galon's thick brows knit. "How do you speak French?"

"I learned it years ago, my lord. Most of us speak a bit of it, though we don't let on."

"Hmph, interesting."

Miles went on. "I knew your father well."

"*You* knew my father? An earl? I find that difficult to believe."

"I was one of his soldiers in Wales, years ago. Circumstances threw us together and we grew quite close."

Galon stared at Miles for a beat, then turned to his brother. "I wish our father had had as much time for his family as he seems to have had for this Englishman." To Miles he said, "Go, now. I'll send you the fellow's name when we catch him. It's an odd custom, but I'll humor you."

Miles was afraid that the name they would send him would be Aelred's. "I'm sorry, my lord, but I must swear an oath to the killer's identity. Before I can do that, I must be certain in my own mind that the man is guilty."

"You must be certain? *You* must be certain?" Galon's dark eyes narrowed. "You're a saucy fellow, Englishman. Would you be so saucy at the end of a rope, I wonder?"

"You can't hang me, my lord. You've no charge."

"Haven't I?" Galon grabbed Miles's left wrist and held up his hand. On the hand was a large silver ring, inlaid with niello. Inside the ring's circular bezel was a cruciform decoration surrounding the artist's impression of a lion.

"What about theft?" Galon said. "A peasant like you could not have come by such a valuable piece of jewelry legally. You must have stolen it, and theft is cause for hanging."

Miles yanked his wrist free. He met the Frenchman's gaze. "This ring was my father's, and his father's before that. The lion is the symbol of my house."

"Your *house*?" Galon threw back his head and roared with laughter. So did Ranulf and most of the other nobles in the clearing. The abbot smiled scornfully, while beside him, Lady Blanche eyed Miles in a contemplative manner.

Galon went on. "Do you expect me to believe that your English dung pile has its own crest? The English may be a vile race, but God's blood, I'd not thought them that vile." He leaned closer to Miles. "I say you took that ring off a traveler. You killed the man, and you hid his body."

"Then why did I keep the ring?" Miles countered. "It does me no good on my hand. Why didn't I sell it?"

Galon shrugged. "Probably because you're too stupid." He turned to Abbot Joscelin. "Since you've been so helpful in explaining English law to me, your grace, let me explain a bit of it to you. As of today, this is my forest. If I catch a thief with the evidence of his crime, I may hang him on the spot. It's an English law, with some ridiculous name—"

"Infangenetheof," the abbot said, somewhat smugly. "But I would advise against such a course of action. I don't particularly like this man, but he's worn that ring since I've known him, and his reputation among the English is—"

"Who cares what the English think?" Galon said. "He's lying about knowing my father. What truck would my father have with a common soldier? He's a thief, and I say hang him."

Some of the other nobles and their ladies agreed. "Hang him!" they cried. "Hang the Englishman!" Earl Thibault's death had made them angry and afraid. They felt alone in an alien land, and they wanted to strike back.

Galon turned to Stigand. "Let us see this rude fellow dance, Stigand. Fetch a rope."

Stigand slung his black bow on his saddle. He picked four of the biggest foresters to help him. "Look lively," he told the men, "or you'll get a taste of the lash."

The foresters, who were English, bracketed Miles reluctantly while Stigand bent a noose onto a length of rope. Miles looked around. There was a small opening in the crowd just behind Stigand. If he could get through that opening, he might be able to lose himself in the forest.

He gathered himself. With his fist, he hit Stigand in the nose as hard as he could, breaking it again. He pushed Stigand aside and ran, aiming for the break in the crowd. But someone tripped him and he went sprawling. Before he could get up again, the foresters were on him. A blow to the temple stunned him. Another blow to his kidney rendered him momentarily helpless. Someone kicked his ribs and pain jolted through his body. His hands were bound behind him, and he was hauled to his feet.

He looked to see who had tripped him. It was Abbot Joscelin. The abbot seemed proud of himself, and Lady Blanche stared at him in surprise.

Stigand stood before Miles, his nose gushing blood over his red tunic. As the foresters gripped Miles's arms, Stigand hit him in the mouth. Miles sagged, but the foresters held him upright. Miles shook his head and spit blood. His teeth felt loose. His ribs ached where he had been kicked.

Stigand slipped the noose over Miles's head and pulled the knot tight. With the foresters' help, he dragged Miles across the clearing. The noose choked Miles, and he let himself be pulled along in order to breathe.

Stigand jerked Miles to a halt at the far side of the clearing, beneath a tree with low branches. As nobles and servants crowded around, Stigand looped the rope's free end over a stout limb. Miles twisted and tried to kick Stigand in the groin, but Stigand managed to avoid the kick.

Galon was enjoying himself hugely. "There's spirit in the fellow," he cried.

Lady Blanche stepped up. "You're not really going to do this, are you?"

"Of course I am," Galon said. "I'm the earl presumptive—it's my duty to provide entertainment for my guests."

As the other nobles roared approval of Galon's statement, Blanche turned away. Abbot Joscelin joined her, and she shook him off.

To Miles, Galon said, “Any last words, thief?”

Miles stared the Frenchman in the eye. “Your father had nothing good to say about you, and now I see why.”

That hit home. Miles could see it in Galon’s eyes. He could see it in the way Galon worked his jaw. Galon tried to cover it up, though. “Not very original,” he sniffed. “But, then, you didn’t have much time to prepare.”

Galon nodded to Stigand, and to the foresters, Stigand said, “Tail on.”

The foresters looked at each other. They did not like this, but what choice did they have? With a decided lack of enthusiasm, they grabbed the rope's free end.

“Pull!” Stigand ordered them. “Pull, damn you!”

The foresters heaved. The rope dug into Miles's windpipe, lifting him. He fought it, rising on his toes, straining. He couldn't breathe. Everything was turning grey. Then his toes left the ground and he was kicking in the air. His mouth opened. He felt his tongue protrude. He heard horrible strangling noises and they were coming from him. His stomach jerked spasmodically, making his entire body twitch. People were laughing. There was a roaring in his ears. He saw bright red spots.

Then blackness.

5

MILES'S feet struck something hard. He fell forward, banging his face on the ground.

He lay there. Air trickled into his lungs.

He was alive.

He began retching and gagging, getting dirt and leaves in his mouth and not caring, tears running down his cheeks. The noose was still tight around his neck.

A horse stamped nearby. Miles rolled onto his side and his eyes swam into focus. He saw young Lord Geoffrey on a mud-splattered bay, sword in hand, angry look on his face. Above Miles, the severed rope dangled from the tree branch.

"What the Devil do you mean, hanging this man?" Geoffrey demanded of Galon.

Galon seemed taken aback. "Why so upset, brother? He's just a peasant."

"Yes, but he's one of *my* peasants, and I don't like them being hung by anyone but me."

"He's also a thief," Galon said. "He stole that ring on his hand."

"Miles isn't a thief, you fool. He got that ring from his father, who was the English thegn of my estate." With his sword, Geoffrey motioned to Stigand. "Untie him."

Stigand hesitated.

"Untie him!" Geoffrey commanded.

Stigand looked to Galon. Galon wasn't happy about being called a fool, but he growled, "Take him, then, if he means so much to you."

Stigand cut Miles's bonds, giving Miles a kick in the back for good measure. Miles wobbled to his feet. He loosened the noose around his neck, sucking in air. He rubbed feeling back into his hands and wrists, which tingled painfully as the blood returned to them. He drew the noose over his head, wincing because the skin of his neck was burned raw and bleeding, and the rope from the noose stuck to it in places as he was pulling it off. He tossed the heavy noose at Stigand. Stigand wasn't expecting that, and the noose hit his broken nose before he recovered and caught it. Stigand sucked in his breath with pain and bristled at Miles, but made no further move.

Geoffrey sheathed his sword and dismounted. He was lithe and blond, and his blue eyes sparkled. He wore a knee-length red shirt and cross-gartered hose. While one of the grooms took his horse, he spoke to Galon. "You should thank me, Galon, I've just done you a favor. Miles, here, is a free man. You cannot hang him out of hand the way you would a villein. He must be tried in the King's Court. King Henry would take offense at you hanging one of his free men."

Galon gave Geoffrey a dubious look. He turned to Miles. "Miles, what kind of name is that? It's not English, is it?"

Defiantly, Miles said. "It's the name I was given. I would ask my father why he chose it, but your people killed him at Sand Lake."

"Good for them," Galon said. "And you claim to be free?"

"It's not a claim."

"Really? How many days do you work in Lord Geoffrey's fields?"

"None," Miles said.

Geoffrey gave Galon a look. "I told you."

Galon rocked back and forth, his eyes on Miles. "A free peasant, how unusual. Well, we'll have to make you unfree, won't we? I'll have no free English on my lands."

Geoffrey started to say something, but Galon stopped him with a raised hand. To Miles, he said, "I'll see you a villein, Englishman, I promise you. When I'm sheriff, I'll fine you every chance I get, until you own nothing but what's in your belly and you have no choice but to commend yourself to servitude."

"That's the way it should be!" Ranulf said, glad to see sanity returning to the world.

Galon indicated Miles's hand. "I'll have that ring, as well."

Miles drew himself up straight. "You people took my father's sword and title, but you'll not take this ring. You'll not take my freedom, either."

Galon raised an amused eyebrow. "We'll see." He turned to Geoffrey. "I take it you failed to find Father's killer."

"Yes," Geoffrey admitted. Like his horse, Geoffrey was splattered with mud. He had lost a glove, and he sucked at a cut across the back of his bare hand. He went on. "There were no tracks, no scent—no sign of the killer at all. I cannot fathom it. Abbot Joscelin's hunting dogs are the finest in the shire, yet they could find no trace of the fellow. Whoever he is, he's an expert in the woods."

"That's all right," Galon said, "I have my own expert. Stigand, I appoint you shire sergeant. For your first duty, I charge you with finding the man who killed my father."

Stigand smiled through the blood on his face. His nasal accent was made more pronounced by his broken nose. "Dead or alive, my lord?"

"Oh, alive—alive, by all means. I intend to have sport with the fellow."

Stigand nodded. "I'll start at dawn, my lord." He retrieved Aelred's arrow from where it lay beside the body. "I'll need this."

"I'll offer a reward, as well," Galon went on, raising his voice. "Fifty marks to the man who brings information about the identity of my father's killer."

There were nods and murmurs of approval from the nobles in the clearing. "You're taking a lot of responsibility upon yourself," Geoffrey told Galon. "As under-sheriff, I am officially in charge of finding Father's killer until the new sheriff is appointed."

"And I am head of the family now," Galon reminded him. "I believe I am within my rights. After all, we both want the same thing, don't we—Father's killer brought to justice?"

Miles's guts roiled. Fifty marks was a small fortune. It was only a matter of time before somebody besides him identified Aelred's arrow. Miles needed to talk to Aelred. He needed to hear Aelred's story. If Aelred hadn't killed Earl Thibault—and Miles couldn't believe that he had—Miles had to learn who had done it, quickly, before the assize.

Galon looked at the sky, but it was nearly impossible to judge the time of day here in the greenish light of the Beeches. "Come," he told the gathering, "we'd best leave this place, or 'twill be dark ere we reach the lodge."

The earl's white horse was brought forth. Its jingling harness bells sounded forlorn. Dried blood was streaked across the horse's neck and down its right shoulder. Geoffrey and the earl's squire lifted the earl's body and laid it across the saddle. The squire was a boy of about fourteen who seemed dazed by what had happened. Geoffrey tied his father's hands and feet together beneath the horse, so that the body would not fall off.

While this was going on, the members of the hunting party retrieved their horses and formed up. When all was ready, the earl's squire rode out, leading the blood-streaked white horse with his master's body. The earl's young widow Blanche followed, head held high. Galon and Ranulf came next, then Abbot Joscelin, then the rest of the nobles and ladies, in order of rank, followed by that gaudily dressed merchant. After them came Stigand, along with squires and ladies maids, huntsmen, grooms, kennelers, and dogs—the whole panoply of the hunt.

Miles stood near Lord Geoffrey, watching them go. As the last member of the hunting party left the Beeches, Geoffrey turned. In English he said, “Miles, a word.”

6

"YES, my lord?" Miles said. Miles's neck was scraped raw and bleeding from the noose. His lips were swollen where Stigand had hit him, and his ribs sent shafts of pain though his chest with every breath.

Ravenswell's young lord wasted no time. "Have you any idea who that arrow belonged to?"

Miles said a silent prayer, asking forgiveness for his sin. "No, my lord, I don't."

"Who is known as a poacher in this neighborhood?"

"Half the men in the shire go poaching at one time or other, you know that."

Geoffrey grunted acknowledgment. When times were bad, which were most times, Geoffrey looked the other way as long as the poaching was not too outrageous.

Miles went on. "That arrow could have belonged to almost anyone."

"I assume Galon was right—my father surprised the poacher in the act, and the fellow panicked?"

"Surprised, my lord? On a horse? With those harness bells? Beg pardon, but even the rawest woodsman would have heard your father coming a mile off."

Geoffrey considered this. "And your point is?"

"My point is, I think Lord Galon was wrong."

"Wrong how? Was it an assassination? The poacher spied my father riding alone in the forest and decided on the spur of the moment to kill him? To strike a blow for the Cause?"

Miles shifted uneasily. Such a description fit Aelred. There had been a time when it would have fit Miles, as well.

"Perhaps it *wasn't* a chance encounter," Geoffrey went on. "Perhaps Ranulf is right, and there's revolt in the offing, though I haven't sensed it."

Miles shook his head. "Something about this doesn't seem right, my lord. It's too . . ." He struggled for the words. "I don't know, it feels like it's been set up."

"Meaning?"

"What if the killer wasn't an Englishman at all? What if he was a member of the hunting party?"

Geoffrey stared at Miles for so long it made Miles uncomfortable. At last Geoffrey said, "I thought better of you, Miles. If that's the best idea you can come up with, perhaps I should have let Galon hang you."

"Sorry, my lord, but can you at least consider the possibility?"

"No, I cannot. You're saying that someone in the hunting party, likely a member of my family, found a poacher's arrow and used it to kill my father?"

"I know it sounds farfetched, but—"

" 'Farfetched' isn't the word I'd use. 'Ridiculous,' maybe. 'Hare brained,' even better."

"But it is possible," Miles persisted.

"Anything is possible. It's possible I'll be made archbishop of Canterbury, but it isn't going to happen."

Miles said nothing. Geoffrey let out his breath, clearly exasperated. “What leads you to believe it could be one of the hunting party?”

Miles lifted his brows. “For one thing, my lord, your father wasn’t killed where he was found.”

Geoffrey frowned.

Miles explained. “There was little blood around the body.”

Geoffrey thought. “You’re right. I should have noticed that.” He rubbed his lower lip. “That suggests he was killed elsewhere and moved to the Beeches. But why would anyone . . .?”

“I don’t know, my lord, but a poacher or an assassin would have no reason to move the body.”

“And a member of the hunting party would?”

“Perhaps, though I confess I’ve no idea why. My lord, I realize it's unlikely, but what if it were somehow true? By law, I’m not allowed to accuse a noble before the court.”

Geoffrey raised his hands in annoyed surrender. “All right, all right, I’ll humor you. If you bring me proof—and I mean real proof—that the killer is Norman, I'll accuse him in court.”

This was no small declaration on Geoffrey's part. Miles said, “That would mean trial by battle, my lord. Between you and the killer, or his—”

“Or his champion—yes, yes, I know the law. But it won’t come to that. If you proceed along that line of thinking, you'll be wasting your time, and time is something we have precious little of. Lord Tutbury's assize is in four days. That means you have four days to find the killer."

"Yes, my lord."

"What are your plans?"

"I've sent word for the tithing men to take their rolls. Anyone not accounted for, we'll have to track down."

Geoffrey stared at him in disbelief. "That's it?"

"Well, I—"

"Stop thinking about the damned hunting party and come up with something useful. This *murdrum* fine won't affect just you English, you know. My own estates of Ravenswell and Dalby will be ruined. I'm in debt enough; I can't afford the loss of rents. There will be no stock left, no money, nothing of value. There will be no men to work my demesne, because many will die and others will move away. Your people will be eating dirt by Lammas, and mine won't be far behind. All of which will, no doubt, bring immense pleasure to my brother Galon. When Galon bragged about turning the hundred into a desert, he wasn't joking. Do you know what they call him in Normandy? 'Galon the Cruel.' Do you know why?"

"No, my lord," Miles said.

"He was besieging a castle in County Maine some years back. At the end of autumn, the castellan ran out of food, so he sent his noncombatants out of the castle. Galon refused to let them through his lines, however. He made them stay outside the castle, without shelter, living on leaves and grass—these were the soldiers' wives and children and servants. Most of them died; the rest went mad before the castle finally surrendered the next spring. Galon executed the survivors." He paused. "This is the man who's going to impose the *murdrum* fine. Now do you see why I'm worried?"

Geoffrey gathered the reins of his bay horse, which had been pawing the leaves, searching for grass. "I need to get back."

Miles held the horse's bridle while Geoffrey mounted. They started down the path, following the tracks of the main party, Miles walking at Geoffrey's knee. "Why was your father in England, my lord? He's not been here in years."

"He was after that damned treasure," Geoffrey said.

Miles's eyes widened. "Wulfhere's Treasure?"

"Do you know of another?"

"But it doesn't exist. I told him that years ago."

"He thinks it does."

"Still?" Miles said.

"Yes. Apparently he received new information about it."

"From where?"

"He wouldn't say. He was afraid someone else would find out and beat him to it. I think Galon has come here for the same reason."

They walked on and Miles said, "I didn't see your wife with the hunting party. I—"

"Are you going to accuse her of being the killer, now?"

"No, my lord. I was just—I just wondered if she was well."

"Lady Matilda did not come to the lodge. She doesn't get along with my family."

"Sorry, my lord. I didn't know."

"Don't be. I'd expect no less from my family."

Geoffrey had done an extraordinary thing—he had married for love. Even more extraordinary, he had married an Englishwoman. His wife, Matilda, came from the ancient ruling house of Mercia; her grandfather had been the last English ealdorman, or earl, of Trent, killed at Sand Lake. The family was now impoverished, however, and she had brought no dowry.

Miles changed the subject. "Who found the earl's body?"

"Abbot Joscelin. He and Lady Blanche."

"They were riding together?"

"They always do."

"Were you nearby?"

Geoffrey hesitated. "Actually, I was lost."

Miles looked up and Geoffrey explained. "The huntsmen had scared up a deer. The dogs were let onto the scent, and we plunged into the forest after them. The chase brought us to Ash Creek. The banks along the creek are steep at that point, with but one ford."

"I know the place," Miles said.

"When we arrived, the ford was blocked by an overturned woodcutters' cart. Some waited for the cart to be cleared away, but I turned north along the creek, looking for another ford. I went for some distance when I realized the path I was on was taking me away from the creek, so I had to retrace my steps and start over." He paused, his voice dropping. "By that time, the horns were blowing the . . . the distress call."

"What about your father? Where did he cross the creek?"

"I'm not sure. He had a good head start on the rest of us, and I didn't see which direction he took."

"Did you see anything untoward while you were in the woods?"

"I saw nothing, save for sign of a hermit. I'd never been in that part of the woods before. It's only open for hunting when Father—when the earl—is at St. Mary's Lodge, or if the lodge is rented out."

They were almost out of the Beeches now. Intermittent sunlight burst through the trees, a welcome relief after the otherworldly twilight. Around them, the undergrowth thickened. The narrow path had been churned up by the hunting party's homeward passage.

This was the first time Miles had ever been alone with Lord Geoffrey. He didn't know Geoffrey well—why should he, Geoffrey was a noble. They talked from time to time, of course—about the weather, about crops, about plans for the new field—but never about anything personal, and they were always surrounded by servants or villagers when they did. Earl Thibault's youngest son had been lord of Ravenswell for four years, but he spent only about a third of that time on the estate. The rest was taken up with knight service for the king or visiting his other manors. Unlike his two brothers, Geoffrey had been born and reared in England. During the rebellion of Robert of Bellême, when most of the kingdom's great lords had urged King Henry to accommodate the rebels, Geoffrey had joined the English infantry outside Bridgenorth and shouted for the king to stand firm. The support of these Englishmen had stiffened Henry's resolve. He had rejected compromise and had confiscated all of Bellême's English possessions, one of which had been

Ravenswell—which had been given to Geoffrey for his services that day.

The two men came to a fork in the path. One way led to St. Mary's Lodge, the other to Ravenswell. The cut on Geoffrey's ungloved hand was still bleeding; he sucked it again and shook out the sting. "Collect the reports of your tithing men. Pray to God that we learn something from them."

"Aye, my lord," said Miles. Miles was praying, all right. He was praying that Aelred would be accounted for.

Geoffrey went on. "I will spend tonight at the lodge. If I do not hear from you, I'll meet you at the manor house tomorrow, just past tierce." Tierce would come when the sun was halfway down in the west.

"Yes, my lord." Miles added, "My lord?"

"Yes?"

"Who was that merchant with the hunting party? I guess he was a merchant. The one with the rich clothes?"

"You must mean Gretch," Geoffrey said. "Morys Gretch." He gave a sour smile. "He was a villein once—a mole catcher, if you can believe it. From Lower Wynchecombe."

Nothing good ever comes out of Lower Wynchecombe, Miles thought, mentally repeating the old saying.

Geoffrey went on. "He made his way to Badford Town, earned his freedom, and cornered the wool trade. He's such a bad horseman they make him ride with the women."

"Why was he in your party?"

"Father owes Gretch a great deal of money and cannot pay. He lets Gretch mix with the nobility as a way of appeasing him. Now stop bothering me about the hunting party, and find the killer."

Geoffrey jerked his horse's reins and started back to the lodge, putting his horse to a trot. Miles took the path to Ravenswell. He crossed the log over the stream, then slowed. Ahead and to his left was Lookout Hill. This was the highest point in the area. On a whim, Miles made the climb; he hadn't been up here in a while. Sweat made the rope burn on his neck sting; his bruised ribs were on fire. Halfway up, he had to stop and catch his breath. He hated getting old.

He reached the top. They used to keep a boy on guard up here, by the lone elm tree, watching for sign of the Danes, but the custom had fallen into disuse. It had been a long time since the last Danish raid, and men said they were over. Still, there had been lulls before, and the Danes could come again.

Miles came upon the charred remains of the Midsummer bonfire. On a clear night, you could see that bonfire clear across the shire. Every year, on Midsummer's Day, there was a race to the bottom of the hill, the reward a silver coin and a wheel of goat's cheese. Men and women, boys and girls participated. Miles and Leofric had done it every year. Most of the racers ended up falling and somersaulting or bouncing to the bottom—great fun if you didn't break your neck. Miles sighed. He was too old for that now.

From this spot, Miles could see a long way over what had once been central Mercia. To the west, where the Leicester Road crossed the River Eal, the whitewashed wooden tower of Badford Castle thrust itself above the trees outside

Badford Town. To the east was Huntley Abbey, with its new church going up.

It was a beautiful midsummer's evening. Long shadows crossed the land. The breeze had died and the air was soft. Insects rose in lazy clouds. Ravenswell lay below, an irregular grouping of cottages dominated in the center by the tiny stone church of St. Wendreda, and on one end by the manor house and its outbuildings. Across the rolling countryside, ripening furlongs of wheat glowed golden in the setting sun, alongside darker blocks of barley and oats, and here and there green strips of peas and beans. Miles's neighbors were making their way home from the fields, bringing ploughs and oxen with them. Distant bells tinkled as the sheep were driven from the pasture. In the meadow, Gilbert the hayward and his assistant were collecting the cattle, which had been put to graze on the stubble left from haymaking. Here and there children played, and snatches of their cries drifted up to Miles.

Miles could not stop thinking about Earl Thibault as he'd seen him in the clearing, shrunken and grey. He pictured him as he'd been in Wales, handsome and strong and commanding. For a second he felt the cold and rain of the Welsh hills again, heard the strange Welsh war cries. Heard Leofric screaming for help.

He shivered and started down the hill toward the village.

7

Wales, 1086 A.D.

THE men rose to their feet, stepping from the shallow indentation in the earth. A few arrows still fell, rattling off shields, scarring leather jacks. The rain blurred Miles's eyes, and he tried to blink it out.

Toki placed Miles and Leofric in the first line, as he had promised. The men stood the way they had been trained, shields overlapping. Leofric was on Miles's right side; Alauric, a cottar from Brandleigh, on his left. Miles's left hand gripped the straps behind his shield's metal boss; another strap hung from his neck, taking much of the shield's heavy weight. In his right hand was a long-hafted axe. He hoped the others couldn't see how scared he was.

Earl Thibault and his squire Etienne mounted. The earl picked ten men from the second line and, through broken English and gestures, gave them to understand that they would form a reserve, to be used should the more numerous Welsh attempt to turn the English flanks.

Through the rain Miles saw the Welsh climbing the hill, moving through the trees. They were lightly armored, with long hair. Many had painted faces—some with swirls of color, some with patterns of dots. There was a huge, red-haired fellow—a giant, almost—with a long red moustache, and his entire face was painted blue. His arm was decorated with a thick gold band. The Welsh beat sword or spear or axe blades on their shields, screaming their strange war cries, trying to scare their enemies.

Now the English took up their own war chant: "Mercia! Mercia!"

Miles glanced behind him and saw a puzzled expression on the earl's face. Miles doubted that the Frenchman knew what Mercia was, though he was earl of a good chunk of it.

About fifty yards away, the Welsh stopped to build a line, locking their own shields. "Get ready," ordered the centenar Eastorwine. "Two paces forward."

Shields clattering, the English line moved over the lip of the hill.

"Mercia! Mercia!"

The Welsh started forward again, screaming, beating their shields. Miles could make out individual faces; he made eye contact with the blue-faced man. The man's eyes were distended, ferocious, filled with hate, and they sent a chill down Miles's spine. Miles's breath came in short bursts. Beside him, Leofric shifted uneasily.

Closer. A volley of Welsh spears. Men fell, replaced by men from the second line. Some of the long, two-handed English axes were thrown—the men had practiced this—and Welsh went down with axe blades in heads and bodies.

The Welsh were almost on them.

"Maintenant!" the earl cried from behind. *"En avant!"*

The English line surged forward, to gain downhill momentum. A last, truncated cry of "Mercia!" and they crashed into the Welsh. As they did, someone deliberately shoved Miles from behind, knocking him off balance—Toki, it must have been. Miles stumbled on the wet hillside and almost fell, and he was horrified because, just as he regained his balance, his shield hit that of the huge, blue-faced Welshman. Miles struggled to keep his footing on the muddy slope. He heard steel hitting wooden shields, cries, screams of pain. The blue-faced Welshman battered Miles's shield with an axe, hacking at it, roaring.

"Push!" yelled Eastorwine. "Keep them off balance!"

Miles ducked behind his shield, praying, pushing against the blue-faced man. The second line pushed the first line from behind, steadying it, adding weight to the English formation. Yells and cries. Miles locked his shield with those of Leofric and Alauric. The blue-faced man's axe came over the top of Miles's shield, knocking Miles's conical helmet askew. The blue-faced man was tremendously strong and Miles made no headway pushing against him. In fact, Miles had trouble keeping his own place in line. Despite help from the man behind him, he was forced back a pace by the blue-faced man, creating a small gap between him and his neighbors. He smelled the blue-faced man's fetid breath, tinged with ale. A spear blade stabbed over Miles's shield on the other side, just missing his face. Miles tried to fight back, to wield his long axe, but he didn't have enough room to swing it. The blue-faced man pushed him back another step. "Miles!" Leofric cried in alarm. Miles dropped the axe. Awkwardly, because he was still pushing with his shield as hard as he could, he pulled his short sword, or scramasax, from its sheath.

The blue-faced man hammered Miles's shield with his axe, hewing chunks out of it, then slamming into the shield with his body, forcing Miles back another step. The gap in the line grew larger. Leofric covered it, sliding back a step, but if Miles was forced back any further, the gap in the line would be too big to cover.

Suddenly the blue-faced man changed tactics. Hoping to catch Miles off guard, he went low, and his axe blade chopped into the ground, missing Miles's foot by inches. Miles saw his chance. He stabbed though the gap in the shields with his scramasax, felt the blade go through mail then hit something soft and yielding. He pushed deeper, heard a groan, yanked the scramasax back and stabbed again. Felt the blade sink in again.

The heavy weight against his shield lessened. He pushed, bringing himself back even with Leofric and Alauric. He reached over the top of his shield and stabbed with the scramasax. This time he caught the blue-faced man in the throat. Blood spurted and the man dropped to the ground, to the wails of the Welsh around him.

"Push!" cried someone.

"Push!"

A Welshman in front of Miles slipped on his butt in the mud and his lower body slid under Miles's shield. Miles reached down and stabbed his scramasax into the man's groin.

"Push!"

Grunting, heaving, the locked lines swayed back and forth, men hacking at each other with axes, stabbing with swords and spears, rolling on the ground with bare hands.

There were more of the Welsh, but the English were facing downhill, which gave them an advantage. Miles stepped on the man he had stabbed in the groin, using the man's face for traction in the mud.

The Welsh tried to force openings in the English shield wall, pairs of them prying shields apart with axe heads or their bare hands, while other men tried to take advantage of the opening. The ground was slippery with mud and blood. Miles saw a severed arm. Trees got in the way. Both sides went around them, quickly reforming before the other side could exploit the opening. A few Welsh scrambled into the trees and dropped from lower branches onto or behind the English line, hacking at the English until they were killed by men in the second line.

A cry to Miles's left. "Look out!"

A brawny Welsh warrior ran up with a barbed spear and stuck it into an English shield. The footmen had been warned about this tactic, but before the Englishman's partner could break the spear, the Welshman pulled the spear back, and the weight of the barbed spear head pulled the Englishman's shield down. Another Welshman rammed a spear blade into the unprotected Englishman's mouth. As the Englishman fell, two more Welsh took on the man to his left. One hit the man's feet, another grabbed his head, and together they wrestled him to the ground. There was a sudden gap in the English line. The Welsh shoved through. Shouts and screaming and confusion. "Hold your ground!" Miles shouted instinctively. He knew that if they turned and ran, they were all dead.

"Hold!" Miles yelled again. "Close up!"

More shouts and screams. Leofric and Alauric bunched close to Miles, Alauric swinging his two-handed axe, Leofric using a scramasax. The English line wavered. There weren't enough men in the second line to replace the casualties. Miles sensed that the line was ready to give way.

Just then, two armored horsemen appeared, swords rising and falling, attacking the Welsh who had broken through the line. They were followed by a section of footmen. It was the reserve, led by Earl Thibault and Etienne. Their sudden attack made the Welsh who had broken through lose their nerve. They turned and ran. The English line reformed.

"Do not pursue!" cried the earl. "Stand your ground!"

The English line steadied, locking shields. Horns blew, and the Welsh retreated down the hill. Toki pushed his way between Miles and Leofric. He threw his axe with both hands. The axe spun end over end, caught a retreating Welshman in the back of the head, split his skull and sent him sprawling into the side of a tree.

Miles was keyed up, breathing hard, still wanting to fight. For a moment he was disappointed that it was over, but that feeling didn't last long. The energy drained out of him until he hardly had the strength to stand. He bent double, heaving for breath, his heavy shield dangling from its neck strap. Beside him, Leofric and Alauric did the same. Miles had no idea how long the fight had lasted. It had seemed to take but a few moments, and it had also seemed to go on forever. Beneath his leather jack, he was soaked with sweat. His shield arm was sore from the blows it had taken, especially from the blue-faced man; his right hand was cramped and covered with blood from gripping the scramasax. His feet were caked with mud. He sank to the ground, raising his face to the cold rain, happy to be alive.

Leofric dropped his shield and helmet and stood with his hands on his hips, gasping. “All right?” Miles asked him.

“I think so,” Leofric said. His knuckles were scraped and bleeding. His thick leather jack was torn and splashed with blood.

Around them, the hillside was littered with dead and wounded, with weapons and armor and bits of gear. Wounded were moaning, crying, thrashing with pain, crawling around in the mud in their own blood and intestines. Men were sitting or standing—dazed, exhausted. Some drank water from clay bottles; others staunched their wounds or tended the wounds of comrades. Still others methodically dispatched the Welsh wounded or—like Toki—looted their bodies. The earl of Trent dismounted near his green and white banner. There was blood on the Frenchman’s sword, more blood on his face and armor. He patted his exhausted young squire’s shoulder and said something reassuring to him.

Below, most of the Welsh had reached the path. *Please don’t let them come again,* Miles thought. But instead of reforming for another attack, the Welsh disappeared up the path, following the main body of the routed English army. Their walking wounded trailed behind as best they could.

“Off for easier pickin’s,” opined Alauric of Brandleigh, pressing a strip of dirty cloth against a deep slice in his neck.

“Christ—look!” said Leofric, pointing.

In the distance, rising above the leafless trees to the east was a column of smoke. Sounds of fighting could be heard, faint screams. That was where the army's baggage train would be. The soldiers' wives and camp followers were there. Men hung their heads or exchanged grim looks.

Toki didn't care about the baggage train. He held aloft the gold arm band he had taken from the blue-faced Welshman. "Some sort of chieftain, this one must of been."

"Miles killed that man," Leofric told him. "That gold is rightfully his."

"Let him take it from me then," Toki said.

Toki, Miles, and Leofric came from the same manor, Ravenswell. Toki hated the other two, especially Miles. When they were boys he had bullied and beaten them unmercifully, until one day a few years back, they had ganged up on him and knocked him silly. He'd left them alone after that, but his feelings hadn't changed.

Miles was too tired to argue. "I don't want it," he said. "Let Toki keep it and pretend he did something in the fight."

Toki started forward. "You—"

"*Arretez*!" Earl Thibault cried.

The earl approached. He regarded the company of axe men critically, as if trying to determine whether they had measured up to his expectations. "*Centenare!*" he cried.

"Centenar!" repeated one of the vintenars, named Merleswegen. "Where's—oh, God."

Men turned. Eastorwine stood off by himself. He was shaking, unable to move. A blade had hacked open his face from his left eye to his jaw. Ragged skin hung down, revealing blood and bone and broken teeth. In his remaining eye was the look of a hurt animal. Swallowing their revulsion at his appearance, Miles and Leofric helped him sit. They would have given him water, but he didn't have enough of a mouth left to drink it with.

The earl looked at Eastorwine matter of factly. "We need a new *centenare,*" he said.

Toki swaggered forward. "I'll do it, my lord." He was always bragging about his warlord Viking ancestors; no doubt he thought he was owed the job.

The earl looked him over. "You ran before. Do you speak French?"

Toki's brow wrinked. "Huh? No, my lord, I don't—"

"I need someone who speaks my language."

Men looked at one another. Then Leofric spoke up. "Miles speaks it, my lord."

"Shhh," Miles hissed, but it was too late.

The earl looked at Miles with a sour expression. "You ran, as well. Is there no one else?"

Before Miles could stop him, Leofric went on. "Miles is a noble, my lord. One of ours."

The earl studied Miles more closely. "This is true?"

Miles shrugged. "My father was a thegn."

Leofric wouldn't shut up. "The men like Miles, my lord. They'll follow him."

Alauric added, "'Twas Miles who killed that Welsh chief with the blue face."

That statement caused the earl to regard Miles with new interest.

Other men who knew Miles's background chimed in: "Miles should be centenar. Let Miles do it!" They started chanting: "Miles! Miles!"

Miles knew they were only saying his name because of his family. They were calling for the ghost of his grandfather Wulfstan, not for him, and that both angered him and made him feel guilty. He had done nothing to deserve the post.

"I don't want the job," he protested. He wanted to kill Frenchmen, not work with them.

The earl frowned. "You are young, English. How do you speak my language so well?"

Sheepishly, Miles said, "I—I picked it up from a girl."

There was laughter. "Miles fucking a French girl," said the carpenter Oslac, not caring that the earl heard. "There's some revenge for our side, anyway."

"Hope there's some little Mileses runnin' around a French court somewhere," said the pedlar Guthric.

To Miles's surprise, the earl smiled at that. "Very well, English. You are *centenare*. For now."

As the earl turned away, Toki swore. "Always the same. Your family gets everything, mine gets nothing. Well, I won't obey you."

Miles ignored him. It was a battle that would have to be fought, but not now. Toki had tried to kill him by pushing him off balance as the fight started, and that would have to be taken care of, as well. Miles turned to Leofric. "Why did you volunteer me?"

Leofric grinned. "You wanted to lead troops. Here's your chance."

8

Wales

RED-BEARDED Earl Thibault surveyed his command. The men were tired from battle and weeks of marching. They were worn down by dysentery and bad food. Their clothes were falling apart. Their tents, rations, and cooking gear had been lost with the baggage train.

Clearly the earl would have rather been with his own kind, mounted knights, instead of peasant footmen—and English footmen at that. And just as clearly, the footmen felt the same. They were uncomfortable being led by this foreigner. They were used to Azo and Eastorwine, men they related to. But they were stuck with each other.

The earl beckoned Miles to stand near him. Miles made a point of not standing too close. He didn't want the others to think he approved of the earl, because he didn't. Miles's lifelong dream was to lead a revolt against the French, to return the country to English rule, and then to secure independence for Mercia. No one else had been successful at rebellion, and since Miles was of noble blood, he figured it was his turn. The flame of freedom burned inside him. He hated the French. He hated their language, hated their customs, hated their food. He intended not only to drive them from power but to kill them—the men of a certainty, the woman and children if it came to that. The French weren't welcome in England. They didn't belong; they never would. Miles had joined the earl of Trent's force to get experience in soldiering, to learn how to beat the oppressors. And now this Frenchman wanted Miles to be his right hand. It was a position Miles did not desire. He'd gladly have left it to Toki, someone only too willing to play up to the French and gain their favor. He was stuck with the job, though, and he'd have to see it through.

The earl addressed the company, with Miles translating the more difficult parts. "*Messieurs*, we must depart this place quickly. The enemy will return, and this time they will bring their entire army. We cannot go back the way we have come. That route is blocked."

"So what do we do?" Toki growled. He left out "my lord," and Miles knew the omission was deliberate.

The earl stared at Toki. Villeins did not address nobles without permission; they did not question nobles' commands. The earl pointed a gloved hand at the rugged mountains behind them, forbidding and half hidden by clouds under the grey sky. "We go that way. We march for our base at Northop. We will find safety there."

Northop was just west of Hawarden. There was a wooden tower and palisade there, built as a base camp during the march into Wales, back when this had still been a game, back when it had been fun. But Northop was far from here—who knew how far on a roundabout route through the mountains? Miles had no idea where they were right now. He doubted any of them did, save perhaps the earl.

The men looked at each other. The prospect of a march through these trackless mountains, with no shelter and no food but the hard bread in their scrips, was not an encouraging one.

It was left to another Frenchman, the squire Etienne, to state the obvious. "We don't know the way, my lord."

Earl Thibault acted confident. "We will capture natives and use them as guides. We will follow the stars if we have to—that is, if we ever see the stars again through this endless rain."

The jest lightened some men's spirits. Miles glared at his new lord with hatred. If all went well, Miles would someday take this man's title. That would be his reward for freeing the country.

"Welsh guides?" Toki mocked. "It was Welsh guides that led us into this ambush. We can't trust them."

The earl didn't understand every word Toki spoke, but he understood Toki's tone. The earl's authority, the authority of his class, was being questioned.

Miles stepped forward. He was Toki's superior now; much as he disliked it. It was his job to keep this from getting out of hand. They needed this French earl. For now. "That's enough, Toki."

"Says who?" Toki shot back. "You? Why? Because some French fuck wants to—?"

Miles punched Toki in the jaw. Miles was exhausted, but he put all his weight into the blow, knocking Toki to the ground. Toki was the miller of Ravenswell's son, lording it over everybody, and Miles knew he wasn't going to stop until he was made to stop.

Toki lay on his back, stunned. The men tensed. Toki's friends shifted. Miles sensed rather than saw Leofric loosen his scramasax in its sheath.

Miles turned, addressing the company, trying to sound like a leader, trying to sound like Wulfstan's grandson. "Anybody else have something to say? Get this straight, we're going to maintain discipline. It's the only way we'll get out of this. Anybody who doesn't like it is free to go their own way. But if you stay, you'll obey orders." He looked around. "Well?"

He knew he was taking a lot on himself, offering to let the disaffected leave without first getting the French earl's permission, but he felt it was the right thing to do. "Who wants to go?" he challenged. "Speak now if you do."

The men glanced at each other, but no one said anything. Toki's friends waited to see what Toki would do. Miles said, "What about you, Toki? Are you leaving?"

Toki shook the cobwebs from his head and smirked at Miles. "I'll stay," he said. "For a while."

Miles held out a hand to help Toki to his feet, but Toki shook it off. At the beginning of the day, Toki had been Miles's vintenar. Now Miles commanded him, and Miles knew that rankled a man's pride. Maybe Toki wouldn't cause more trouble, but Miles doubted it. In fact, he would almost bet on it. Toki was of Danish descent, and he liked to put on the airs of a Viking warlord. Miles hadn't forgotten how Toki had tried to kill him during the battle, and he had no doubt that Toki would try again were he given the chance.

Miles turned to the earl. The Frenchman regarded him with what might have been approval. It was hard to tell, and

Miles didn't care. He didn't want the approval of a Frenchman.

The earl spoke to the company. "We must start now. My horse and that of my squire will each carry two of the wounded."

Miles was surprised, so were the others. The earl didn't have to give up his horse, not for common footmen. Not many French nobles, and even fewer of the earl's rank, would have done such a thing. Miles said, "And the rest of the wounded my lord?"

"Those who can walk must do so. As for the others, we cannot leave them to the mercies of the Welsh. We have seen what that is like."

The wooded hillside grew quiet. Everyone remembered the men who had been taken prisoner by the Welsh on the march west—tortured, mutilated, burned alive. Shrewsbury's army had done the same to the few Welsh they had captured—this was war without quarter. Miles said, "Perhaps we could fashion litters, my lord. Carry them."

"They would slow us down," said the earl. "The Welsh would catch us."

Miles wiped a hand across his dry mouth. The men were looking at him. He was centenar. He had to lead. Whatever was to be done, Miles had to set the example. He had to be like Wulfstan. "Very well, my lord."

God forgive me.

He took a deep breath and drew his scramasax. He moved toward Eastorwine. The veteran centenar sat where Miles and Leofric had left him, shaking uncontrollably, covered with his own blood. Miles was shaking as well; he hoped he could keep his hand steady. He was aware of everyone's gaze upon him. Eastorwine followed Miles with his remaining eye, and Miles thought—or did he wish it?—that he saw a look of thanks there. He made a sign of the cross and stepped behind Eastorwine. He had to do this quickly or he wouldn't be able to do it at all. He tried to think of happier days—of his wife Alice and his son Garth. He pulled Eastorwine's head back, stabbed his scramasax deep into the centenar's neck, then ripped it forward and across.

He stepped back as Eastorwine's body jerked and fell forward, spurting blood. All those years of loyal service and this was how it ended—slaughtered by one of his own men on a muddy Welsh hillside. Eastorwine had no family as far as Miles knew, just a woman who followed him with the baggage train. She was probably dead now, or wishing she was dead. The scramasax was shaking in Miles's hand, a hand wet with the centenar's hot blood. He wiped his bloody hand on his cloak—he could have used Eastorwine's cloak, but he thought that would dishonor the man—then wiped the scramasax blade and sheathed it. His eyes met Leofric's, but he couldn't read what his friend was thinking.

He looked at the rest of the men, many of them ashen faced at what they had just witnessed. "You know what to do," he barked at them. "Get on with it. We haven't got all day." His stomach heaved, and he fought to keep from vomiting, from looking weak in front of the men he was supposed to lead.

The wounded who could not walk were killed. For the most part, they were men who would have died anyway—

men with limbs that had been hacked off, or part way off, men with their guts split open. Logic told Miles that this was the right thing to to, but logic does not allow for feelings.

"*Plus rapide!*" the earl ordered. "The Welsh will be here." In the distance, the sound of battle from the baggage train had died down. The fighting there was nearly over. More smoke rose; more screams—some of them plainly female—carried on the wind.

Some of the men began digging a mass grave. "*Non*," the earl told Miles.

Miles repeated the order. "No time for that," he told the gravediggers.

The men bristled. "It's not Christian to leave them unburied," said a skinny fellow named Wat o' Riseby.

"Bad luck, too," Alauric added.

The earl looked at Miles impatiently. "We can't help that," Miles told the men, and he spoke bitterly, because he knew the men were right. If he were in charge, he would have buried them, prayed over them. "Form up and let's get out of here while we still can."

Four wounded men had been tied on the earl's and Etienne's horses. The rest of the men hurried into line. There had been about two hundred of them when they left Trentshire, a hundred and seventy-odd at the start of today's fight. There were perhaps a hundred left. Some wore rough bandages, seeping blood. Some hobbled or leaned on comrades' shoulders for support. A few hurriedly stuffed loot from Welsh bodies into their leather scrips or hung captured weapons from their belts. They slung their long axes across their backs, those who still had them. They untied their cloaks and drew them close against the rain and November chill, tugging the hoods over their heads.

Miles picked two men to scout ahead, and they started off. They were experienced foresters, and they would find a trail through the mountains. Next, he told off five men for the rear guard. That done, he took a place at the head of the line, by the banner with the white swan, feeling like a traitor in this spot, feeling somehow unclean. He noticed Leofric watching him, and he felt bad about dragging Leofric into this. Then Leofric winked at him, and the two friends grinned at each other in spite of themselves.

A few rows behind Miles, Toki complained in a low voice to his friend Burgred the Black, so named because of the color of his hair and beard. Toki must not have thought Miles could hear him. "Here we are, in the middle of bloody nowhere, putting our lives in the hands of a Frenchman."

"And of Miles," Burgred reminded him.

Toki spit. "We'll see how long that part lasts."

Burgred laughed.

Miles should have said something but he was too tired. Besides, the earl and Etienne were approaching, wrapped in their cloaks of Trentshire green. The earl looked over his assembled men. "This will be a hard march, harder than any you have ever experienced. Those who do not keep up will be left behind. Our task is simple. If we reach Northop, we will be safe. If we do not, we will die. Is that understood?"

No answer. A few heads bobbed in acknowledgement.

"*Tres bien.*" The earl turned his head and nodded to Miles.

"All right," Miles said, raising his voice. "Left turn, by twos. Let's go."

As a cold swirling mist descended on the hilltop, the company set off. Miles marched beside the earl's banner, reflecting on the irony of his situation. He had joined the army to learn how to defeat the French. Now he was depending on a Frenchman to save him.

9

Trentshire, 1106 A.D.

MILES reached the sunken path that led to the village. The path was as old as the village itself, and no one knew how old the village was. There was a circle of large rectangular stones in a clearing nearby, erected by the Old Folk, and the village was probably at least as old as the stones.

Miles was thirsty—he couldn't remember the last time he'd had anything to drink. The rope burn on his neck stung, and his ribs still hurt like the Devil. Around him, the fields were nearly empty; most everyone had gone home by now. He smelled flowers, honeysuckle in the hedges, fresh grass, trees. He smelled food cooking, and he realized how hungry he was. He hoped Garth's wife, Mary, had made some of her cheese-and-legume pasties. He loved those. In the autumn, after the animals had been slaughtered, the pasties would contain pork or lamb; in the winter, ham or bacon. Meat was exhausted at this time of year, though, save for the occasional poached rabbit or pigeon from the lord's dovecot.

Ravenswell was located where the paths from St. Mary's Lodge and Riseby joined. From that point, the road ran south to Badford Town, the same road down which Miles's father had marched on his way to Sand Lake. His father had never returned. In his stead had come the French.

He passed the first houses—huts, really, or shacks, tiny buildings with angled roofs, holes in the ground, some of them. These were the homes of the poorest cottars. How did people live there and raise families? But they did.

The path became the village street. Around him, children played, yelled, laughed. Dogs barked and chased each other, while cats prowled for mice or observed dogs and people with lofty disdain. Villagers went about their chores, shapeless men and women in shapeless clothing.

"There he is!" the cottar Talbott cried. "There's Miles. He's back."

Miles made his way up the street, avoiding the puddles from last night's rain. On either side of him were timber-framed cottages with thatched roofs and crofts extending behind them that contained vegetable gardens and apple and pear trees. Some of the houses were built close to the street, others were set back from it.

Men and women clustered around him, worried. Leofric's son, Peter, saw Miles's neck and torn clothes. "Miles, what happened to you? What did they do?"

"Do they know who killed the earl?" said a woman, not caring about Miles. "Have they caught him?"

"Is it *murdrum*?" said another man. They didn't care about the earl, either; he was an abstract to them. They cared about themselves, about how the earl's killing would affect them.

Miles shouldered his way through them. "Looks that way."

"But you'll get the bugger what done it, right?" said Wat's father, Tom.

"'Course he will," Peter said. "It's Miles."

Miles saw Grim, the miller, leaning against a fence with a couple of his friends. Grim bowed his head to Miles with a mocking smile.

Osbert the reeve came up and fell in beside Miles, the inevitable stalk of straw in the side of his mouth. People crowded around them, eager to hear what they said. "Did you see the body?" Osbert asked.

"I did," Miles said.

"And?"

"Young Wat was right. Looks to be a poacher's work."

"Did you recognize the arrow?" They both knew what Osbert meant: *Was the arrow Aelred's?*

"No," Miles lied.

"You forming a search party?"

"Lord Geoffrey's already done that. They found nothing. Lord Galon has his man Stigand looking for the killer."

"Galon?" said Four-Fingered Hugh. "Galon, what they call the Cruel? He's here?" A buzz went through the crowd. "I heard of Galon when I was in France. A bad 'un, he is." Hugh had done some soldiering in France. He'd lost his finger in an accident here at home, chopping firewood when he was drunk.

Osbert rubbed his grizzled jaw. "Convenient, ain't it?" he said to Miles. "Now this Galon fellow can be made earl right away. God help us if he's as bad as Hugh says he is."

"He may be worse." Miles lifted his neck and showed Osbert the rope burn. "He gave me this."

Osbert's eyes widened; some of the villagers made noises. "He hanged me," Miles explained.

"Hanged you? Why?"

"Because he felt like it. Lord Geoffrey saved me—cut me down just as I breathed my last. Wasn't for Geoffrey, I'd be food for the worms."

"Christ's stones," Osbert said. "That don't bode well for us—or for Lord Geoffrey, I'll wager." He lowered his voice so those around them wouldn't hear. "D'ye think the Beardmen did for the earl? I hear they're active again. But you'd know more about that than me."

Miles knew about the Beardmen because his son Aelred was one of them. The society of Beardmen had sworn not to cut their beards until the French were driven from England. The group had been quite active at one time. They had been responsible for killing dozens of French nobles and men of lower ranks—mostly slain from ambush, as Earl Thibault had been, or stabbed in their gardens, like the old bishop of Badford. Indeed, the *murdrum* law had been enacted primarily to curb their actions. It had proved largely successful—until now, perhaps.

"I don't think it was the Beardmen," Miles said. "They're mostly talk these days." Osbert gave him a questioning look, and Miles changed the subject. "We should hear from the tithing men by tomorrow. Maybe we'll have some luck there."

"Let's hope so," Osbert said.

The crowd approached the squat, whitewashed stone church of St Wendreda, with its small tower. Ravenswell's previous lord, Aimerie, had been a tyrant who cared nothing for the lives or property of his villagers. Geoffrey's first act on replacing him had been to present the village with a new church, taking the place of the wooden one that had stood in that spot since long before Miles was born. The stone church was the pride of the neighborhood. Riseby didn't have one, nor did Dalby or Newton or West Woodwell. You had to go all the way to Badford to find a church of stone. Across the street from the church was the well. There weren't many people at the well at this time of day, but the trampled ground around it was muddy from spilled water and last night's rain.

"Miles!" Father John, the church's tall, stooped vicar, hurried from the church yard, followed by Agnes, his housekeeper. The priest dressed no different than his flock, and he spent nearly as much time in the fields as they did. He took Miles's hand, and his grip was not strong. He started to speak but was stopped by a series of wracking coughs, as if something was slowly being torn apart in his chest. Miles doubted he would last the winter. Father John caught his breath, wiped specks of blood from his lips, and went on. "I want you to know that we're all behind you."

"Thank you, Father," Miles said.

"We're counting on you, as well," stocky Gilbert the hayward told Miles, and there was a note of warning in his voice. "We can't afford a *murdrum* fine here." There were words of approval from the crowd.

Father John went on. "If there's anything you need, let me know."

Miles arched his brows. "I need the name of the earl's killer. I don't suppose God's given you that?"

"No, more's the pity." The priest coughed again and said, "I'm praying for you, Miles.

"Pray for all of us," shouted Four-Fingered Hugh. "We'll need it if Galon the Cruel's about."

Miles's daughter Aethelwynn pushed through the crowd, followed by his son, Garth. Garth was built much like his father, tall and rugged. Aethelwynn was sixteen, beautiful like her mother, with reddish-blonde hair. "What happened to you, Father?" she asked, worry on her face as she took his arm. "Were you in a fight? Your shirt's torn, and look at your—"

"Where's Aelred?" Miles asked Garth.

"He's not home yet," Garth said.

Miles swore to himself. Aethelwynn pressed on, her blue eyes wide. "Your neck, Father. It looks like you were . . ."

"Hanged?" Miles said. "I was. Our new earl, Galon, did the honors."

"What!" Aethelwynn and Garth said together.

"I'll tell you about it later," Miles said.

"Pity he didn't finish the job," said a deep voice.

Miles didn't have to turn to know who the voice belonged to—Grim the miller, Toki's son. Grim was twenty-five, squat and dark with a black beard, a thatch of black hair, and scaly red patches all over his face. He and the cronies who were with him were of Danish, or partial Danish, blood, descendants of families who had once lorded it over the estate and the village.

Miles ignored Grim. The crowd, which now included most of the village adults, had reached Miles's house. Garth's wife, Mary, stood beneath the doorway's thatched awning, looking worried. At the gate, Miles turned. "Osbert, can you send to the manors tomorrow? Have each reeve question his bailiff. See if there's been strangers about. Father John, I'd like you to visit Huntley Abbey and talk to the hospitaller. He'll know of any untoward travelers. Peter, see what you can learn about the woodcutters whose cart blocked the ford during the hunt. I'll speak to William the Beardman, see what he knows of this matter."

Osbert took his leave and went to his house, which was next to Miles's. Peter and Father John departed, as well, though the rest of the crowd remained. "When will you know who did it?" a woman shouted at Miles. "Tomorrow?"

"You have to find him, Miles," shouted someone else.

As Garth opened the gate, Grim ambled up to Miles's fence. He lifted his shirt, lowered his braies, and urinated against the fence, the urine splashing off the willow fence and onto the ground.

"Ah, that felt food." The miller breathed with relief and re-tied his braies, looking thoughtfully first at Miles, then at the crowd. "Come now, Miles," he said, raising his voice so that everyone could hear, "stop pretending. Your son Aelred killed the earl. We all know it, and so do you."

There, it was out.

The villagers all started talking at once, but Grim's voice rose above them. "Just like you killed my father. Just like your grandfather killed mine. Killing's in your family's blood. And don't think we're going to suffer a *murdrum* fine for the sake of your boy. 'Cause we're not."

There were scattered shouts of approval.

"Aside from your big mouth, there's nothing to say Aelred did it," Miles lied again.

Grim played to the villagers. "Really? Then maybe we'll find proof."

"Do that," Miles told him.

Grim was about to turn away, then he stopped. He gazed at Aethelwynn, looking her up and down, taking his time, openly admiring her figure. He bowed elaborately to her. "Good evening, Mistress Aethelwynn. My, but you get prettier every day. Girl like you should be married off by now and breeding pups, keeping some lad warm at night."

"And a man like you should be minding his own business," Aethelwynn shot back.

Grim laughed and looked her over again, slowly, as if he were undressing her in his mind. He turned to Miles and smiled. "Be seeing you."

He and his friends started back up the street, laughing.

10

THE crowd dispersed and Miles opened the gate. His big dog Chieftain ran up to greet him and Garth, then tore off again and began barking at Osbert's dogs through the fence that separated their properties.

Miles had lived here all his life, save for a brief period at the hall when he was a babe. His mother, Ediva, had built the house on land owned by her family, along with two uncles, his father's younger brothers. One uncle had been falsely charged as a traitor and hanged, as the French exterminated the English nobility. The other uncle had fought with Hereward. He had disappeared after the last stand at Ely, and was presumed dead. Ediva had raised Miles by herself, filling his head with the deeds of his father, Edwulf, and his grandfather, Wulfstan. Miles had rebuilt the house twice, once after a flood, and once after the Great Wind Storm of St. Jude's Day, eight years back.

Miles's house looked like most of the others, only larger, timber framed with wattle and daub filling and a thatched roof. He had re-thatched the roof last spring, removed the smoke hole from the roof's middle and added new holes at each end. His croft ran from the street to the common fields in the rear of the village. At this time of day, the chickens were in their coop, the oxen fed and bedded in the north end of the house. The big grey cat prowled around the hayrick, seeking mice.

Garth's three children waited in the yard. "Grandpa, you're late. We're hungry."

"Sorry," Miles told them. "I'll do better next time."

He got water from the barrel under the roof eave, drinking deeply from the wooden cup. He drank again. While he slaked his thirst, he told Garth, Mary, and Aethelwynn about the day's events and about how he had been hanged by Galon.

Garth shook his head. "Sounds like the kind of thing Lord Aimerie used to do."

"Praise God Lord Geoffrey was there," Mary said. After bearing three children, Mary was still a fine figure of a woman, tall and willowy. "I can't abide the French, but Geoffrey seems decent enough. Must be, he married one of us. Now, we'd best eat, or the children will revolt and lay siege to the house. Where is Aelred?"

"No idea," Garth said.

"I can guess," she said archly.

They went inside. The house was neat, the hard-pack floor swept twice daily. There was more furniture than most of the neighbors had—a trestle table, a workbench, a distaff and loom, a small sideboard for dishes and utensils, chests for clothes. The wall that divided the house proper from the ox pen had been made solid a few years ago. Before that there had been a half-wall, with the animals hanging their heads into the living quarters.

The stone fire pit was in the room's center, the fire damped down now, and the cookpot over it, with porridge cooling inside. The family sat at the trestle table, Miles fighting off the children, who liked to climb on him and pummel him. Chieftain plopped himself at Miles's side expectantly, as though Miles would magically produce a haunch of venison for him to gnaw on.

They said grace, and the porridge was served. The porridge was made from peas and barley, accompanied by rye bread and cheese. What was left of the porridge would be saved in the pot for the morrow, and fresh ingredients added to it. The adults drank watered ale; the ale was watered even further for the children.

Mary ladled porridge into Miles's bowl with a knowing smile that revealed a missing molar. "You were hoping for pasties, weren't you, Father?"

Miles cleared his throat. "Well . . ."

"I was too busy with the children to do extra baking today. Sunday perhaps." Because Miles was free, he was allowed an oven; the rest of the villagers had to use Lord Geoffrey's bake house.

Miles and Garth broke the bread with their hands. They had knives, but in Trentshire it was considered bad luck to let iron pass through bread.

Mary had no such superstition. She used her belt knife to cut bread and cheese, passing some to the children before getting her own portion. Garth sliced a piece of cheese and ate it with the thick bread. "Grim's a right bastard, looking at Wynn like he did."

To his daughter, Miles said, "You keep clear of Grim. I don't trust him."

"Hard to do in a small village," Aethelwynn said.

"Well, try. If he does anything to you . . ."

"What?" Aethelwynn said. "You'll get no help, save from Garth and Peter. Everyone's scared of Grim and his friends."

Garth said, "Then he goes telling everyone that Aelred killed the earl."

Mary spread her hands. "If a poacher did it, like they're saying, Aelred's the obvious suspect."

"Mary!" said Garth.

"Why do you two always take up for him?" Mary said. "We face ruin if a *murdrum* fine is levied on the hundred. I won't have my children starve to protect your brother."

"There's no proof that Aelred committed the crime," Miles told her. He'd gotten so comfortable with the lie that he was starting to accept it.

"You can't believe Aelred would do something like that," Garth added, speaking to Mary.

"Why not? He belongs to those stupid Beardmen."

"He's not the only Beardman in the hundred," Miles pointed out.

"No, but he's the one with the biggest mouth, and he's a dead shot with an arrow."

Garth said, "You don't like Aelred, do you?"

"I like him," Mary said. "I think he's a good boy at heart. He just thinks he's better than everybody else, like your family are still nobles. How often does he put in a full day's work in the fields?"

Miles said, "He's only eighteen, he's—"

"See, more excuses. When you were eighteen, you were married, so was Garth. Married with a family."

Miles grumbled, "I've not found him a wife who brings a suitable dowry."

"Then maybe you should lower your expectations. He'll need a place to go after . . . after you've left us."

"Mary," Garth said again, but it sounded like his heart wasn't in it, and Miles realized they must have spoken about this subject before.

"I'm serious," Mary went on. "Garth and I have our own family to look after. We can't provide for Aelred, as well, especially when he doesn't pull his weight."

Garth's three children shifted uneasily as they ate, trying to pretend they didn't hear. Chieftain laid his head on Miles's lap, and Miles stroked it.

"Well," said Aethelwynn brightly, setting down her spoon, "this is a cheery meal. What about me, fair Sister? Do I pull my weight?"

Mary patted Aethelwynn's hand. "Of course you do, Wynn. You do more than your share, in fact." She cast an eye at Miles. "Still . . ."

Miles finished for her. "Still, she should be married. I know."

"God knows she's pretty enough, and there's plenty of boys—and men—who'd be eager to have her. Some of them quite well off."

"But they're not free," Miles said.

"Freedom, freedom," Mary said, throwing up her hands, "that's all you're ever on about. What difference does it make?"

"It makes a lot of difference if you lose it. If Aethelwynn marries a villein, by law her children will be villeins."

Aethelwynn took up the argument. "So what? Villeins draw water from the same well as we do, they live on the same street, worship in the same church. It's just a word. Mary's a villein."

Miles eyed her closely. So did Garth. Was there something they did not know? Miles narrowed his eyes. "Are you in love?"

Aethelwynn didn't answer. She matched his gaze resolutely.

Miles's jaw set. "Who with?" he demanded.

"I won't say."

"Who with!"

"No!"

Miles tried to check his rising anger. Mary put a steadying hand on his arm.

"Don't my feelings count for anything?" Aethelwynn cried. "He's a hard worker, maybe he'll win his freedom some day."

"The number of free men in this shire is getting smaller, not larger," Miles told her. "I won't have my grandchildren be villeins."

"You let Aethel marry a villein," she said.

"Yes, and look how that worked out," Miles said. Miles's eldest daughter, Aethelgifu, had married Martin Above the Brook. Martin wasn't free, but Aethel was adamant and pleading, and because Miles loved her, he gave in. He wasn't overly fond of Martin. Martin was prosperous and ambitious, but he was conceited, the type of person who thought he knew more than he did. He treated Aethelgifu like a servant. Aethel had died in childbirth, and Miles always blamed himself for allowing her to marry Martin.

"So who am I supposed to marry?" Aethelwynn went on. "Tell me that. Where do I find one of these magical freemen—or am I supposed to remain in this house all my life? You heard Mary, I should be gone by now. All my friends are married."

Garth rose. "I think that's enough for one night," he said. "Let us conclude, before we say something we regret."

There was a brief silence, then Miles rose as well. "I agree."

Aethelwynn got up from the table and left the house, near tears.

"What's wrong with her?" Miles asked.

Mary sighed and gave Miles a look that said he would never understand women. "She'll be all right. She's got a lot on her mind."

"Do you know who she's in love with?" Miles said.

Mary rose as well. "I think Garth is right. We should leave this subject for another day."

Frustrated, Miles went outside and took a turn around the yard. There was no sign of Aethelwynn. The summer sun was setting; the breeze rustled his shaggy hair. Mary cut his hair, but he would have to wait till she was in a better mood before he asked her to do it again. From inside came the sound of children laughing. Amazing how quickly they recovered from the tension in the house. He wondered if God designed them that way.

Chieftain joined him, and he scratched the dog's neck. There was more grey in the dog's muzzle. "Getting on in years, too, aren't you, old friend? We've had some good times, haven't we?"

Chieftain poked his muzzle under Miles's hand. Miles laughed and petted him.

Miles leaned on the gate, taking in the evening air, looking both ways down the peaceful, nearly deserted street, Chieftain next to him. But the person he hoped to see wasn't there.

He stayed for a bit, then: "Come on, boy, let's go inside."

The twilight sky faded to grey, but the door would be left open until full dark to provide light inside. Miles sat at the work bench by the window, mending his torn shirt with needle and thread, squinting as he did, while Mary cleared up. After that, Mary readied the children for bed, while Garth saw to the sheds, making sure tools and harness and Miles's plough were cleaned and put away.

Miles stared at the floor. He would have preferred rushes on the floor, to soak up moisture and provide a bit of warmth, the way they had it when Alice was alive, but Mary wanted it this way, saying rushes brought dirt and disease. Was he really that old, that Garth and Mary were making plans for when he was gone? He knew how they felt. Garth was no doubt eager to be head of his own household instead of caretaker of his father's. Mary likely felt the same. She knew that everything she did was judged against the way Alice had done it.

Miles finished with the shirt and put it back on. As he did, his attention was caught by wisps of smoke drifting up from the damped fire. He'd have to wait till winter, when the fire burned all day, to see whether the two-hole system was better at getting smoke out of the house than the old center hole had been. At this point it seemed the smoke hung in the rafters more with two holes, where it had seemed lower to the floor with one hole. He hoped the new system cut down on red eyes and coughing on cold days when the windows were closed and the door could not be opened.

On the other side of the wall, one of the oxen lowed. Miles couldn't smell the oxen as much with the new wall, but he sometimes missed them sticking their noses into family affairs. He remembered once, when Aethelwynn was little, one of the beasts had started eating her shirt when she stood too close to the wall . . .

Beside him, Chieftain came alert, tail wagging.

A shadow filled the doorway, and into the house slouched Aelred.

11

THE house went quiet. Mary was standing on a stool; she paused as she lifted her hand mill, or quern, from its hiding place in the roof beams. Aethelwynn waited for Mary with a sack and a bowl. They would go out back and grind grain for the morrow's bread. They always waited till dusk lest wagging tongues inform Grim, the miller, who held exclusive rights to grinding grain on the manor.

Chieftain ran over and jumped up on Aelred, licking the boy's face. Laughing, Aelred pushed the dog down. Aelred was tall and slender. His blue eyes could charm the birds out of the trees and the girls out of their tunics, and he knew it. He wore an old-style pointed cap of green leather. His beard was thin and scraggly, made even worse looking because of its length.

"Why all the gloom?" he said, looking around.

"Where have you been?" Miles demanded.

Aelred grinned. "In the forest, of course."

"Dunham or St. John's?"

"St. Johns."

"Poaching?"

Aelred started to make a joke, but stopped. "What's wrong with everyone? It's not like I haven't killed a deer before. I gave the meat to the Widow—"

"Did you know that the earl of Trent was killed today in St. John's Wood?" Miles asked him.

The humor drained from Aelred's face. "No."

Mary hopped down from her stool. “Did you do it?”

“No!” Aelred looked surprised to be asked the question. Garth returned to the house at that moment; his eyes widened when he saw his brother.

Aelred went on. “I mean, he’s French, so I’m not sorry he’s dead, but—”

“Let’s go outside,” Miles said, “so the children may sleep.”

The adults gathered by the cottage door in the fading light. Miles studied Aelred closely, and in a low voice he said, “The earl was killed by one of your arrows.”

Aelred blanched.

Aethelwynn put a hand to her mouth.

“What!” said Garth.

“I knew it!” Mary said. “You stupid . . .” She was so angry, she couldn’t finish.

To his father, Garth said, “You didn’t tell us this.”

Miles continued, his eyes on Aelred. “I saw the arrow. I recognized it right away, but I didn’t tell anyone. Now, do you wish to change your story?”

“No!” Aelred said, and he took a step back. “I . . . I . . .” He looked at the ground, unable to meet Miles’s eyes. “Two arrows were stolen from my camp.” He had a camp in Dunham Wood where he kept his bow and arrows and tools for dressing animals.

“When did this happen?” Miles said.

“Three days past.”

“And you’re just now telling us?”

“I—I didn’t think much of it . . .”

Mary looked ready to throttle Aelred. "Do you realize how ridiculous that story sounds?"

Aethelwynn rounded on her. "Why would Aelred lie?"

"Why do you think?" Mary snapped.

Aethelwynn said, "You can't believe that Aelred—?"

"How can you *not* believe?" Mary said. "Admit it, Aelred, you killed him."

"I didn't," Aelred protested. "I swear. You believe me, don't you, Father?"

There was a pause, and Miles said, "I believe you."

Mary made a face and swore under her breath in disgust. She turned to Garth. "And you?"

"I'm with Father," Garth said. "It's not the kind of thing Aelred would do. Besides, Aelred's no liar. If he did it, he'd admit it. He'd probably brag about it."

Mary was incredulous. "Do you *want* to see us impoverished?" she asked Garth. "Do you want to see your children starve?"

"No, but—"

"Then do the right thing and surrender your brother to the authorities."

"But I didn't do it!" Aelred was almost crying. Aelred, who tried so hard to act bluff and hearty.

Miles rubbed his chin. What he was going to say went against all his principles. "You'll have to run for it, Aelred."

"No!" Mary said.

Miles went on. "The bailiffs will be here for you soon—if Grim and his friends don't get hold of you first. If you're caught, you'll likely be hanged and no questions asked."

Aelred said, "I'll go to my camp and wait—"

"No. Don't tarry in Trentshire. Go to our relations in Wiltshire."

"If he runs, it will look like an admission of guilt," Garth said.

"It's the best we can do," Miles said. To Aelred, he said, "I'll send word when I find the real killer."

"What if you don't find the killer?" Aelred said.

"I don't know. You could go for a soldier, maybe. The kingdom of Jerusalem needs men. That merchant Saewulf is outfitting another voyage to the Holy Land from Bristol; you could go with him."

"No, I won't leave England. Why should I, it's my home."

Aethelwynn grabbed Aelred's arm. "The important thing is that you go. Now, while there's still time."

Mary turned, tight faced, fists on hips. "Miles, you're making a—"

"I do what I must," he told her.

"So will I," she shot back. "Don't count on living in this house when this is over." She turned on her heel and left.

Garth scraped together leftover bread and cheese and stuffed them into Aelred's scrip. Miles took some coins from a purse in the chest and gave them to his son. Aethelwynn hugged Aelred, but Mary pointedly refused to wish him well. She took her quern and started for the rear of the house. Aethelwynn made to accompany her, but Mary held up a warning hand. "I'll do it myself."

Miles and Garth accompanied Aelred from the village to the edge of Dunham Wood. When they reached the wood, Miles embraced Aelred. "Good luck, son."

"Goodbye, Father. Garth."

Garth hugged Aelred as well. "Get rid of that damned hat. And cut that beard—it looks horrible."

Aelred laughed, showing a flash of his old bravado. "That I'll never do."

Aelred turned and vanished into the forest.

Miles and Garth started home. Garth was quiet, staring at the ground as they walked. "What is it?" Miles asked him.

"Mary's right, you know. Aelred's story is the most ridiculous thing I've ever heard."

"I know," Miles said. "That's why I believe it. Only an idiot would make up a tale like that, and Aelred's no idiot."

"Then who stole his arrows?" Garth said. "And how did they know where to find them?"

"That's what we must learn."

Garth looked back and let out his breath. "I pray we haven't made a mistake in letting him go."

"You're not the only one," Miles said.

12

MILES was in bed, listening to mice scrabbling in the thatched roof. Nearby, Garth lay on the trestle table, wrapped in a blanket and snoring, using his cloak for a pillow.

They slept in their underclothes, Miles covered by his old cloak of rabbit skins. The beds were sacks of straw, raised on wooden frames to keep them from the drafts that blew under the door. The beds were crammed along two of the cottage walls. The three children slept together, though that arrangement would not last much longer. Mary was bound to conceive again, and when the next baby was out of the cradle, the oldest boy, Alfred, would share the present bed with the youngest, Alfstan, while the middle child, Cecily, would share a yet-to-be-built bed with the newcomer. Garth and Mary's bed was given privacy by a linen screen that hung from a cord. When Miles and Garth had returned to the house from seeing Aelred off, Garth had drawn the bed screen only to be greeted by Mary's curt: "Sleep elsewhere."

Miles was tired, but his mind raced. If Aelred didn't kill Earl Thibault, who did, and how did whoever it was know where to find Aelred's arrows?

On the floor beside him, Chieftain raised his head and growled.

Miles heard horses. Distant, but coming closer. Moving fast. Must be important, for them to be out after dark.

Chieftain's growls grew louder as the horses reached the village street, and Miles swung out of bed in alarm.

Garth stirred on the table top. "What is it?"

Chieftain leaped up and bounded to the door, barking, as the horses stopped in front of Miles's house. Miles heard his gate being kicked open. He went to the door, joined by Garth. Mary and Aethelwynn were awake now; the three children as well, Cecily with a protective arm around little Alfstan.

Before Miles could open the door, someone began banging on it with a heavy object, like a sword hilt. Chieftain was barking furiously.

"Miles!" came a voice. "Open up!"

More banging.

Miles held Chieftain by the collar, barely restraining him, while Garth unbarred the door.

It was Stigand, with a party of armed men, one of them carrying a torch. Stigand pushed past Garth into the house. Stigand's broken nose had been splinted and bandaged; there were dark circles under his eyes and dried blood down the front of his tunic.

Chieftain reared on his hind legs, fangs bared, foam slobbering from his jaws as he snapped and barked, Miles holding him back as best he could. "Chieftain, down!"

"Get control of that dog," Stigand said, "or I'll have one of my men put a spear through its guts."

"You do that, and you'll find a knife in yours," Miles told him.

They stared at each other a long moment.

"Chieftain, down," Miles said again. The dog calmed somewhat and Miles handed it to Garth.

Mary had drawn a cloak around her chemise. Her hair hung loose. She gathered Aethelwynn behind her and confronted Stigand. "Who are you, and what do you want here?"

Stigand ignored her. He looked around the house, then said to his men, "Search the shed and the grounds. Then the village."

Men left the house to obey.

"Where is your son Aelred?" Stigand asked Miles.

"I don't know," Miles told him. "He didn't come home last night."

"Interesting. By the way, the arrow that killed Earl Thibault has been identified as belonging to Aelred. Odd that you didn't recognize it, isn't it?"

Miles tried to brazen it out, scoffing, "Identified by who?"

"You're charged with aiding a criminal, Miles. I'm to deliver you to Lord Galon."

"No!" said Aethelwynn. She started forward but Mary held her back. The three children cowered in a corner, their shadows flickering in the torch light.

Garth pulled on the growling dog's collar. "You can't just—"

"Get dressed," Stigand told Miles.

Miles threw on his hose and shoes, his shirt and woolen overshirt.

"Take him!" Stigand said.

Men grabbed Miles's arms and led him out the door.

Outside, Stigand turned. "By the way, I owe you this." With his gloved hand, he punched Miles in the face. Miles was just able to turn away so that the blow didn't break his nose, the intended target, but the force of the blow made him see bright lights. His legs sagged, and the men had to hold him up.

"Let's go," Stigand said.

13

MILES was jolted into consciousness by the bouncing of the horse. Stigand's men had tied him across the animal's back like a sack of grain, hands and feet bound together beneath the saddle. He was slammed up and down as the party rode along the darkened road, guided by the rider with the torch. Mud splashed his face from the horse's hoofs. When it wasn't mud, it was dirt. As fast as he spit bits of earth from his mouth, more came in. He squinted because of all the grit being thrown into his eyes. Not that it mattered, because he couldn't see much in the dark. Once and a while, one of the riders said something in French or laughed. Otherwise, they kept quiet.

They reached St. Mary's Lodge just before dawn. Miles's bonds were loosened and he was thrown to the ground. Stigand kicked him in his already sore ribs. "Get up."

Rubbing life back into his chafed wrists, Miles dragged himself to his feet. Stigand shoved him toward the hall. "Move."

"Who identified the arrow?" Miles said.

"None of your business." Stigand shoved him again. "Move."

The lodge was laid out like a manor house, with a timbered hall and half-timbered outbuildings. Earl Thibault had built it and had once spent a lot of time here, though he rarely came anymore. Now, when it was used at all, it was rented out by the local nobility.

Stigand pushed Miles forward. "Stop looking around."

The eastern sky held a hint of grey as they entered the hall. The building had aisles on both sides, a dais at the far end and a fire pit, now cold, in the center beneath the smoke hole. Trestle tables were laid out with food—bread, cheese, fruit, and watered wine—and men and women were catching a quick breakfast before the day's hunt. The building hummed with conversation. Heads turned as Stigand and his party entered. Miles saw Ranulf's tanned face in the crowd. Galon was in a group on the dais. There was no sign of Lady Blanche or Abbot Joscelin. Stigand left Miles with the guards and went to report.

"Miles!" cried a voice.

Miles turned. It was Etienne, the earl's steward. He hugged Miles, awkwardly because Miles's wrists were bound. "I thought you'd have found that treasure by now," Etienne said, "be living like a king somewhere. Always had an idea you knew where it was."

Miles said, "I told you then that—"

"That it didn't exist. I know. Didn't believe you, though. You mean to say you've never looked for it at all?"

"I've never even thought about it."

Etienne turned to the guard. "Bring this man food and drink."

The guard, a burly Englishman Miles didn't know, said, "Can't do that, my lord. Stigand, he said—"

"I don't care what Stigand said. I'm telling you to do it."

The guard hesitated, then drew off.

"Insolent fellow," Etienne said.

Time had not been kind to Etienne. His curly blond locks had thinned, and he had cut his hair short as a result. His boyish looks had settled into middle-aged resignation. He looked unhappy, unsatisfied. Part of that could have been because of the earl's death—he had been with the man for over twenty years—but part seemed permanent.

"A bad business about Earl Thibault," Miles said.

Etienne shrugged. "It's for the best in a way. I don't think he had long to live. He was in a lot of pain."

"He looked shocking. Nothing like I remembered."

"He was sick. No idea what it was. It was like something was eating him up from the inside. He changed a lot these last years. Speaking of looks, you appear to have been roughly handled." He smiled. "Again."

Miles smiled in return. "I'm beginning to think Lord Galon doesn't like me."

The guard brought Miles bread and ale. Etienne motioned the guard to leave. "Sorry I can't cut your bonds," Etienne said.

"That's all right." Miles gulped the ale and gnawed at the bread, tilting his chin toward the crowd at breakfast. "Surprised they're going hunting with all that's happened."

"People have to eat," Etienne pointed out. "Besides, I doubt Galon's all that broken up about his father's death."

"He's probably happy about it. Now he gets to be earl."

Etienne raised his brows. "Perhaps."

"What do you mean?"

Etienne lowered his voice, glanced to see if anyone was listening. "Earl Thibault recently revised his will. He left his title and the estates that come with it to Lord Geoffrey."

Miles's eyes widened.

"The will has to be heard in court, of course, but . . ." Etienne spread his hands.

"Does Galon know?"

"I'm not sure. Hard to keep anything a secret these days. Modern times, you know."

"What about Lord Geoffrey?"

"He's been informed of the change."

Miles thought about that. Geoffrey an earl. With an English wife. That would be something. He said, "What will you do now? Geoffrey will need a seneschal."

Etienne shook his head. "I'm done with all that. Geoffrey can appoint his own man. I'm going off to live my life. What I should have done years ago."

Miles gave him a look.

"I've spent my entire career in Thibault's service," Etienne explained. "I had expected more from life somehow. I expected to make a name for myself, not be a glorified servant. Oh, I was rewarded. The earl gave me lands and money, plus I have lands I inherited from my father or obtained from my marriage, but I've never had time to look after them properly, to enjoy them. I've always been with Thibault. My wife runs the estates, along with my steward, and I suspect the two of them are more than just working partners. I barely know my children, assuming all of them are even mine."

While Miles finished the bread and ale, Etienne went on. "Frankly, the earl was not as generous as I might have wished. I suspect he'd have done better by you, had you stayed with him. He always had a fond spot for you, you know. Mentioned you often, on campaigns, when things got tough. 'Wish Miles was here,' he'd say. Well, I was there, wasn't that enough?"

Miles said, "I think you're reading something into his actions that wasn't there."

"Oh, no, no. It was there, no mistake. It's not that he was disappointed with me, exactly, it's just that he thought you'd have done better."

"I don't know what to say."

Etienne clapped his shoulder. "Say nothing, old friend. It's over now. Life moves on."

On the dais, Galon and Stigand were talking, looking Miles's way. Etienne grew serious. "I can't believe your boy killed Thibault."

"He didn't," Miles said.

"They have evidence."

"Their evidence is wrong."

"You'll have the Devil of a time proving it." Etienne sighed. "It was so simple in Wales, wasn't it? The only thing we had to worry about was staying alive. Kill or be killed. It was actually kind of fun in a way. It's all gotten so complicated since then."

Miles kept watching the dais. "What do you know about Stigand?"

"Only what I've heard. His mother was English, a survivor of King William's destruction of the North. Apparently there was nothing left of her village, so she did the only thing she could and became a camp follower. Stigand's father was a soldier, though I'm not sure if he—or his mother—ever knew which one. He grew up in army camps, mainly in France. Became a soldier himself and came to Galon's attention as somebody willing to do the dirty work."

"Can he use that bow he carries?"

"None better, they say."

"Lord Geoffrey told me that the earl was here to look for the treasure."

"He was. There, you see—the treasure again. You're the only one who doesn't believe in it. Thibault received word from someone who claimed to know where it was. He wouldn't tell me who."

"Why didn't this person just dig it up himself?"

Etienne shrugged. "Don't know. It's what I would have done. Maybe he was worried about attracting attention with such sudden wealth and was prepared to settle for a reward."

"Or maybe he was trying to lure the earl here," Miles mused. "Galon and Ranulf are here for the treasure as well, aren't they?"

"Yes. I'm sure Thibault wasn't happy about that."

Stigand approached, bowing to Etienne. "A word to the wise, my lord. Don't get too chummy with this one. He's not likely to be with us long."

Etienne drew himself up. "A word to the *wise*, sir. I'll get 'chummy,' as you call it, with whomever I chose. And in the future do not address me unless you've been invited to do so."

Stigand glared, then said, "Yes, my lord." He took Miles by the arm. "Lord Galon's ready for you."

14

STIGAND dragged Miles through the hall. Breakfasting nobles turned to stare. Miles knew he was a rarity to most of these people. Their main experience with the English was as servants or peasants they passed in the fields.

They halted at the foot of the dais, where Galon stood talking to a pregnant woman who must be his wife, Rosamunde. Beside her was another woman, plain looking but richly dressed, her clothing unsuited for the hunt.

Rosamunde was talking. ". . . can you get this cleared up quickly? I want to make sure my baby is born in Normandy, not this English pest hole."

Galon was patient with her. He sounded like he had heard this before. "I'll do my best, my dear, but circumstances here have changed, and I'm afraid I may—"

Stigand cleared his throat. "My lord?"

Galon turned, saw Stigand and Miles. Galon wore the same plain clothing as he had the previous day. His bowl haircut and drooping moustache seemed sinister in the early light creeping into the hall.

"Excuse me, lady," Galon said to his wife. He hopped from the dais and planted his fists on his hips. "Well, well, well, what have we here? Miles, the Free Man." He laughed and added, "What am I going to do with you, Miles? I try to hang you, but my brother saves you, and here you are a day later, back again. You intrigue me, I don't know why. It's unlikely to prove healthy for you, however."

He slapped Miles heartily on the shoulder. "I don't think I've ever touched a peasant before, save with sword or spear." He looked at his hand. "Hope I didn't catch anything. Now to business. Your son killed my father, yet you pretended not to recognize his arrow yesterday. That makes you either monumentally stupid or part of the conspiracy. Which is it?"

"There is a third option, my lord," Miles said. "Aelred did not kill your father."

"Ah. His arrow shot itself, perhaps?"

Miles said, "May I ask who identified the arrow?"

"You may not. Answer the question."

Miles persisted. "How do you know your informant was telling the truth?"

"By the expression on your face. If it wasn't your boy's arrow, you wouldn't look so worried. And you still haven't answered my question. How did your son's arrow find its way into my father's throat? Magic? A sudden gust of wind?"

Ranulf, Galon's wife Rosamunde, and some of the nobles laughed at that. Galon said, "Your son's as good as declared his guilt. Why else would he skulk off in the middle of the night?"

"Aelred is a free man," Miles said. "He has a right to leave the land. He's committed no crime by so doing."

" 'Free man'—there's that term again," Galon said, wagging a finger. "It's beginning to irritate me, and I don't like being irritated." He turned. "Stigand, shouldn't you be chasing the killer?"

"Yes, my lord," Stigand said.

Stigand bowed to Galon and departed the hall, taking his men. That left Miles with Galon, Ranulf, and a crowd of vengeful French nobles. Miles felt hatred around him. It would take little for these men—and the women—to tear him apart. Aelred was probably far away by now, thank God. Miles wondered if he would ever see the boy again.

Galon stuffed a chunk of black bread in his mouth, crumbs dropping to the floor. "Etienne, do you remember the size of the last *murdrum* fine levied here?"

Etienne answered promptly. "Forty-five marks, my lord."

"Only forty-five? A paltry sum. Hardly befitting the life of an earl. Two hundred would be more suitable, don't you agree?"

Etienne's jaw dropped. "Two hundred? My lord, such a fine would ruin every manor in Guildford, including a very rich one belonging to you. They'll be—"

"I have over eighty manors," Galon said, "from Pevensey to Courtomer. What is the loss of one? It will be worth it to teach these English a lesson."

"What of the other nobles with holdings in the hundred?"

"That's their lookout," Galon said.

Etienne crossed himself. "Please God, we'll find the killer first."

Galon rubbed his stubbled jaw. "What if I hang the killer *and* impose the fine?"

"You can't do that, my lord," Etienne said.

"Says who?"

"The law."

"I make my own law," Galon told him.

Outside the hall, horns blew. Dogs barked as the huntsmen led them from the kennel. Horses' hoofs clumped.

Galon finished his bread and drew on his gloves. The other nobles followed his lead and prepared to leave the hall. "Beautiful day," Galon said. "We should have good sport." He started away, then stopped and snapped his fingers as if he'd just had an idea. There was mischief in his eyes as he turned to Miles. "I understand you have a daughter of marriage age. Can't remember her name, some English nonsense."

The bugger was remarkably well informed. Galon waited, but Miles didn't tell him the name.

"Why is she not married?" Galon said.

"I haven't found anyone suitable, my lord."

"Pity. Can't have the poor girl becoming a spinster, now, can we? Tell you what. Pay me *merchet*—pay it to me, not to Geoffrey, I don't trust that bastard—and I won't impose the *murdrum* fine."

No *murdrum* fine! There was a gasp in the room. *Merchet* was the fee paid by villeins to their lord when a daughter married.

"I'll even make the fee a penny," Galon went on, smiling jovially. "What could be fairer than that?"

"Paying *merchet* would mean that I am no longer free," Miles told him.

Galon spread his arms. "A small price, don't you think? I'm certain the other residents of your hundred would agree."

Miles's jaw set, because Galon was right. Miles's freedom didn't interest his neighbors. It interested only him and his family, and if last night's events were to be believed, even some of his family weren't that concerned with it.

Galson's smile widened. "Now, we must find a place to hold you until the assize. People here are so fond of telling me that you can only be tried in King's Court. We'll see what the court has to say about you abetting a criminal. Etienne, where do you keep prisoners in this place?"

"There's no gaol at the lodge, my lord. Not much call for one. When we have a prisoner, we usually lock him in the warehouse."

"Very well, take this fellow there."

"Must we, my lord?" Etienne said. "I know Miles. I can vouch that he won't leave the—"

"I've had as much of this fellow's insolence as I'm prepared to take. Lock him up."

Etienne bowed as Galon left the hall, followed by Ranulf and the other nobles. To the delight of those who saw it, Ranulf threw an elbow into Miles's sore ribs as he passed.

Etienne beckoned a couple of guards. Miles knew the guards. Viel and Eanred, their names were. They were local lads pressed into duty because the Flemish mercenaries who usually performed that service had gone south to join the king near London, where he was mustering an army to invade Normandy. The guards carried spears but wore no armor, only their regular clothes.

"Sorry, old friend," Etienne told Miles. "I cannot go against Galon's orders.

Miles shrugged.

Viel, a sturdy ploughman, took Miles by the elbow. “Sorry to do this to you, Miles. Come on, let’s go.”

15

THE three men left the hall. Viel was from Lower Newton. Eanred, the other guard, was from Riseby. Miles had known both men for years, from fyrd musters and markets and hundred courts. They felt comfortable around him, and they walked easily with him toward the warehouse, spears resting on their shoulders.

"It won't be so bad, you'll see," Viel told Miles. "We'll bring you some food and ale. How's your family doing, with all this business about Aelred?"

"They're coping as best they can," Miles said. "How's your family?"

"Little Robbie's feelin' poorly, but I reckon he'll get over it. Everybody else is fine. Crops is comin' in. Not a bumper year, but not a bad one, neither. Life goes on, eh?"

Eanred, heavy set and good natured, grumbled in his gravelly voice, "I'd rather be home, getting' ready for the harvest, than be stuck here, doin' guard duty. I got too much work to do."

"I know," Miles said. "I hope Garth remembers to send Alfstan into the barley to throw stones at the crows. Buggers'll be out in force on a nice day like this."

"How old is little Alfie now?" Eanred said.

"Four."

Eanred shook his head. "They grow up quick, don't they? Good on Garth for puttin' him to work. There's some these days want to wait till their kids are—"

Miles turned, grabbed the spear off Viel's shoulder and rammed the butt into his stomach. Viel doubled over, retching. Miles pivoted with the spear and cracked Eanred alongside the head. Eanred dropped to the ground.

"Sorry, lads," Miles told them. He dropped the spear and ran.

Viel was on his hands and knees. "Damn it, Miles, come back! You'll get us in trouble with Galon."

Miles knew that, but he couldn't help it. He kept running, headed for the lodge walls. He would scale them, cross the field and get into the woods. As he passed the fish pond, he heard Viel's cry behind him. "Prisoner's escaped! He's getting away!" Excited cries in response.

The wooden wall was low, with sharpened ends on the logs to discourage intruders. Miles scrambled up, swung between two of the sharpened ends, getting splinters in his hands, and dropped into the ditch.

He landed awkwardly, bending an ankle, in water and muck and indescribable filth. A frog hopped in surprise. On the wall's other side, horns blew. "Muster the guard!"

Miles limped from the ditch and began running through the pasture used for grazing the horses. He couldn't move fast because of his ankle. The lodge's gate was on the far side of the wall from him. He heard horses thundering through it.

He'd never beat them to the woods, not on this ankle.

Ahead and to the left was the recently built garden, with its low stone wall. Miles limped to the wall. He heaved himself over awkwardly, fell on his injured ankle again, and was stabbed with pain. Behind him, the sound of horses grew louder.

The garden was filled with neatly lined apple and pear trees, with beds of fragrant roses and lilies. Birds flew. Bees buzzed.

He had to hide. Where?

Ahead was a trellised arbor, covered with climbing roses. Miles headed toward it.

As he approached, he heard voices from inside.

". . .you don't want to be the king's ward." It was Abbot Joscelin. "He'll sell you to the highest bidder. Mt. Carmel is a good priory. The rules are relaxed for those from the right families. You can—"

"I don't want to join the Church," said a woman—Earl Thibault's wife, Blanche.

"Perhaps I can buy your wardship, then."

"With what? You've told me the abbey is in debt."

The pursuing horses were almost at the garden. Miles stepped into the arbor. Before him was Abbot Joscelin in his tailored brown robe. His back was to Miles, and his arms were around Blanche, his head close to hers.

"I can get money," Joscelin continued.

"How?" Blanche said. "That treasure?"

"With your help, y—"

They stopped as they realized someone was behind them. They turned and saw Miles.

"You!" Blanche said, blushing beneath her olive skin.

Miles bowed, trying to act nonchalant. "Good day, my lady. Lord Abbott."

From outside the garden came the sound of horses pulling up. Voices. Banging on the barred garden gate. "Open up!"

Joscelin started to say something, but Blanche spoke first. "Who is it?" she demanded in a loud voice.

"The guard, my lady. We—"

"What do you want?"

"A prisoner's escaped. That Miles fellow. We need to see if he's in there."

The abbot stepped forward, but Blanche caught his arm. "He's not here," she called.

"You're sure, my lady?"

"Of course I'm sure, you dunce. I'd see him if he was here, wouldn't I?"

"Where could he have gone then?"

"How the Devil do I know? That's your job. Now go away and leave me to my devotions. My husband just died."

"Yes, my lady. Sorry."

Muted voices outside. "He ain't here," said the guard.

Another said, "But his tracks—"

"He tricked us somehow. Her ladyship'd know if he was in there, wouldn't she? Better double back."

The guards rode away.

Blanche and the abbot drew away from one another, Blanche looking guilty, the abbot angry. "Why did you do that?" Joscelin asked her.

"You want them to see us together?" Blanche said. "There's enough talk as it is."

A grass-covered earthen bench ran around the inside of the arbor. Miles sat on it and propped up his ankle, easing the pain. "Sorry, my lady. Bit of a sprain."

The abbot glowered at Miles. "You make a habit of showing up where you're not wanted."

Miles looked from one to the other. "Just doing my duty, my lord."

Beneath her linen veil, Blanche's arched brows betrayed a hint of amusement. "Your duty is to barge in on us?"

"My duty is to find your husband's killer, my lady. Lord Galon is trying to stop me from doing that."

Joscelin said, "That's because the killer is known. It is your son."

"I don't believe that," Miles said.

"Who cares what you believe? The evidence—"

"Evidence can be manipulated."

"Manipulated?"

"Aye, my lord." Miles said blandly. "Sort of like how you manipulated the charter that gives you possession of Morton Chase."

Blanche couldn't help but smile at that. Huntley Abbey and the earl of Trent were engaged in a long-standing law suit over possession of Morton Chase. The earl held a charter from William I giving the manor to him, but the abbey had a similar charter from the Mercian king Offa. The manor had previously belonged to the English earl of Trent, Lady Matilda's grandfather. Wulfstan of Ravenswell's name was on the charter as a witness, so there was a possibility that

Miles, as Wulfstan's descendant, would have to testify about the suit in court.

Rage filled the abbot's face. "Are you saying our charter is . . .?"

"I'm not saying anything, my lord. Just giving an example."

"I can make it hard for you, Miles. Very hard. You hold a half-yardland of me, and—"

"Beg pardon, my lord, but you make it hard on all your tenants. No need to make an exception of me."

Blanche smiled again. Not so the abbot. If the abbot had worn a sword, Miles was certain he would have drawn it at that moment and cut Miles down.

"You're a rude fellow," Blanche told Miles, "even for a peasant."

Miles said, "I'll take that as a compliment, my lady."

"It wasn't meant to be."

"We peasants must take our compliments where we can get them."

Blanche's brow clouded. "Perhaps Galon was right to hang you."

Miles waved a hand toward the arbor's entrance. "All you have to do is cry out, and he'll try it again."

Blanche thought about that. "Mmmm. Lucky for you I don't want to give him that satisfaction."

"Why not?" Joscelin fumed. "I've never encountered such insolence. This wouldn't be tolerated in France." To Miles, he said, "I knew you thought yourself above your station, but I never dreamed you were this deluded."

Lady Blanche touched the abbot's arm. "Forget him, we should go. We've been out here a while. Someone will notice."

"Let them. I don't care."

"I do. And it's best we leave separately." She covered her nose with her flowing sleeve. "I'll go first. If I remain any longer in this creature's pestilential presence, I'll throw up."

Still covering her nose, and averting her face from Miles, Lady Blanche left the arbor. Miles heard the garden gate squeal open, then close.

Miles and the abbot waited uncomfortably, the handsome abbot uneasy at being in such proximity to a simple ploughman. Joscelin was a man marked for advancement. He had studied with Anselm at Bec, and he had come to Huntley from the prestigious abbey at Cluny, where he had been sub-prior. He was widely expected to be made a bishop within a few years.

Miles picked the splinters from his hands. "How goes the suit over Morton Chase, my lord?"

"None of your damned business," the abbot replied. "And I'll thank you not to speak to me."

"As you wish, my lord."

The abbot stuffed his hands in his long sleeves and left the arbor, where he waited among the pear trees. After a decent interval, he opened the gate and left. Miles heard distant horns in the forest—the huntsmen, maybe, or the guards pursuing Miles. Maybe both.

Miles rested on the bench in the drowsy heat. The scent of roses was overpowering, like a drug. Was this what Heaven was like?

He snapped to. He couldn't stay here long. Someone might come. Or the abbot might give him away. The chapel bell tolled terce. Miles went over the wall again and hobbled for the forest. He had to hurry or he would be late for his meeting with Lord Geoffrey.

16

MILES limped from the lodge to Ravenswell manor house, which was a half-mile west of the village. His ankle started feeling better the longer he walked on it, but he knew it would tighten up as soon as he stopped.

He crossed the plank bridge over the ditch. There was no guard at the manor house gate; there never was. People who worked at the manor knew Miles, and they waved or called greetings. Word that he was on the run must not have reached this far yet. The guards were probably still searching the woods, thinking he'd gone to ground there. It was only by the greatest good fortune that he'd gotten away from the garden, Lady Blanche being more concerned with her reputation than with apprehending a fugitive.

They'd be looking for him here soon, though. He had to keep moving. If they caught him, they were liable to hang him on the spot. Miles doubted he could reason with them—Viel and Eanred weren't likely to be in a bargaining mood, and the others would be too terrified of Galon to listen to Miles.

The manor house was laid out much as St. Mary's Lodge, save on a smaller scale, with a hall and outbuildings, fish pond and garden and orchard, kitchen, stables, and quarters for those who lived here permanently. The only difference was the addition of the home farm—demesne, the French called it—with its barn and additional stables and equipment. Upon entering the gate, Miles never failed to remark that, had the battle at Sand Lake gone the other way, all this would have been his. It might have been his anyway, had the rebellion he had once planned come to fruition. Involuntarily, he glanced at his ring . . .

"Miles!" It was Pierre Courtenay, the manor's steward. Gruff and burly, with thinning dark hair and a short beard, Pierre was in charge of the estate's day-to-day operations. Lord Geoffrey might travel, but Pierre lived here full time. He was the man the villagers worked with. He was a former soldier with an English wife, and he and Miles had shared many a cup together. As a free man, Miles had more in common with Pierre than he did with most of the villagers.

The two men shook hands and Pierre put an arm around Miles's shoulder sympathetically. "A bad business about Aelred, *mon ami*. I heard they took you away last night. I'm surprised Lord Galon let you go so quickly."

"He did so reluctantly," Miles said. Which, in a way, was true.

"You're limping."

"I twisted my ankle while crossing a brook on my way here."

Pierre laughed heartily. "You're getting old, *mon vieux*. We both are. I'm guessing you wouldn't say no to a cup of ale?"

"You're guessing correctly," Miles told him.

"Come, let's get out of the sun."

They went to the manor brew house, where Pierre drew them wooden cups of ale. They sat on a bench beneath an elm tree, letting the breeze cool them on this warm day. Miles kept an eye on the manor gate, watching for riders.

"Where is Lord Geoffrey?" Miles asked. "I'm supposed to meet him here."

"He's touring the estate. Talking with Osbert and some of the others about the New Field."

"You didn't go with him?"

Pierre shrugged. "He said he wanted to go himself. I have enough to do here, getting the demesne farm ready for the harvest, sorting out the men who didn't show up for work in the fields today and setting the beadle after them. You'd think these fellows would learn, but they never do."

From the timbered manor house, Lady Matilda appeared. She was carrying a bolt of cloth, showing the young seamstress beside her what was wrong with the warp. She saw Miles sitting with Pierre and a smile crossed her face. She sent the seamstress on her way and came over. "Miles."

Miles got to his feet, bowing. "My lady."

She gestured with a hand. "Don't 'my lady' me. You've got as much noble blood in your veins as I do. I'm living in what should be your house. Had circumstances been different, you and I might even have been married. Did you ever think of that?"

"It has crossed my mind," Miles said.

"That would have been interesting."

"Aye, but you can't dwell on what might have been."

Miles had a comfortable relationship with Lady Matilda, perhaps because he was the closest thing to English nobility in the district. Matilda was open faced and in the early stages of pregnancy. She wore a white chemise and, over that, a red kirtle. A belt was passed twice round her waist and loosely knotted in front. From beneath her linen headdress, blonde braids hung down her chest. She seemed genuinely pleased to see Miles. "Pierre, might I borrow your friend for a bit?"

"Certainly, my lady," Pierre said. He finished his ale and left, patting Miles on the shoulder. "Talk to you later, *mon vieux.*"

"Geoffrey should be home soon," Matilda told Miles. "I know he wants to speak with you. Have you eaten? You missed dinner, but I can probably find you a leftover pasty or two."

Miles was famished. "That would be most kind, my lady."

Matilda beckoned a servant and sent her to the hall for food. "You look a bit worse for wear," she told Miles.

"It's Lord Galon's way of introducing himself," Miles said.

"Yes, Geoffrey told me he tried to hang you. What a world we live in." She grew serious. "I heard about Aelred."

Miles nodded.

"You don't believe he killed the earl, do you." It was a statement of fact, not a question.

"No," said Miles.

"Neither do I."

Thank God.

Matilda went on. "The problem, of course, is proving it. And the only way you can prove it is by finding the real killer."

"Aye," Miles said.

"That won't be an easy task."

"No." Especially with him on the run. "You didn't know Earl Thibault very well, did you? He was a good man."

"I knew him hardly at all. He's been in France since our wedding. Geoffrey's been over there a few times to see him, but not me. Thibault was quite nice to me when I did meet him." She paused. "Unlike the rest of his family."

Miles grinned. "I remember. It was a famous affair at the time."

She grinned back. "Shocking, actually. Arranging one's own marriage is unheard of." Matilda had been the local beauty. All the young men had pursued her, including a number of French knights, despite her lack of social status. But she had sworn to marry English—until she met Geoffrey.

She shrugged. "We were in love. We still are. Geoffrey believes the French should mingle with the English. Until they join their blood with ours, they'll never have a secure power base here. King Henry himself realizes that—why else did he marry an Englishwoman?"

She rubbed the bulge of her stomach. "This child will have the first English blood in the Monteaux family. They're very proud of their 'blood purity,' as they call it. They'll be doubly unhappy when they find out Geoffrey is to be made the new earl, and not Galon."

"Does Galon know he's been cut out of the title?" Miles said.

"I'm not sure. He'd do anything to stop it, if he did."

They shared a meaningful glance at that.

Matilda continued. "Galon wants Wulfhere's Treasure, as well. Fellow's greedy as a bishop."

"The treasure doesn't exist," Miles said.

"You and I know that, but Galon doesn't."

"Why does he want it so badly?"

"Castles. Soldiers. War. He wants to be the balance of power in the kingdom, and if that treasure was as rich as it's supposed to be, he'd be in a fair way to achieving his goal."

"Do you think Galon killed the earl?"

"He'd be my first choice," Matilda said. "Though there's others who'd like to have seen the old man dead."

Miles raised his brows. "Who?"

"I don't mean to sound like the village gossip, but you could start with the earl's wife."

"Lady Blanche?"

"Or her lover. She collects lovers like some people collect relics, but the current favorite is Abbot Joscelin."

Miles remembered the hunting lodge arbor and Joscelin's arms around Blanche. He remembered them together at the hunt. The abbot had discovered the earl's body, and Blanche had been with him when he did. But if Blanche was so openly unfaithful, why had she been concerned about being seen with Abbot Joscelin in the garden? Why had she, because of that, let Miles escape?

Matilda went on. "With Thibault's death, Joscelin will try to keep Blanche from going back to France. The fool's besotted with her. More importantly for Joscelin, the suit over Morton Chase is likely to go against him—his charter is an obvious forgery—and naming a new earl will give him the chance to play for time."

"You mean to bribe someone in authority?"

"That's a polite way of putting it."

The serving girl brought Miles a wooden plate, upon which were three pasties. Matilda laughed. "Meat in summer—the wages of aristocracy. Our huntsmen had a good morning."

Miles took a bite; the venison had been simmered in some kind of sauce. "This is good."

"I'll tell the cook you like it. He has a way with pastry, don't you think? At least the French are good for something."

Miles smiled, had another bite, sipped his ale. Still no sign of alarm at the gate. Pigeons flapped and cooed around the nearby dovecote. There were not nearly as many of the birds as there used to be. In Lord Aimerie's day, the pigeons were protected and allowed to descend on the crops by the hundreds. The villagers hated them, and the dovecote had become a symbol of Aimerie's oppression. One of Geoffrey's first acts on assuming the manor had been to drastically reduce the pigeon population, and the villagers had been treated to pigeon pies for a week.

Matilda breathed deeply and sighed. "Ravenswell is my favorite manor. I wish we could spend more time here. I hate traveling from one place to another, staying long enough to exhaust the food, then packing everything up and moving on. You're fortunate you don't have to put up with it."

"Aye, my lady." Miles got back to the subject at hand. "I've thought all along that the earl's killer was a member of the hunting party. The problem is, whoever did it had access to Aelred's arrows, and how would one of the hunting party have gotten that?"

Matilda considered. "Maybe it wasn't one of the hunting party. Could Aelred have given the arrows to someone—one of the Beardmen, perhaps—and be covering for them?"

"He says not. He claims they were stolen from him."

"That explanation won't go over very well at the assize. Thank God Aelred got away, though I fear the rest of us will pay the price for his escape."

Miles grunted assent. Then he said, "There was a fancily dressed fellow in the hunting party who kept off to himself. He was English—Morys Gretch your husband said his name was. Do you know anything about him?"

It was Matilda's turn to raise her brows. "You've never heard of Morys?"

"We don't get much news in the fields, I'm afraid. Some kind of merchant, isn't he?"

" 'Merchant' is what he calls himself. Morys Gretch is a criminal. He runs Badford Town. Nothing happens there without his approval. Don't let his gaudy get-up fool you, he's a dangerous man. He gets invited to events like the hunt because people wish to keep on his good side."

"I understand the earl owes—or owed—him money."

"A good deal, from what Geoffrey says. He actually threatened Thibault once."

Miles was surprised. "He threatened a noble?"

Matilda laughed. "You really are naïve in the ways of the world, Miles. Morys Gretch wasn't scared of Thibault. He might be scared of Galon—*I'm* scared of Galon—but not of most other men. Galon would go into Badford and cut Morys's head off, then burn the town for fun. Thibault would never do that."

Miles started on the last pasty. "So . . . if Galon became earl, Morys might lose the money he was owed."

"Unless it was worth the loss for him to show people that he can't be crossed, even by a member of the nobility."

"And now that Geoffrey inherits the title? Will he inherit the debt with it?"

"I pray not," Matilda said.

"Could Morys get Aelred's arrows?"

Matilda canted her head, as if she hadn't thought of that before. "Morys Gretch can get anything."

Miles sucked venison juice from his fingers, then wiped his hands on his rough wool hose. He was tired, and he didn't feel like walking all the way to Badford on this bad ankle. He'd have to take the back roads, too, to avoid the men who were looking for him. "I should talk to this Morys."

"By yourself? You'd be safer having your skull trepanned."

"I don't see that I have a choice."

"Really, Miles. I'd advise against it."

"It's three days to the assize," Miles pointed out. "I need to find the killer."

"What about your meeting with Geoffrey?"

"Tell him where I've gone. I'll talk with him when I return."

"*If* you return," Matilda said.

17

MILES hated towns. He never understood why people lived in them. They were dirty, smelly, disease ridden—a blot on God's landscape. You couldn't stretch your legs or get a breath of fresh air in town. You couldn't run the soil through your fingers, watch the crops grow, tend the animals. You couldn't hear the call of birds, the wind's whisper through a waving field of grain.

There were eight, maybe nine hundred people crammed inside Badford Town's wooden walls. The only stone building was the cathedral, whose rectangular tower dominated the massed humanity. The town had become so full that houses were being built outside its walls, gobbling up the surrounding farmland. Miles wondered where the evicted villagers went, and he felt sorry for them. He felt almost as sorry for the villagers who remained, villagers whose once-quiet country lanes were now clogged with people going to and from the town, with townsfolk coming outside the walls to take the air—and sometimes to steal, or commit other crimes.

Miles entered Badford through the River Gate. He was footsore and tired, hungry and thirsty. He wanted nothing more than to lie down and sleep. Yet he was alert, remembering how Lady Matilda had warned him against coming here, how she'd said it was dangerous.

The street leading to the market place and cathedral was cobbled. The other streets were dirt, which meant mud, churned with animal and human droppings, with urine and garbage and blood from slaughtered animals, with bones and rushes and stones and bits of wood thrown haphazardly to provide footing.

Miles asked people in the street how to find Morys Gretch, but they seemed reluctant to answer or acted as though they'd never heard of him. At last, someone furtively directed him to Mory's shop, a nondescript building on the Street of Wool Merchants.

Miles went in. The shop's ground floor was nearly empty of goods, and those goods in the window seemed to be placed there more for show than for sale. The four men inside didn't look much like merchants, either. They were big, scarred, and rough—albeit well dressed—with long daggers in their belts. They regarded Miles without welcome.

"I'm looking for Morys Gretch," Miles told them.

A fellow with pointed, elfin-like ears drew his dagger and picked his nails with its tip. "Why?"

"I need to speak with him. I'm Miles Edwulfson, pledge for Guildford Hundred."

The elfin-eared man considered, and while he did, the other men in the shop edged closer to Miles, surrounding him, and he understood that he could disappear from this place and that no one would ever be the wiser.

The elfin-eared man made a decision. *Live, or die?* Miles wondered.

The man sheathed his dagger. "Come on, then."

Miles expected the man to lead him to the northeast corner of town, where the bigger houses were, or to one of the new houses outside the gates. Instead, they passed under an ancient arch onto Shitte Lane, the vilest part of town. They were surrounded by ragged urchins covered in filth, by malnourished adults with festering sores and feral eyes. By tattered whores and drunks. Houses, if you could call them houses, crowded in upon one another, and the latrines were the streets. Wild dogs roamed the garbage along with cats, who found good hunting amongst the rodents. The stench was appalling, and Miles breathed through his mouth, though that didn't help much. His feet squelched in God only knew what muck.

They passed into a courtyard. In startling contrast to the misery outside, the buildings around the courtyard were clean and well maintained. The courtyard grounds were raked dry and swept. Opposite the gate stood a fine house, shaded by an elm tree. More well-dressed ruffians loitered on benches outside the house.

Miles and his escort approached the house. " 'E's come to see Morys," the elfin-eared man told one of the ruffians, a scarred cove missing part of an ear. "It's the hundred pledge."

The scarred fellow looked Miles up and down, and once again Miles felt like a decision was being made about his fate. The fellow beckoned curtly and ushered Miles through the door. "Wipe your feet," he cautioned.

On the house's sparsely furnished ground floor, a trio of men sat at a table, tossing dice in a bored fashion. Miles and his companion went up a flight of stairs to the first floor.

Baskets of fragrant flowers stood on stands around the room, making it resemble a lush garden. Fresh rushes, scented with herbs, were piled on the floor. On a table in one corner were piled bolts of expensive cloth, in another corner was a table with stacks of coins and a set of measuring weights. More stairs led to sleeping quarters on the second floor. There was no sign of a wife or children.

Morys Gretch was by the window overlooking the courtyard, arranging a basket of yellow roses, smelling them. He glanced over his shoulder as Miles came in. “Been wondering when you’d show up.”

18

MILES was surprised. "You know who I am?"

" 'Course I do," Morys said, turning from the flowers. "You're Miles Edwulfson, the hundred pledge. I seen you when Galon put that rope burn on your neck yesterday, though it looks like you been beat up more since then. Figured you'd be along to speak to me. Cerdic, fetch us some refreshment, would you? My friend Miles, here, looks like he could use it."

The scarred man raised his brows as though he did not wish to leave Morys and Miles alone.

"We'll be all right," Morys assured him. "Go on."

Cerdic left the room.

Up close, Morys was older than he had looked when Miles saw him in the Beeches. His greying hair was cut short and covered with a linen coif to keep dirt off. He had a raspy voice, a face like a fist, and a body to match. He went on, showing off. "I also know that you hold three yardlands from the lord of Ravenswell and a half-yardland from the abbot of Huntley. You pay Ravenswell three shillings, seven pence in rent, plus a chicken and a sheep at Christmas. You pay the abbot ten pence and a dozen painted eggs at Easter."

"Impressive," Miles acknowledged.

Morys shrugged modestly. "I make it a point to know about men I may have to deal with."

"And I pay Ravenswell three shillings, eight pence. It went up."

"I'll make a note of that."

Morys wore a long red tunic—a richer red than Miles had ever seen—over a white shirt, along with deep blue hose. Heavy rings crusted his fingers. "You like this tunic?" he asked Miles. "Kermes, they call it, dunno why. Dye comes from Spain. Made from crushed bugs or something. Amazing, isn't it?"

Miles didn't know what to say, so he said nothing.

Morys plucked one of the yellow roses and sniffed it. "Ah, I love roses. I assume you don't believe that dimwitted son of yours killed the earl, and you're trying to find out who did."

"That's right. I was hoping you could help me."

"What you mean is, you're wondering if I killed him." Morys put the rose back in the basket and stepped away from it. "If I'd done it, you'd be dead by now."

"So I take it you're innocent?" Miles said.

"It's no secret I threatened the old goat, but I didn't kill him. I wish he'd told me where that damned treasure is before he croaked, though."

"There is no treasure," Miles said.

"Whoever told you that is wrong. It's there."

Miles sighed. He didn't want to get into that argument again.

Morys went on. "Think about it. If I killed the earl, would I have done it that way? Make a big show of it? Go to the trouble of putting the blame on someone else? Why? There's men, professionals, who'd do the deed for a price. They'd kill the bugger, then disappear. Better yet, they'd kill him and make his body disappear, and no one would ever know what become of him. Someone wanted Thibault's body to be found. That's why they moved it."

"So you noticed that it had been moved, too?"

" 'Course I did. I've moved a few bodies meself in my day."

Cerdic returned with a tray containing ale, bread and cheese, along with bowls heaped with cherries and strawberries. "Thank you, Cerdic," Morys said. He indicated the tray. "Help yourself," he told Miles. "Bread's fresh baked. Fruit was picked this morning."

Miles's pride wanted him to say no, but he couldn't help himself. It had been a long walk. He poured some ale, broke off a piece of bread and topped it with a slice of cheese. "Good bread," he mumbled between mouthfuls.

"Why do you think I can help you?" Morys asked him.

"You were there. Plus, you know the people who were in the hunt."

Morys took a turn round the room while Miles ate. Morys's shoes were of expensive white leather, with pointed toes, and Miles wondered how he made it through the muck of Shitte Lane, or did he change shoes when he went out?

Morys stopped. "Why *should* I help you? What's it to me if your son hangs?"

Miles might have anticipated that question, but hadn't, and his answer was weak. "If I find the real killer, perhaps it may somehow prove to your advantage."

Morys mulled that over, shook his head. "Can't see how." A sly grin crept over his face. "But it would be fun to see one o' them French turds on the gallows for once, and not our own people. You like the strawberries, by the way? I own the farm they come from. Never had strawberries in Lower Wynchecombe. I was a mole catcher there, didn't have land enough to shit on. Didn't fancy that life much."

"Don't imagine you would," Miles said.

"So I run away and come here. If you can stay in town a year and a day without being caught, you're a free man. A free man, Miles, just like you. How 'bout that? My old lord, he sent men to get me back, but I hid from 'em. Damn near starved to death, but at last he gave up. So I stayed, and I went into business, and here I am."

Miles looked at the counting table, piled with coins and clipped pieces of coins. "What exactly *is* your business?"

"This and that. Started out doin' whatever needed to be done. Diggin' building foundations, working as a porter." He winked. "Other things, too. I moved on to gambling and running whores. Then selling protection to merchants."

"Protection from what?"

"From me," Morys said. "After that, I went into wool. Then I run the Jews out of town and took over their money-lending business. At considerably steeper rates, I might add."

"And if people can't pay back the money you lend them?"

Morys smiled. "There are . . . 'consequences.' "

"How does the law feel about what you do?"

The smile grew wider. "When you have money, you are the law."

Miles looked out the back window at a well-tended garden with vegetables and apple trees. "Why live on this street? Surely there are better neighborhoods?"

"Because I'm safe here. I have enemies, but they can't get within a hundred yards of me when I'm here. Every man, woman, and child on Shitte Lane works for me, and there's good coin if they report outsiders."

"Was I reported?"

"The moment you walked through the town gate."

Miles turned away from the window. "So who do you think killed the earl?"

Morys made a face. "Have you considered Lady Blanche?"

"You're the second person who's said that. Her by herself, or her and Abbot Joscelin?"

"Her and just about anybody. There's few she hasn't been with, maybe fewer still who wouldn't kill to enjoy her—ah—favors. She has her eyes set on young Lord Geoffrey, from what I hear, and she wouldn't be able to get him if Thibault dragged her back to France. She, or whoever she's in it with, could have hired somebody to do it."

Miles shook his head. "Geoffrey's loyal to his wife."

"Is he? Really? Or was his marriage a calculated move to get our people on his side? With the support of the English, he's better able to ride out any potential troubles that come up. Would he be receptive to Blanche's advances? I don't know, but I'd wager most men would."

"Would you?"

Morys smiled. "If she stays in England, I'll have her, and, believe me, it won't take long. I'll pound that meat till she screams for mercy."

Miles put aside that disquieting thought. "If Blanche did it, why would she blame Aelred?"

"To throw suspicion on our people and away from her."

"You got to the Beeches right after Blanche and Abbot Joscelin, didn't you?"

"I did."

"What did you see?"

"Joscelin was there, bending over the earl's body, while Blanche watched."

"Did Blanche seem upset?"

Morys snorted. "She did, but it was an act. And Joscelin, he was grinning from ear to ear. Happy as the proverbial clam at high tide."

"Could Joscelin have killed the earl, or arranged it?"

"He could. The earl's death solves a lot of problems for him, what with that suit over Morton Chase and all."

"Does Joscelin owe you money?"

Morys grinned. " 'Course he does. The idiot's spent so much on building projects—and on women—that he's run Huntley into the ground. I have a charter that promises me Upper Stourbridge if he can't pay, and when I have Stourbridge, I'll control every sheep farm in the shire. Then I can sell wool to the Flemings with no competition, and won't I just charge 'em for it."

There was a noise on the stairs from the second floor. A young woman, attractive in a tawdry way and wearing the thinnest of shifts, started down. "Are you going to be long?" she asked Morys with a pout. She saw Miles, and her eyes widened. "Who's this? He's cute for an old man." She smiled archly, looking Miles over. "Big, too."

The play on words made Miles blush. It had been a long time since he'd been with a woman.

With a nod of the head, Morys motioned her back up the ladder. She sighed and went back. Miles watched her bottom as she climbed. He couldn't help it, the shift was so thin.

"You like that?" Morys asked him.

"I suppose."

"You can have her if you want. I know you're not married, must get pretty lonely for you."

"Not now, thanks."

Morys grinned. "All business, eh?"

Miles ate some cherries and tried to put the woman out of his mind. The cherries were dark and sweet, and for some reason that made him think about the woman even more. "What about Lord Galon? Could he have killed his father?"

"Dunno," Morys said. "Don't seem his style somehow. Galon's the type likes to kill you face to face, likes everybody to know he done it."

"The last king, Rufus, was killed the same way. Shot with an arrow while hunting. Maybe that's where Galon got the idea."

"Could be. Tell you what, though, I'd be happy if it was Galon. Last thing I want is that bastard in power around here. Cut off his head or ship him back to France, I say, and the sooner the better." Morys seemed to be warming to the idea of Galon as the killer. "If Galon killed the old man, Stigand would have shot the arrow. Stigand don't miss with the bow, they say. Stigand's weak point is he thinks he's cleverer than he really is. Planting your son's arrow on the body is exactly the kind of show-off thing he'd do." He stroked his short beard. "Now I think on it, it's the kind of thing Ranulf's witch of a wife, Mathilde, might do, too."

"Ranulf's wife is a witch?"

"She's from Breton, they're all witches there. Apprenticed under Marie of Alexandria, the most famous witch in France. Mathilde prefers using poison for her deeds, but I'm sure an arrow would work just as well. And she's an accomplished archer, I've seen her on the hunt."

"Mathilde," Miles said. "Plain looking, dark hair, flashy dresser?"

"That's her."

That's who Miles had seen at the lodge earlier with Galon and Rosamunde. "Why would she do it?"

"Revenge for her husband. Ranulf's been cut off. Thibault's tired of wasting money on him."

Miles nodded. It was a lot to consider. "Tell me something. On the hunt they make you ride with the women 'cause you're a bad horseman. You don't seem the type to tolerate such an insult. Why do you do it?"

Morys smiled broadly. "I'm not as bad a horseman as I let on. I like to ride with the women. I *want* to ride with the women. Later, I ride the women themselves. French women are no different than any other. They like money and gifts, and they'll spread their legs to get them. This way, not only do I get back at the husbands, I take their wives—and their daughters. How do you think I know so much about Mathilde?" He cleared his throat. "Now, is there anything else you need?" He inclined his head toward the second floor. "I have business."

"No," Miles said. He was ready to leave. He had a long walk back, and he needed to get home before dark. "I suppose not."

"Before you go, I have a proposal for you."

Miles gave him a look.

"I'd like you to work for me."

"What?" Miles said.

"I could use a man like you, Miles. I've got muscle, like Cerdic, but I need brains, and that's what you've got. Besides, you'd add some class to the organization. You're descended from nobility—real nobility, not that French trash."

"Is that the only reason?"

Morys laughed. "See, I said you had brains. I want respectability—I want what you have—and you can help me get that. I don't want to be mayor of Badford, it's too much work and I already run the town, but I do want to be an alderman. Even more, I want to be one of the twelve jurors of Guildford. A word from you would go a long way toward both of those. Also, there's some fellows from Leicester pushin' to take over my business, and havin' a hero soldier like you on my side might make 'em think twice."

Miles hadn't expected this, "I don't—"

"You're wasted in that village, Miles. You could live like a king here—better than a king. You could be important. Why, with your brains and background, might be you could take over the business one day, when I'm gone or retire."

Miles said nothing, still digesting what he'd heard.

"You wouldn't have to give up your lands," Morys told him. "Rent 'em out or let your boys run 'em. Every man is free in the towns. The towns are where the future lies, Miles. The towns are where the power will be."

That's ridiculous, Miles thought.

"Think it over," Morys told him.

"I will," Miles promised.

"Just remember—I don't like it when somebody refuses my offer."

Miles said nothing.

"Cerdic will show you out." Morys paused and smiled. "Oh, and Miles?"

Miles stopped.

Morys smiled, and this time the smile wasn't friendly. "Unless you're planning to accept my offer, don't come here again. You were lucky this time."

19

Wales, 1086 A.D.

"HOW would you describe this country?" Leofric asked Miles.

They were marching through a desolate valley, beside a rushing, boulder-strewn stream. Rain pelted down.

"Bleak," Miles replied.

"That's it? Just 'bleak?'" Leofric looked around. "I think it's kind of pretty, in a way."

From behind them, Alauric said, "All right, then, 'pretty bleak.'"

Alauric's laughter at his own joke was cut short by an arrow that entered his skull from the left and transfixed it, the tip of the arrowhead protruding next to Alauric's right eye. He gave a surprised cry and fell.

All eyes turned up the hill to their left. Halfway up, a lone figure left the cover of some rocks and climbed for the top.

"There he is!" Burgred cried.

Toki shouted, "After him, lads!"

A number of men broke ranks and started up the hill. Earl Thibault, who must have anticipated their move, got in front of them, arms outstretched. "*Arretez*—halt! Get back!"

Toki dodged around the earl and kept going. Miles caught Toki, grabbed his arm, and pulled him back. Toki shoved Miles away, knocking him off balance so that he almost fell. "Don't touch me, Miles. Nobody touches me. Not you, not that French fuck. You may think you're some kind of lord, but you're not."

"He's getting away," Burgred shouted at the earl, pointing.

Other men growled angrily as the Welshman disappeared over the hill, but the earl was firm. "*Arretez.*"

"You heard him," Miles said. "Stay in your ranks."

"What's the matter with you, Miles?" said Oslac, a carpenter from Dalby. "Alauric's from Guildford Hundred. He's one of us. And you just stand there and let his killer get away."

Miles said nothing. He hated being in the position of defending actions by this French earl. He hated defending a Frenchman for anything, but in this case he suspected the Frenchman might be right.

"Miles is a coward," Toki said. "He's only centenar 'cause him and Little Dick sucked up to the Frenchy."

Miles reddened.

The earl cut in. "We do not have time to chase one man. We can't afford to slow our march."

"What march?" Toki shot back. "You talk about time, yet here we are, wasting it. Swanning around the back of beyond when the road to England lies over there to the north."

"And that road is where the Welsh will be looking for us," Earl Thibault explained. "We need to keep away from them. To hide."

"I'm tired of this shit," Toki grumbled to Burgred, another man with Danish blood. "We'll be wandering around these hills till the Second Coming. I'm ready to strike out on my own."

"I'm with you when you go," Burgred said.

Others within earshot muttered assent.

The earl, who had not heard Toki, turned a cold eye on Miles. "I am not used to being addressed in this manner by commoners, English. You must do a better job of keeping your men in order."

"Aye, my lord," Miles said, but keeping them in order was becoming increasingly difficult. The men were tired, hungry, wet, and cold, and after days of marching they didn't seem to be getting any closer to safety. In truth, Miles would have been just as happy to follow Toki's idea and abandon this Frenchman, but something told him not to. Not just yet.

"All right, men," Miles said wearily. "Let's get going, before that fellow who killed Alauric comes back with some of his friends."

"What about Alauric?" Wat o' Riseby said, indicating the body. "What do we do with him?"

Miles knew how the French earl would have replied, and as much as he hated to admit it, he now knew the earl would have been right.

"Leave him," Miles said.

The dispirited company lumbered along in the rain.

* * *

The expedition had begun as an afterthought. That summer, levies had been called up to repel an expected invasion by King Canute of Denmark. When Canute died and it became obvious no invasion was forthcoming, the earls of Shrewsbury and Chester had decided to use their men and launch an expedition into Wales, to chastise the Welsh king, Gryffd.

The army had mustered outside Chester in August and marched west. The expedition started out well enough. The weather was good, the going easy. In addition to knights and footmen, there were a large number of priests and other clerics, along with camp followers—washerwomen, prostitutes, and victuallers. King Gryffd's army faced them at Northop and was routed. The English built a fort and base at Northop, garrisoned it, and moved on after the fleeing Welsh.

The land grew hilly, and as the march slowed, the English left their siege engines behind—there was nothing to besiege in this country. The weather tuned bad, and the going slowed even more. Men were picked off. Scouting and foraging parties vanished. Granaries ahead of the English force were burned; there was no food to be had. Men died of sickness. The Welsh that were captured were put to death, as were the English, Flemish, and Normans who were captured by the Welsh. Always Gryffd and what remained of his army were just ahead of them. Always one last effort would see the Welsh king brought to bay.

October drew to a close amidst rain and cold and lack of roads, or even footpaths in some places. The army was penned in by woods and hills. Armor and weapons rusted. Horses starved for lack of grain. Some argued for turning back, but Shrewsbury and Chester were reluctant to do so without showing any results for the expedition, whose cost had been considerable.

Then they had come upon the Welsh army drawn up for battle at last, and they had rushed into the disastrous ambush . . .

* * *

The day was drawing to a close, though one could hardly tell because the sky was so dark and heavy with rain. The scouts came back. "Men up ahead," they announced, breathless.

"Form up!" the earl cried.

The men clattered into a battle line, their energy suddenly renewed by fear.

The earl turned to Miles. "English, see who these men are."

"Aye, my lord," Miles said. He turned. "Leofric, with me."

The two men started up the darkening valley, the rain-swollen stream to their right. They were tense. Leofric had his long-handled axe at the ready; Miles drew his scramasax.

"Maybe it's somebody selling food," Leofric said hopefully.

"With our luck, the food'll be poisoned," Miles said.

"Cheer up. We're not dead yet."

"Then why does it feel that way?" Miles said.

Leofric pointed. "Look."

A disordered band of people was headed toward them. By their dress and equipment, they were Flemish and Norman mercenaries, crossbowmen some of them, along with a couple knights and two women. Many of the party were hurt or sick. Some had weapons, some did not.

The rag-tag party halted when they saw Miles and Leofric. Miles raised a hand and called to them. "We're English."

Some of the men sank to the wet ground in exhaustion. "*Grâce à Dieu*," murmured one.

The two knights advanced. "Waleran of St. Just," announced the taller one, whose left arm was wrapped in a bloody sling. "This is Pierre of Caen."

Miles noted how beaten down Waleran must be to address a footman like Miles as an equal. "You were with the earl of Shrewsbury's column?" Miles asked Waleran.

"We're all that's left of it," Waleran said. Some of the blood on his dirty sling was wet, which meant his wound was still seeping blood. "Shrewsbury and Chester and their retainers hopped it to safety, damn their souls, and abandoned us. The Welsh have been chasing us for two days."

"We're with the earl of Trent," Miles told them.

"Trent?" Pierre of Caen said. He was a burly, dark-haired fellow, who had lost, or thrown away, his helmet and shield. "He didn't run with the rest?"

"No. We'll take you to him."

Miles and Leofric led the little group back to the column. Trent greeted them and assigned them places in the line of march. The two females were washerwomen—one tall and sturdy, the other a stocky peasant—who had somehow avoided being killed in the massacre of the supply train. "You can be cooks," Trent told them in their Norman tongue, "assuming we ever get anything to cook. Now, hurry. We have to change our course and keep moving."

"The earl doesn't seem too happy to see these folks," Leofric observed. "Don't know why. Give us a few extra fighters at least."

Miles surprised himself, because he could guess what the earl was thinking. "He's unhappy because they've led the Welsh right to us."

20

Trentshire, 1106 A.D.

"SO you think the earl's killer is French?" Garth said.

"I've thought it likely from the start," Miles told him.

"Why?"

They were heading home along the Mill Field, heads tilted against the rain. It had been a beautiful day, then out of nowhere dark clouds piled up and, just like that, it was raining. Not hard rain, more of a heavy drizzle. After a long walk from Badford Town, Miles had reached the fields, hoping to find Lord Geoffrey, had instead run into Garth on his way home. It was Saturday, and it was a manor tradition for people to leave work at mid-day on Saturday instead of late afternoon, but Garth had stayed late.

Miles hobbled on his throbbing ankle; he was getting too old to be jumping off walls. "Because of the wound, for one thing," he said. "The arrow entered Thibault's throat from straight ahead, like Thibault was facing the person, like it was someone he knew. It didn't come from the side or back, like it might have done had he been shot from ambush. Also, the arrow's course was flat, as though he had been shot from horseback, not upward and through the back of his head as it would have been had it been shot by a man on foot."

Garth said, "Which means it wasn't Aelred?"

"Aelred doesn't ride."

They walked around Four-Fingered Hugh, who was meandering along, a hoe and rake on his shoulder. "Hello, Hugh," Miles said as they passed, but Hugh failed to reply and gave Miles an odd look.

Miles stared back at Hugh for a moment, then continued with Garth. "Plus, there's the question of why the body was moved."

"That part makes no sense to me," Garth said.

"Apparently the earl left the lodge early and rode far ahead of the rest of the hunt, not waiting for the others to catch up. Why?"

"Maybe he was going to meet someone," Garth said. "An assignation?"

"Perhaps, though with a wife who looks like Lady Blanche, that's hard to believe. Or perhaps it was something else."

Garth understood what his father was driving at. "Not the treasure?" he said.

"Yes, the treasure. I think that was it, and whoever killed him moved the body because the body might not be found otherwise."

"The killer wanted it to be found?"

"I believe he did."

"Why?"

"Because the killing took place at a remote location; a location that would reveal where the treasure was, or where the killer thought it to be. If the earl was missing and there was a search, finding the body where he was killed might give some hint to the killer's identity."

"So it was staged to look like a poacher did it?"

"Yes."

Garth said, "But why did the killer pick Aelred to take the blame?"

"Aelred was convenient, I guess. A known malcontent."

Garth said, "How can I help you?"

"By staying here in the fields," Miles said.

"I love Aelred, too, you know. We can't let the killer—"

"Who's going to do the work if you're not here?" Miles told him.

Garth gave no reply, but his lips tightened and he looked away.

The path ran where the wheat field bordered the common pasture. They passed the head of one of Miles's strips of land. "Look at this." Miles pulled at a loose fence post. Each strip owner was required to fence his end of the strip, thus eliminating the need for one person to fence the whole field off from the pasture. "This post wasn't like this two days ago. Why hasn't it been fixed? If those cattle get into the fields, we'll be paying damages to half of Ravenswell."

"I told Talbott to do it," Garth said. "I was ploughing all morning, then I had to check the eel traps. I can't be in two places at once."

"You can't be in one if you're helping me find the killer," Miles told him. "When we get home, get a mallet and come back and hammer this in."

Garth withdrew into his hood. The rain fell.

Miles knew he was hard on Garth, and he hated to hurt him. But Garth sometimes wanted more from his father than

Miles was prepared to give. Miles needed distance between them. He knew Garth couldn't understand his father's attitude—Garth had lost none of his own children yet.

Miles remembered his second son, Arthur, a bright, blond, bouncing boy. Miles had loved that boy; he'd never imagined he could lose him. Then a plague swept the shire. It was gone quickly, like a dark cloud on a sunny day, but it took Arthur with it. Miles's third son, Aedric, was spared, but Aedric had been born simple.

Miles never told Garth how he had prayed for Aedric to die. Never told him how relieved he'd been when, two years later, his prayers were answered. Miles knew it was a mortal sin to wish someone dead, but he'd been happy when it happened, happy that the child didn't have to face a world for which he was so unfit.

And yet . . . yet there had been love there, behind the lolling head and the overlarge eyes. Miles could still feel the pressure of the misshapen little fist around his finger, so full of trust and warmth . . .

Miles remembered his wife, Alice, dying while giving birth to Aethelwynn, and his eyes misted. He'd given too much, lost too much. He would never get that close to anyone again. Too much of his life lay buried in St. Wendreda's churchyard. Soon, perhaps, he would be buried there himself . . .

He halted and faced his son. "Garth, I know you think I favor Aelred, but I don't."

Garth said nothing, but his expression said he was unconvinced.

Miles went on. "I've given Aelred more time than I gave you because I had to. You were always the son I could trust, the one who did the right thing. I never had to worry about you, and I guess I . . . I guess I took you for granted. Aelred's a good boy, but he's a dreamer. Always in trouble. Never for anything serious—not until now, anyway—but I always had to keep after him, and I wasn't able to give you the attention you deserved."

"Why are you telling me this now?" Garth said.

"Because I should have told you earlier, and for that I apologize. You've gotten all the work because I could give you responsibility and know you'd carry it out. If I give Aelred responsibility, he's like to go off in the woods by himself or be skylarking with his friends. I thought he'd change, but he never has, and I've always had to keep an eye on him. I don't love you less or love him more."

Garth pursed his lips. "Thank you for saying that, Father. I've waited a long time to hear it."

"I'm not good at talking about feelings, I guess," Miles said.

They embraced, and Garth slapped his father's back. When they drew apart, Garth's eyes were moist. "Come on," he said. "If we miss the ale brewing, Mary'll chuck us both out of the house."

With all that had happened the last two days, Miles had completely forgotten about the ale brewing. The village had an alewife, but others were allowed to brew from time to time as long as they paid the prescribed tax. Mary's ale was regarded as particularly good. This brewing had been scheduled for some time, and she refused to change it because of the turmoil brought on by the earl's death.

Miles said, "About the house . . ."

Garth waited.

"Maybe Mary's right, and it's best I go. Leave you two on your own."

"Or we'll build our own house," Garth said. "There's land on the way to the manor house, we could build there."

"It's best I go," Miles said. "It's the least I can do for—"

A rock bounced off Miles's shoulder.

He turned, but there was no obvious culprit, though a knot of giggling boys stood not far away.

"Better get used to that," Garth said. "Everyone knows Aelred's arrow killed the earl. They figured it out when Stigand and his men were here last night."

They came abreast of the church. "Go ahead," Miles told him. "I'll be home directly."

21

MILES entered the churchyard. The church of St. Wendreda was heavy and low, God's fortress in a hostile world. Miles didn't know why it had been named after St. Wendreda. Wendreda was Anglian, not Mercian. She had been daughter to a king and a healer of note who had established a nunnery in the Fens. The church had originally been named for St. Guthlac, but that had changed after the Danes were driven out. Miles's grandfather, Wulfstan, would surely have been involved in the decision, but what caused it, no one knew.

Miles remembered the plain wooden structure that had stood here before, not much larger than his own cottage, sweating villagers crammed cheek to jowl during services. Lord Geoffrey had hired Badford Cathedral's stone masons for the new church's construction, and the small entrance arch was ornamented with the dog-toothed design so favored by the French, painted in alternating colors of red and blue.

The building was large enough to accommodate the hundred-and-fifty-odd souls of Ravenswell. Right now, the only flooring was beneath the choir, but there were plans to fix that. Miles stood in the center of the room, facing the altar. Light from the tiny slit windows filtered through the dimness, glinting dully off the lead crucifix on the back wall and off the brass tabernacle, where Christ lived. Along the whitewashed walls, Ulic, the village artist for thirty years, had painted scenes from the life of St. Wendreda. He didn't know anything about Wendreda, of course, so he made them up. There were scenes from the Old Testament, as well, and from the life of Christ. In fact, Ulic had gotten carried away before he died, and the walls were crowded, the scenes overlapping one another in a riot of fantastical figures in red and blue and green. Ulic had lived at the edge of the village, where he had told Miles and Leofric tales of old Mercia, of Offa and Ethelbald, and the glittering court at Tamworth, when Mercia had been the bright jewel of the English kingdoms. Tales that were being forgotten by the younger generation.

Miles stood facing the altar and prayed for guidance. He prayed for Aelred, for his family, for the village, for the strength to see this through and the wisdom to do the right thing. He closed his eyes and felt at peace, as he always did when he came here. He liked to come when no one else was about, liked the solitude, the feeling of being alone with God . . .

From the baptistry came a series of wracking coughs. Father John entered, brushing dirt from his hands. "Hello, Miles," he said. "I've just come from the tithing barn. Getting it fixed up for the harvest. Never too early to start. St. Peter in Chains will be here before you know it."

Ten percent of the manor's crops went to the Church—to the rector, really; Father John was just a vicar, who lived on a stipend. The villagers never tithed as much as they were supposed to; they had families to feed, and times were usually hard. Father John knew this and didn't mind. He understood his parishioners' worries and, like them, he was content with not contributing to the further enrichment of some wealthy lord's son. Ravenswell's rector was a Frenchman. They saw him once a year, when he descended on the manor with his entourage to go over the accounts, always complaining that Father John wasn't milking enough out of the villagers—and out of Lord Geoffrey.

Father John went on. "Thought you'd be home, getting ready for Mary's ale brewing."

"I'm going there in a moment. I just stopped by to pray."

"The lodge bailiffs were in the village earlier, looking for you. Apparently you were made prisoner at the lodge and escaped?"

"I did, Father." To the priest's questioning look, Miles added, "I can't very well find the earl's killer if I'm in the lodge gaol."

Father John rubbed his hands as though they were cold. He coughed again and sniffled. "You've a difficult task, Miles. I've prayed for you, I've prayed for you since Earl Thibault's body was found. I've prayed that the Lord would aid you in finding the man you seek."

"Thank you, Father."

"Open your heart and God will tell you what to do. Obey Him, though the road be difficult."

"No matter where it leads?" Miles said.

"No matter where it leads. God has chosen you as His instrument of justice. If you fail, justice will not be done. Accept that, embrace it. Be at peace with yourself."

"I'll try, Father."

Father John started coughing and bent over. Miles went to aid him, but he waved Miles off. Miles wondered if they'd get a priest when John died or a man of minor orders, unable to say Mass or administer the Sacraments. Lord Geoffrey would want a priest, but priests were scarce in the countryside. Few Englishmen could afford Holy Orders for their sons; even fewer Frenchmen would take a post as insignificant as Ravenswell.

The coughing died. Father John straightened and smiled. "Now, you'd best get ready for that ale brewing."

"Aye, Father."

Feeling refreshed and strengthened, Miles genuflected before the altar and left the church.

22

GARTH'S wife, Mary, was raising the ale broom beside the gate as Miles approached. "Men from the lodge were here looking for you," she told Miles as he entered the gate.

"I heard," Miles said.

"You're not very popular with the French or the English right now. Word's out that Aelred's arrow killed the earl, and people are furious with you."

"I'd probably be furious, too, were I them," Miles admitted.

"I don't have to tell you how I feel."

"No. You've made that obvious."

Miles eased his weary body onto the bench beside the house, while Garth attempted to lighten the air. "I'll pour us some ale."

But Mary wouldn't let it go. "What do you plan to do now?" she demanded.

"I plan to find the earl's killer," Miles said.

"We know who the killer is."

"No, we don't," Miles shot back.

"Why is it so hard for you to admit the truth?" Mary said. "Is it because you blame yourself? Is it because you made Aelred what he is?"

Miles glared at her, and she went on. "Don't try to deny it. You wouldn't give your children the new French names like everyone else—no, they had to have the old English ones, to remind them of days that are lost forever."

"You gave your children—"

"Garth did that, not me. You disinherited Aelred so he'd be poor—"

"I did that so my land wouldn't be divided—"

"Then you filled his head with all your nonsense about freedom. Is it any wonder he's turned out the way he has? Mary's milk, you should be proud of him. He's only tried to be like you!"

Garth set two mugs on the bench. Mary went on, shrugging off her husband's attempt to stop her. "I'll not have you destroy my family. I'll not have you destroy my children's future. We have to live in this village. We have to see these people every day. We're not going to be shunned because of your pigheadedness. You're a self-centered old man who cares for nothing save that wastrel son of yours."

"What would you have me do?" Miles asked her. "Watch Aelred hang for something he didn't do?"

"He *did* do it!" Mary looked to her husband for help.

"I don't believe Aelred did it, either," Garth said. "I told you that."

"My God!" Mary blurted. "You're as stupid as he is." She turned back to Miles, and her eyes were hard. "If there's a *murdrum* fine levied on this hundred, I'll slit your throat myself and save the rest of our neighbors the trouble."

Miles stood. "I will continue until I know the real killer."

"Why?" Mary threw up her hands. "Why persist in this folly?"

"Because someone has to stand for the truth. And because I owe it to Lord Thibault. If not for Thibault, I'd be dead these many years. He saved my life in Wales. He made me the man I am."

"Then a pox upon him," Mary said, "because he did a piss poor job."

Miles steadied his voice. "It is my duty to find the killer, Mary. If I deny my duty, I deny part of myself."

"You—"

"Here come the neighbors for ale," Garth interrupted, "and they don't look happy."

23

THE villagers filed into the yard, carrying wooden mugs or drinking horns, most of them looking decidedly less than festive. There were men, women, and children. The older children would drink along with the adults, though they were not supposed to. Mary welcomed them individually, and she and Aethelwynn, who had just appeared with Peter, poured them ale from the cask.

"Thought you were going to get that mallet," Miles reminded Garth.

Garth hoisted his mug. "Reckoned I'd have a—"

"Time enough to drink when you're done."

Garth sighed. He put down the mug and started around back, to the tool shed.

Most of the villagers were there, even the regular alewife, Gunhild, and her husband, Ivo. Gunhild was glad for a day she didn't have to work. She and her husband would likely get drunk, then go off to the woods and have sex, as would many of the other couples who were present. A lot of babies were conceived on ale nights.

They gathered under a spreading elm. Father John arrived with his housekeeper, Agnes. Duncan Brown of the Guildford jurors was there, as well. So was peg-legged William the Beardman, whose presence saved Miles a long walk to Sudbroke. Duncan and William being here meant that serious business would be conducted, and the scowl on Mary's face said that she realized the evening was unlikely to be a pleasant one.

A table and benches and a couple stools had been set out. Those who could, sat; the others stood. The smaller children ran around the croft with Chieftain, who loved children. No one paid heed to the drizzle. It would have to be raining very hard for them to go indoors before dark.

At first they kept the mood light. "Excellent ale," the portly Gunhild told Mary. "You'll be taking my job from me, I don't watch out."

"Good as always," said William the Beardman, wiping foam from his lips. "Well worth the trip."

"Fill us up again, will you?" asked the cottar Talbott.

Miles was tired, and he declined further pleasantries. There were things he needed to know before the gathering got out of hand, as it inevitably would. To the reeve, he said, "Osbert, did you send to the manors?"

Osbert had been about to say something, and he looked irritated at being put off. "I did. There's been no strangers about. None out of the ordinary, at least. The only result was lost work time for the men I sent. Your French friend Pierre ain't happy about that. 'Course that don't bother you none, you don't work the lord's strips."

Miles ignored the jibe. "Father—anything at the abbey?"

Father John coughed and shook his head. "Nothing, Miles. Sorry."

"Peter, did you find those woodcutters?"

"I did," Peter said. "Aelfsige and Aelfhere, their names are. Brothers. They live outside Lower Wynchecombe. Seems they do a bit of cattle thieving on the side."

" 'Course they do," muttered Miles's former son-in-law, Martin Above the Brook, "they're from Lower Wynchecombe."

There was nervous laughter, and Peter went on. "Outside of that, there's nothing suspicious about them. The breakdown was legitimate—wheel fell off the cart. They didn't see anything that would be useful to us. They were too busy trying to get their cart upright, afraid the foresters were going to start beating them if they held up the hunt too long."

Miles turned to William the Beardman. "William, could the earl's killer be one of your fellows?"

The Beardman shifted his wooden leg, wincing. As a young man, William had been walking in the king's forest one day, when he was arrested on suspicion of poaching and thrown in gaol. After months in gaol, his right foot putrefied, and his leg was cut off below the knee. When at last his trial came, there was no evidence against him, so he was released. That was when he had joined the Beardmen. His leathery face, with its forked beard reaching well below his waist, wore a perpetually sour expression. "That's why I come here today, Miles. There's no plans on, not in Guildford—nor anywhere else in England that I knows of."

Slyly, Four-Fingered Hugh said, "Aelred's a Beardman. He'd do it, right?"

William wiped a hand across his mouth. "He's a funny one, Aelred. Young compared to the rest of the lads. Hates the French like the very Devil, too. But, no, I don't see him— "

"Stop!" Osbert said. Osbert's jaw was set; he'd been waiting for this. So had his wife, Leticia; so had everyone.

Osbert banged the table with the flat of his hand. "You lied to us, Miles. You told us you didn't recognize the arrow that killed Earl Thibault. But you did. It belonged to Aelred."

Gilbert the hayward said, "What's worse, you helped Aelred escape."

Miles was firm. "I did that because I don't believe Aelred is guilty. You all know him. He couldn't have done this."

Barrel-chested Weland, the smith, said, "Don't feed us that shit. It's his arrow, who else could it have been?"

Miles said, "I—"

"Do you know what's in store for us because of what you did?" Osbert pressed.

"Of course I know, just as I know what would have been in store for Aelred."

Four-Fingered Hugh snorted. "Not much as it turns out. The little fuck run off, leaving us in the shit."

Osbert said, "We go back a long way, Miles, but you've put your family above the village welfare, and that ain't right."

Osbert's wife, Leticia, added, "It's God's own blessing your family's not up at the manor house no more. You've done us worse than the Frenchies ever did—even old Aimerie."

Miles said, "I understand your—"

"No, you don't!" Gilbert said. Gilbert was a younger man. He would probably be reeve one day, when Osbert died or retired. "The only thing you understand is being free. It's all that matters to you, that and your brat's life."

These were people Miles had known all his life. He was surprised how quick they were to turn on him and his family. *Maybe I shouldn't be.*

Leticia said, "Mary, can't you talk some sense into him?"

Mary folded her arms. "I tried. He won't listen."

Aethelwynn was near tears. "It's horrid, the way you're talking about my brother."

"He should of thought about that before he put an arrow in the earl," Weland said.

Miles replied patiently. "I'll be hit by a *murdrum* fine as hard as any of you. If I believed Aelred was the killer, I'd have turned him in."

"I don't believe that," said Martin Above the Brook.

"I would," Miles repeated, but he wasn't sure he believed it, either. In his deepest heart, he wasn't sure he believed that Aelred wasn't the killer. Was Osbert right—was family loyalty blinding him to the obvious truth?

Osbert drank some ale. "All right, Miles. If Aelred didn't kill the earl, who did?"

"One of the hunting party," Miles said. "Had to be."

People stared at him as though he were mad. Father John's housekeeper, Agnes, said, "You're saying the killer was French?"

"That's my belief."

Duncan the juror looked away in disgust. "That's bloody great, that is."

"And how are you going to prove that?" Leticia asked.

"I don't know," Miles admitted. "I've got two more days."

"You can't accuse a Frenchman in court," Duncan reminded him.

"I've got someone who can," Miles said.

"Who?" Gilbert demanded.

"His grandfather, old Wulfstan," Leticia cackled, and everyone laughed.

The cottar Oswold said, "Don't go accusin' Lord Galon whatever you do."

Miles said, "I will if he—"

"I don't care if he did do it. Accuse him and lose—and you're bound to lose—and we're all dead."

"Galon'll skin us like eels," Tom the swineherd added. "I hear he done it to people in France—skinned 'em alive."

"Miles is full of shit," Four-Fingered Hugh said. "He don't have no one to accuse the French." He shook his mug, spilling ale over his hand. "I won't see my family die because you failed to surrender Aelred, Miles. This is on your head, not ours."

"What can we do?" said the swineherd Tom. "Aelred got away."

Gilbert the hayward said, "We can get rid of Miles as hundred pledge, for a start."

There was general agreement to that.

Miles was stung. He had never liked the job of hundred pledge, but it made him feel respected. Looked up to. Maybe they were right—maybe he did think he was better than everyone else.

Osbert shifted the ever-present straw in his mouth and sipped his ale. "Duncan, can we get a vote before the assize?"

Duncan gave Miles a hard look. Duncan was a ploughman from Riseby. Like Miles, Duncan had connections to the old English aristocracy, which was why he'd been elected president of the jurors. Unlike Miles, he wasn't free, and he envied Miles for that. "I'll try to arrange it. By rights the job should go to Garth, but I don't think the others would accept that, the way things are now."

"I'll do it if you need someone," said Martin Above the Brook.

"Time enough for that later," Osbert told him.

Father John came over and put a hand on Miles's shoulder. "Sorry, Miles."

"It's all right," Miles said. "It's probably for the best."

Father John gave Miles a pointed look. "Remember what I told you. It won't be easy, but—"

Just then there was a commotion at the gate, and heads turned.

Grim the miller had arrived, along with his wife, Diote, and his friends Ralf and Asmundr.

24

"TIE up the dog," Miles told Garth's oldest boy, Alfred. "He doesn't fancy Grim."

The newcomers all carried elaborately carved drinking horns, as though flaunting their Danish heritage. "Greetings, all!" Grim cried brightly. "Sorry we're late. Work, you know." He bowed. "Mistress Mary, 'tis ever a treat to sample your excellent ale." He bowed even more elaborately to Aethelwynn. "Lady Aethelwynn, your beauty enchants."

Aethelwynn nodded curtly.

Grim turned to Miles. "Miles. Surprised the bailiffs haven't been back again, looking for you."

Miles said nothing. He was a bit surprised about that, as well. It was probably because Stigand was out after Aelred with his best men, and those that were left had no leadership. Like as not, they'd be back tomorrow. He'd make himself scarce by then.

Mary poured ale for the newcomers, glaring at Diote, whom she disliked. Grim drank, belched with satisfaction, and looked over the group, which had fallen silent upon his arrival. "This gathering seems a bit . . . heated. I wonder why?" He put a finger to his lip and tapped it thoughtfully. "Could it be because our esteemed hundred pledge has let the earl's killer get away, leaving the rest of us facing ruin?"

Mary might be on the outs with Miles, but she wasn't going to let Grim interfere. "Look here, Grim. We don't want none o' your—"

Grim held up a hand. "I'll bet Miles didn't tell you the best part." He took a long drink and belched again. "Damn, that's good ale. Now, where was I? Oh, yes. Lord Galon has offered to drop the *murdrum* fine if Miles will pay *merchet* on young Aethelwynn here."

Mary and Aethelwynn stared at Miles in shock. Around them, there was at first a stunned silence, then an uproar. Men and women shouted over each other.

"What!

"Are you serious?"

"Why didn't you tell us, Miles?"

Miles wondered how Grim had found out, but the miller was considered the "lord's man" in any village, and he always had information first.

Grinning, Grim held up his hand again for silence. "It gets better, it gets better. Galon offered to make the *merchet* a penny."

This time the yard exploded with noise. Duncan the juror turned to Miles. "Say this isn't true."

Miles was silent.

Osbert was livid. "What did you tell him?"

Grim was enjoying himself. "Don't be modest, Miles," he cried. "Tell them your answer."

Miles clenched his jaw. "I said 'no.' "

Loudest uproar of all. Gilbert the hayward hurled his mug to the ground. "Why?"

Miles stood. "To pay *merchet* is to surrender my freedom, and that I will never do."

"What about the rest of us?" Mary said, shoving Miles. "Have you thought about us?"

"He never thinks about no one 'cept himself," Leticia said.

"Thinks he's better than us," said the ale wife's husband, Ivo.

Gilbert seethed. "You bastard, Miles."

Aethelwynn pushed through the crowd and stood in front of Miles. "Take his offer, Father. It doesn't bother me to be unfree. All my friends are—"

"It bothers *me*," Miles said. "There will be no *merchet* on your head, not while I live."

"That part can be arranged," said Grim's sleepy-eyed friend Asmundr.

"Shut up, Asmundr," Mary said. "You're not one of us." Asmundr was regarded as a newcomer to the village, though he had been there fourteen years. He was the only male villager not born there.

Grim went on, grinning, addressing Aethelwynn. "Better talk him into it quick, lass. You're turning into a right old spinster."

Diote and Ralf, who were siblings, laughed at that. Diote regarded Aethelwynn with hard blue eyes "Young Wynn's got a wet, ripe field in serious need of ploughin'," she observed. "Got anybody in mind, sweetie?"

"As a matter of fact, I do," Aethelwynn said defiantly.

Peter stepped up beside her and took her hand.

"No," Miles said.

He felt betrayed. Peter, son of his oldest friend. How could he do this? "This is how freedom is lost, Aethelwynn," he told his daughter, "and once you've lost it, you can't get it back again. I won't—"

"You won't descend to our level, Miles?" Grim interrupted. "Or should I say, *Lord* Miles? Still think you're lord of the manor, don't you? Still trying to be something you're not."

Miles stepped closer to Grim. "At least I'm not a thief, like you. You cheat these people every day. They know your weights aren't accurate, but they're too afraid of you and your bully boys to complain."

"They follow manor law," Grim said, "unlike you. You think I don't know that you don't bring all your grain to my mill? I'll prove it one day and have you in court. You killed my father, and I'll see you—"

"That's right, I killed him," Miles said, "and I'm glad I did. I never seen a man needed killing more. Except you."

Snarling, Grim threw his horn at Miles. Miles ducked it and Grim lunged at him with his knife. Screams and shouts. Miles didn't have time to draw his own knife. He dodged the thrust and grabbed the miller's wrists with both hands.

The two men stumbled around the yard, muscles straining, grunting, each trying to trip the other, the younger man slowly gaining the advantage. They bumped off the table, then Grim reached around and slammed a thumb into Miles's right eye.

A sun exploded in Miles's' skull; he wondered if he'd lost the eye. Desperately he tried to maintain a grip on Grim's knife hand and he swung his knee into the miller's groin. Grim whooshed out his breath and dropped the knife.

Miles stumbled backward, bile in his throat, trying to get his bearings. He felt his eye swelling, knew it would be closed soon. Dimly he saw Grim moving forward again, and he set himself to receive the younger man's charge. With surprising quickness for a man his size, Grim picked up a stool and swung it at Mile's head.

Miles dodged the full force of the blow, but he couldn't avoid it entirely. The heavy stool grazed the side of his head, laying it open. Miles fell to the wet grass. Instinctively he rolled over as Grim brought the stool down with both hands, missing Miles's head and breaking the stool on the ground.

Miles raised an arm to ward off kicks he knew were coming and was rewarded with a sharp blow to his already damaged ribs. He waved his arm again, in desperation, and this time he caught the swinging foot. He got his other hand round the foot and twisted. Grim staggered, turned off balance and fell on his stomach.

Miles scrambled up, dropped a knee on the miller's back and locked Grim's head in his powerful grip. He twisted Grim's head, levering it upward from the chin. Grim's cries became a strangled gurgle.

"Stop it!" cried Osbert. "You'll tear his head off."

Which was exactly what Miles intended to do.

He twisted the miller's head as hard as he could, trying to rip it from Grim's body. He heard bones cracking.

Someone grabbed Miles's arm. "Stop!" It was Father John.

Others grabbed Miles's arms, as well, prying his fingers from Grim's chin.

At last they got Miles off Grim and pulled him back, Grim fell face forward onto the wet grass with Miles struggling to get at him and finish the job.

"Miles, Miles. Calm down." Strong arms pinned him and kept him still.

Wild eyed, Miles looked around. Near the table, Grim's friend Asmundr leaned against a table, holding his broken arm in pain, a knife on the ground beside him. Near him stood Garth, with a mallet.

Garth looked at Miles. "You told me to get the mallet," he said innocently.

Grim's brother-in-law, Ralf, was being held with a hand twisted behind his back by Peter. Grim's wife, Diote, sat on the ground, hand to her head. "Ow," she moaned. "That hurt."

"It was supposed to," Mary told her.

By the house, Chieftain strained against his leash, foaming at the mouth and barking furiously.

"Can we let you go?" Osbert asked Miles.

The left side of Miles's face ran with blood where he had been hit by the stool. "If you do, I'll kill that—"

"You'll already be hauled before the manor court on charges of causing an affray," Osbert said. "Don't make it any—"

There were sounds of horses in the lane. Heads turned. "It's Pierre Courtenay! Lord Geoffrey's with him!"

The party rode up to Miles's gate, harness jingling, Pierre in front, Geoffrey and a squire in the rear. Pierre took in the carnage, then announced: "Aelred has been captured. Stigand got him."

The villagers cheered.

25

MILES was stunned.

Aelred captured? How? He should have been far away by now.

"What happened?" he asked Pierre.

"He has a camp in Dunham Wood, as we both know, and Stigand apprehended him there. They've taken him to Badford Castle until the assize."

Pierre cast an eye at the villagers, who were leaving Miles's yard. Many had topped off their drinking vessels before they left. More than a few were unsteady on their feet, despite the evening having ended prematurely. Some of them muttered at Miles. Gilbert the hayward started forward angrily, but Osbert intercepted him, and Osbert and Pierre hurried them all along to avoid further trouble.

"Why was Aelred in Dunham Wood?" Garth whispered to his father.

Miles spread his arms helplessly.

Pierre came back. "So what happened here?" he asked Miles. "I've seen men carted off the battlefield who looked better than you."

Miles could barely see out of his left eye. Blood still ran down his face from where he'd been hit by the stool. He tried to wipe the blood out of his swollen eye, succeeded only in smearing it over his face. "There was a disagreement," he said.

"More than a disagreement, I'd say. Lucky someone wasn't killed."

Grim passed just then, in obvious pain, propped up by Ralg and Diote. Asmundr brought up the rear of the little group, his broken right arm at an angle. Diote cast a spiteful glance at Mary as she went by. "Bitch."

"Move it, or I'll bash you another one," Mary told her. She advanced toward Diote, but Garth held her back. Chieftain was still barking, upset that he hadn't gotten to bite somebody.

Pierre sighed. "There'll be a nice helping of fines at manor court for this one. I'd best talk to Father John, get his version of what happened."

Pierre started away. Miles turned and put an arm around Garth's shoulder. "Thanks, son."

Garth put the mallet down. "Bugger was going to stab you in the back. You believe that?"

"Unfortunately, I do." Peter stood next to Aethelwynn. Miles went over and shook the boy's hand. "Thanks, Peter."

"Happy to help," Peter said.

"I'm sorry I said what I did about you marrying Wynn. It's just that—"

"It's just that you want her and her children to be free, I know."

Aethelwynn put an arm through Peter's. Her eyes were wet.

"You'll understand one day," Miles told her, and even as he said it, he knew how inadequate it sounded.

Aethelwynn wiped her nose. "All I understand is that you're a mean-spirited old—"

"Shhh," Peter told her, stroking her hand.

"Peter's father was my best friend," Miles said. "I knew him almost literally from the day I was born. Don't you think I'd want you to be with Peter if circumstances were different? It would be a dream come true for me. But we have to accept reality. Leofric would understand, if he were here. He'd agree with me."

"I hate you!" Aethelwynn said. She yanked her arm away from Peter, spun on her heel, and left.

Peter watched her go, unsure what to do.

Miles felt awkward. He wanted to tell Peter to go after her, but he couldn't. He had to stop them—

"Why didn't you tell us that Galon offered to drop the *murdrum* fine?" Mary demanded.

Miles was taken unaware. "I—"

"I never thought I'd agree with Grim about anything, but this time he's right. You'll pay that *merchet* or—"

"Or what?" Miles said. "You'll kick me out of the house? You've already done that."

"You are the most stubborn—"

Garth put his arm around her waist. "We'll talk about this later."

"We'll talk about it now," she said.

But from beyond the gate came a cry. "Miles!" It was Lord Geoffrey, and from his tone, he wasn't happy.

With a look at Garth and Mary, Miles passed through his gate. Geoffrey had dismounted and waited in the lane, his horse held by the squire. He bowed to Mary. "Madame." Then he beckoned Miles curtly, and the two men walked past the church and turned down the lane that led to the manor house. When they were out of earshot of the village, the young lord rounded on Miles. "What the Devil are you playing at? Do you take me for a fool? You knew all along that your boy was my father's killer."

"Beg pardon, my lord, but I—"

"I should strip the hide off your back and nail it to the church door."

"My lord, I—"

"You've put us all at risk."

"But—"

"Shut up! My father's will might not be upheld by the king. Even if it is, and I'm made earl, there's no guarantee I'll be made sheriff, as well. That post might yet go to Galon. And even if I was sheriff, I would have to levy a *murdrum* fine. What, did you think I could exempt Ravenswell because it's one of my own manors? The king wouldn't hear of it. Thank God we have your boy in custody. By rights, I should put you—"

"Aelred didn't do it," Miles blurted.

Geoffrey stared, wide eyed with rage.

Miles went on quickly. "Someone stole his arrows and used them to kill your father."

Geoffrey kept staring. "That's absurd. A child could make up a better story than that. And who are you saying took the arrows?"

"I—I'm not sure."

Geoffrey's anger flared again. "You're not sure because your son is the killer, and you're trying to talk him out of the noose. I don't want to hear—"

"I think it's your brother, Galon."

Geoffrey stared again, and Miles went on. "Galon had the most to gain from your father's death. No one can account for his presence during the hunt—him or Stigand."

Geoffrey took a deep breath, composing himself. "You need to accept what really happened and get on with your life. Your son is a rotten apple, and he's going to get what he deserves."

"My lord, I must remind you, you promised that if I came up with proof that—"

"That promise is withdrawn," Geoffrey snapped. "I should never have given it, I should never have trusted you. There is no proof, there never was any. They'll hang your boy at the assize, and that will be the end of it. And if you're lucky, they won't hang you as well, for trying to help him escape."

Miles tried to say something, but Geoffrey cut him off. "Get out of my sight. Go!"

26

CHIEFTAIN was barking.

Miles came awake.

He smelled smoke.

Thick tendrils drifted down from the roof. Red flames crackled in the thatch.

"Fire!" he cried, swinging from his bed. "Everybody up!"

Garth and Mary woke at that moment; Chieftain's barking had roused them, as well, and they had smelled the smoke. "What's going on?" Aethelwynn mumbled, and then she realized, and she jumped to her feet.

Chieftain barked madly. The smoke had grown thicker in just these few moments. The fire overhead was louder; red flames spread.

"Outside!" Miles shouted. "Get out! Where are the children?"

Garth's oldest boy, Alfred, was up and shaking Cecily and Alfstan awake. Garth and Mary dragged the younger two from the bed. Frightened lowing came from the oxen in the next room.

Flames raged overhead. Smoke billowed, with nowhere for it to exit save the smoke holes and the few small windows. A piece of the roof fell to the floor. The house timbers were on fire.

"The door!" Miles cried.

He put an arm around his nose and mouth. His good eye burned; the smoke was so thick he could barely see. He was coughing and choking; so were the others. He felt his way through the smoke to the door. Chieftain barked ahead of him, as if showing him the way to go.

Miles found the door. The outside of the door was on fire, and the heat scorched him. Ignoring the pain, he lifted the smoldering bar and pushed the door open. Chieftain ran out. Air was sucked into the house, feeding the fire, making it burn stronger. "The children!" Miles cried.

Someone—Miles couldn't tell who because of the smoke—thrust little Alfstan at him from out of the blaze. The boy was coughing and crying. Miles grabbed him by the collar and literally threw him through the open door. Cecily got the same treatment. Chieftain grabbed them by their shirts, tugging them away from the house. Alfred made it out on his own, pushed by Aethelwynn, who followed him.

Miles drew a deep breath. Big mistake. Hot smoke poured into his lungs, making him cough and choke and forcing him to bend over. "Father!" Garth cried, grabbing Miles's back and holding him up.

"Get out!" Miles sputtered.

Garth helped Mary outside, Mary wearing only her chemise, then turned and pulled Miles through the door. More of the roof fell. There was a loud crash as the terrified oxen smashed down the wall of their room and lumbered to safety. Miles heard cheers and laughter from nearby.

Choking, retching, good eye burning, Miles stumbled into the cool night air. There was a tub with water and buckets outside the house for use in case of fire, but it was too late for that. Behind him the house was an inferno. Father John and Peter were in Miles's yard, assisting

Aethelwynn and the children. But they were the only ones helping. A large crowd was outside the fence. Many yelled and cheered as Miles's house and everything in it were destroyed, these people whom Miles had counted as friends, men and women, children as well, their faces contorted, flushed with anger and hatred.

The rest of the roof fell with a crash and a roar of flames. The fire cast the crowd in a Hellish red glow. Miles saw Grim and his wife, Diote, along with Ralf. He saw Gilbert the hayward, Four-Fingered Hugh, Will the baker, the alewife's husband, Ivo. Some, like Osbert, looked on glumly, or in terror, or in sympathy for Miles and his family, but no one helped. Rocks flew toward the group in the yard.

"Come on, Miles!" Grim cried. "Come out here and get what's coming to you!"

"Bastard's betrayed us!" yelled someone else.

Reflexively Garth started away from the heat of the fire and toward the gate, but Miles didn't trust the villagers, and he grabbed Garth's shoulder, stopping him. Little Alfstan was struck in the head by a rock, and he started crying.

"It's too dangerous that way," Miles yelled over the noise of the crowd and the fire. "Out the back the back of the croft. Make your way to the manor house, you'll be safe there. Quick now."

Aethelwynn didn't understand. She looked for her friends in the crowd. "But—"

Miles shoved her. "Go!"

Father John, Peter, and Mary hurried the children off, followed by Aethelwynn. Miles and Garth stayed for a last look at the crowd, which was advancing through the gate now, kicking it down, along with the fence. Some were reluctant to join in, but others were emboldened by rage and the spirit of the mob.

"Hurry!" Miles said.

They made for the end of the croft, Chieftain running ahead, then coming back, then running ahead again. They were aided by the smoke, which drifted in the direction of Dunham Wood and hid their escape. Miles tried to keep track of his family, to keep them together, but it was impossible, not with everyone running as fast as they dared in the dark and smoke. He and Garth went last, keeping themselves between the mob and the rest of the family. Behind them were whoops and cries as the villagers looted whatever of value could be found in Miles's yard.

Grim's voice came through the smoke. "Find him!"

Miles and Garth reached the end of the croft. They shouldered through the hedge, getting cut up in the process. The rest of the family, along with Peter and Father John, were gathered in the sunken path, breathless. Cecily wanted to cry, but Mary held a hand across her mouth lest she give away their position. Father John was wracked by coughs, though he tried to hold them down, so their pursuers wouldn't hear. Through the smoke they saw figures advancing.

"To the manor?" Garth said.

Miles looked down the narrow path. Something told him Grim had sent people down there to wait for them. "No, they may be waiting for us in the lane. Cross the field and hide in the woods. If we can't stay together, wait till it's quiet, then make your way to the manor house as best you can."

"There they are!" cried a teenaged boy—Gilbert's son, Henry.

"Run!" Miles yelled.

Garth and Peter hoisted the children over the fence, while Miles kept guard. Miles went over the fence last, and they fled across the wheat field. Miles was running, hobbling on his bad ankle, trying to keep the others in sight, but it was hard to see in the dark, with only one good eye. The smoke in his lungs made it hard to breathe. The dog ran by his side. Miles tripped in a furrow and went sprawling into the wheat stalks. *Part of somebody's harvest ruined.*

He scrambled up. There was no sign of the others. Chieftain panted beside him.

Men and women crashed through the wheat behind him. "After them!"

Miles had to draw them away from the children. He stopped and yelled, "I'll get you, Grim!"

"There he is! Come on!"

The bulk of the pursuers followed Miles and Chieftain. Miles ran through the crops and furrows toward the wood, heaving for breath and feeling every one of his forty years. The villagers piled after him. Then he was in the trees, blundering around in the darkness. He found a thicket and burrowed into it. "Chieftain!" he called in a harsh whisper.

The dog sniffed at the thicket, peed on it. Miles grabbed him by the collar, dragged him inside and clamped a hand across his muzzle. "Quiet, boy. Shhhh."

Miles's ragged breathing sounded unnaturally loud in the sudden quiet. He hoped the pursuers didn't hear him.

Here they came, crashing into the wood. Searching. The dog wanted to get loose and attack, and Miles struggled to hold him back. "No."

"Can't find the bastard," cried a voice. It was Martin Above the Brook, who had once been family.

"Can't see shit in here," complained Henry.

Weland the smith said, "We'll never find him in the dark."

There was a pause, then Grim shouted, "I know you're out there, Miles, and by God's bones, I'll get you. My father's blood is on your hands, and I mean to have your blood in return."

It was quiet for a moment, then came the sound of men and women and boys retreating through the trees and underbrush, cursing as they stumbled into unseen holes or were scratched by thorns.

Miles listened until all was still, then waited some more lest someone had remained as a trap. At last he rose, followed by Chieftain, who peed on the thicket again. There were no shouts of triumph to be heard, so Miles dared to hope that the others had gotten away. He wore only his shirt and braies. His swollen eye throbbed, so did his ankle. His throat was baked raw from inhaling hot smoke. But his thoughts weren't on his own condition.

That fire had been no accident. It had been set. And Miles could guess who had set it. Garth's family and Aethelwynn could have been killed in the fire—they would have been, had not Chieftain alerted them. They could have been killed by the mob that had chased them, as well.

This went far beyond jealousy or anger at Miles. This called for revenge.

And revenge there would be.

27

Wales, 1086 A.D.

DUSK.

The company halted in the cover of a little hollow. The rain was still falling. The Welsh hadn't caught up to them yet, and Miles grudgingly attributed that to the earl's taking a back route. That could change, though, if the Welsh had been following the newcomers, and the newcomers said they had been. It was hard to believe that these men in the hollow were all that remained of the force that had set out so confidently from Chester in August.

Miles marveled at the earl's energy, at his positive attitude. He never seemed to tire, never seemed to believe they wouldn't make it. As much as Miles hated to admit it, this Frenchman was a good soldier.

From beneath their cloaks, the men produced bits of dry or mostly dry wood they'd collected during the day and bundled them together.

"No fires," the earl ordered, walking around the camp.

"Why not?" Toki said. "It's freezing, and we're wet."

The earl ignored yet another breach of protocol on Toki's part, though he threw a reproving glance at Miles for allowing it. "The Welsh will see our fires in the dark," he explained. "It will draw them to us like flies to a corpse."

Toki threw his handful of firewood to the ground in disgust. The earl went off with his squire, Etienne, looking for a suitable place to try to sleep. Finding a dry spot was impossible, with rain water flowing into the hollow, so the men hacked pine branches from a nearby copse, carried them back, and used them to sit or lie on. The knights Waleran and Pierre went with the earl, as did the washerwomen. The earl wanted the two women near him, where they would be safe from the footmen.

"Wants to fuck 'em himself, more likely," Toki grumbled. "I tell you, I've had it with Lord High-and-Mighty Thibault."

Miles tried to assert his authority. "Stop complaining, Toki. The earl's doing his best."

"I had it with you, too," Toki said. "You're no more qualified to be a centenar than I am to be a nun."

Miles grinned. "I don't know, you might make a good nun. I hear you like it in the ass."

Toki leaped to his feet and came at Miles.

Merleswegen, the vintenar, stepped between them, grabbing Toki's arms and pushing him back. "Stop! We've got enough problems. We can't be fighting among ourselves."

Toki and Miles glared at each other, as Merleswegen, then Leofric and Burgred, held them apart. Young Etienne came back to them, sent by the earl, who had seen the commotion. "What's going on?"

"Fuck off," Toki told him and turned away.

Miles knew he should discipline Toki for speaking to a noble like that, but something made him hesitate, and he missed his chance. "Nothing," he told Etienne. "A little disagreement. Everything's all right now."

Etienne had been insulted by a peasant, but he was seventeen years old and obviously unsure what to do about it. He gave Toki a look that was meant to be stern, then returned to the earl's position.

Guards were set. The two horses were picketed and stood disconsolately in the rain with their heads down. Darkness settled over the hollow, though it was already so dark from the rain clouds that full night came almost unnoticed. Miles sat on a pile of pine branches—there weren't enough to make a proper bed to lie on. He huddled with his cloak around him, the hood pulled over his head. Raindrops pattered on his helmet through the wool of the hood. He was hungry and shivering with cold and fever—they all were.

Men hurried back and forth from the makeshift camp to attend to the endless demands of dysentery, and there were curses as they stepped in other men's leavings. The wounded, both those who had been riding and those who had been walking, settled in as best they could. Five of their number had succumbed since the march started and had been left unburied in the brush, to give them a little cover from the Welsh.

"No fires, no food, no nothing," jut-jawed Oslac complained. "No burials, neither, nor proper prayers for the dead. It ain't right."

"Aye," said the pedlar Guthric. "This expedition's been marked from the beginning. It started when Father Damien died."

The company's chaplain, Damien, and his assistant, Thomas, had died of fever while the army was still in camp in Chester.

“That were a sign,” Guthric went on, and the men around him nodded earnestly. “Showed God didn’t approve of the expedition.”

“God don’t give a toss one way or the other,” Merleswegen told them. Merleswegen was the stolid type who was the backbone of every army. “He’s got better things to do than worry about us.”

“That’s not what Father Damien said,” Guthric retorted.

Leofric ignored the talk and stuffed his fists in his armpits to warm them. He hunkered down. “Damn, it’s cold,” he told Miles. “This weather reminds me of that last foot-ball match between us and Riseby.”

“Aye,” Miles said. So that only Leofric could hear, he added, “Only time in my life I ever liked Toki.”

Leofric laughed.

The annual foot-ball match between Ravenswell and Riseby was held on Shrove Tuesday. It was a huge rivalry, and the match three years ago had been especially memorable. Played in a cold, driving rain, it had begun in a meadow halfway between the two villages and lasted almost the entire day until at last Toki kicked the pig’s bladder through the open door of St. Guthlac’s church in Riseby. During the course of the match, one man was killed, one lost an eye, and numerous others suffered broken bones or other injuries. The men of Ravenswell were drunk for days afterward. Church authorities had been so horrified by the violence that they had banned future matches and threatened to excommunicate anyone who tried to play.

Leofric went on. "All our lives, you and me waited to be in that match. Only the second time we get to play, and they go and ban it on us."

"They'll bring it back someday," Miles assured him.

"Won't do us no good if we're dead here in Wales," said skinny Wat o' Riseby, who had been listening. "Anyway, your lot were lucky that day. Our Tam, God rest his soul, he kicked the ball at your church door, but that damned priest of yours cheated and shut the door on him before it could go through."

Miles and Leofric, along with Oslac, who had also been listening, laughed. Leofric spread his arms innocently. "Divine intervention, I'd say."

While Oslac and Wat continued to yarn about foot-ball, Miles turned to Leofric. "Sorry I dragged you into this."

Leofric shrugged. "Too late to do anything about it now. Besides, you never went anywhere without me before, I wasn't going to let you do it this time." Miles and Leofric had been born nine days apart. Their mothers were best friends, and the two of them had been inseparable their entire lives. Leofric went on. "Hope it was worth it, though. You got ideas how to beat the French now?"

"I do," Miles said. "We'll fight 'em like the Welsh do. Hit and run. Ambushes. We won't risk a full-on battle till we've whittled 'em down. Then we'll kill them all and take the country back."

"And who's to be king when we succeed? Not the Aetheling."

Edgar the Aetheling was the last heir to the house of Wessex. Since the conquest of England, he had been kept in compliant semi-captivity by the French. “No, he’s spineless,” Miles said. “Anyway, I’m not interested in England. I want to restore Mercia, you know that.”

Leofric raised his brows. “Going to be hard to find somebody from the Mercian royal line.”

“I know that. Must be somebody out there, though. We just have to figure out who. The French have done a good job of killing off all our nobility.”

“Sure you don’t want to do it?”

“Me? King of Mercia? There’s no way. All I want is Ravenswell back.” He paused. “All right, and maybe to be earl of Trent. Figure being earl is my reward.”

“That would make you one of the most powerful nobles in Mercia.”

“I still don’t want to be king,” Miles said.

“Old Thibault won’t like it if he knows you’re after his job,” Leofric joked.

Miles snorted. “He doesn’t even know what Mercia is.”

They looked over at where the earl huddled with Etienne and Pierre of Caen, trying to sleep. The two washerwomen, who were Flemish, sat nearby, looking scared. The Flemish mercenaries, about fifteen of them, who had not been accepted by the English footmen, were grouped nearby as well.

“What about England?” Leofric said. “The other kingdoms?”

“What *about* England? The other kingdoms can look after themselves, especially those bastards in Wessex.”

“Is that realistic with the French around?”

"There's not that many of the French. Once they're gone, they're gone. They won't be coming back. When the other kingdoms see what we've done, they'll revolt too."

"And when the French are gone, our kingdoms will start fighting each other again, just like they always did. That was the whole point of making it one country—to stop the fighting."

Miles sighed. "You're not making this any easier, you know."

Leofric said, "Seriously, Miles, do you really think you can lead a rebellion? You can't even command this company. You're losing them, you know."

If anyone else had said that, Miles would have hit them. But for Leofric, he answered honestly. "I know." And he felt defeated, because suddenly his dream of freeing the country seemed like just that—a dream.

28

Wales

DAWN brought watery sunshine. It had finally stopped raining, though the ground had become a bog. Miles had slept fitfully because he was shivering so badly. His hands and feet were so cold he could barely feel them. Like the men around him, he dragged himself to his feet, his body protesting.

A cry of alarm sounded from one of the guards.

Miles climbed to the lip of the hollow, from whence the cry had emanated, hobbling painfully as blood flowed into his legs again. He found the guard standing over the knight Pierre of Caen, who had been in charge of the last guard shift. Pierre lay face down in the mud, his throat slit. Blood turned the ground beneath him a watery red.

"Welsh bastards," the guard swore. "He was robbed, too—look. Purse is gone, and so are the rings on his fingers."

"How'd they get so close?" said the vintenar Merleswegen, coming up with more of the men.

"It was easy with the rain," said the guard. "Couldn't hear shit."

Merleswegen said, "They've caught up to us, then."

"Might only be one or two," offered Leofric. "Locals, maybe, not the main body."

Miles noticed Toki leaning on his long axe, a smirk on his face. He had been joined by Burgred and a couple of their friends. None of them looked surprised by Pierre's death. None of them looked upset.

Miles should challenge Toki, he should accuse him of killing Pierre, search for Pierre's purse and rings, but he lacked the energy. He didn't want to confront Toki. He didn't want to be a damned centenar. He remembered what Leofric had said last night about him losing the company, and he swore. He just wanted to go home.

The earl, Waleran of St. Just, and Etienne had come up. If the earl had suspicions about what had happened, he kept them to himself. Bowing his head, he recited a brief prayer over Pierre's body, then said, "We must go." To Miles, he said, "Ready your men."

"All right, men," Miles called. "Get your things and form up."

The men moved slowly.

"Quickly, now," Miles said. But he spoke without enthusiasm and no one seemed to pay him attention. They certainly didn't move any faster.

The men wrapped their cloaks around their waists, slung their scrips, and formed up. The Flemish footmen were behind the earl, Waleran of St. Just, Etienne, and the two washerwomen. Miles and the rest of the company went next. The earl took his mail hauberk, which had grown stiff with mud and rust, and threw it into a pool of dirty water at the bottom of the hollow. "If some Welshman wants to put this in fighting shape, he's got his work cut out for him."

The earl's squire, Etienne, did the same with his hauberk. Waleran of St. Just, who had gotten rid of his hauberk earlier, left his conical helmet behind, choosing to wear only an arming cap. Etienne removed the earl's standard from its staff, folded it, and stuffed it inside his padded leather gambeson. He tossed the staff away. Miles got rid of his long-handled axe. It was heavy to carry, and he'd never liked it much. He preferred to use his scramasax. He would keep his large shield for now.

"How is your arm?" Earl Thibault asked Waleran.

Waleran sniffed at his soaking wet bandage and wrinkled his nose. The arm was swollen. He unwrapped the bandage. The wound and the arm around it were black. The arm must hurt like the very Devil, but Waleran acted nonchalant. "It'll do," he said. He peeled off the old bandage and threw it away, and one of the washerwomen—the tall one—put on a new bandage fashioned from a relatively dry piece of her shift.

The earl stepped in front of the company and drew on the ground with a stick. With Miles again translating the difficult parts, the earl said, "Here is Northop, and here we are. We can assume the Welsh are behind us, and we know that we must stay ahead of them. What we do not know is what is ahead of us. The main road, here—" he pointed with the stick— "will likely be blocked by the Welsh. So we will go this way." He drew a line running southeast of Northop, then up and hooking around, coming in on the fort from the west.

"That'll take days," Toki complained.

"Oh, give it a rest, Toki," Miles said.

"Or what? You and Leofric will beat me up? Why don't you try it? I got help, this time."

The earl threw down the stick. "Enough of this fighting among ourselves. You can do that when we reach Northop. *En avant*."

They started off. Miles walked alongside his men. Toki was nearby and didn't care who heard him as he grumbled. "So he thinks we're going to wander round these hills till the buggers stop looking for us? Great plan, that is. Me, I ain't about to die in some Welsh shithole."

There were murmurs of approval from the men in line near him.

"What are you going to do?" Merleswegen asked.

"First chance we get, we're going to take off on our own—me and Burgred, and anybody else who wants to live."

"I'm with you," Oslac said, and he was joined by some others. Many wavered, though, reluctant to challenge the God-like authority of an earl, even if he was French.

"We'll take them two women with us," Toki added. "They can warm us up, especially that tall one."

"Till they get too wore out," Burgred the Black added, and a couple of the men laughed.

"Leave the women out of it," Merleswegen warned. He turned. "What about you, Miles? Are you with us?"

Toki cut in. "Nah, Miles is Frenchy's pet. He won't leave his hero. Neither will Little Dick. We don't want them with us, anyway."

They slogged on. There was no sense in trying to hide their tracks, it was too muddy. Besides, a child could follow their trail of discarded equipment and the pools of watery excrement left by the men with dysentery. All they could rely on was speed, to go as fast as they could and stay ahead of the pursuit.

Men tossed aside helmets, shields, even their leather jacks, anything to make their loads lighter. Another wounded man died and his body was left behind. One of the horses, Etienne's, could go no further. The wounded man riding him was forced to walk and the horse was left to fend for itself.

"Nice horse," Leofric remarked as they marched by. "Hope the Welsh don't eat him."

"Faster, men," the earl called from the head of the line.

"Doesn't he ever get tired?" Leofric said.

Miles paid no attention. He stumbled along, chest heavy, weak from fever and lack of sleep. He no longer paid attention to his men. He was lost in himself, lost in self-pity. He was not meant to be a leader of men. He no longer had confidence in himself, in the earl, in anything. He tried to pray, but no prayers came.

They weren't going to reach safety. They were going to die here in this sodden wasteland. Why go on? He wished he had never come, wished he had never thought of being a soldier, of leading a stupid rebellion. It wasn't right, to die like this, so far from home and family.

Family . . .

He thought of Alice and Garth, Alice with a child on the way. How would they remember him? Would they remember him at all?

He was tired and light headed, and his feet didn't want to work anymore. He couldn't take another step. He stumbled. The world was spinning . . .

He found himself sitting on the ground, the wet and cold seeping through him. He tried to get up, but couldn't. He tried to take off his ring and throw it away, because he did not deserve to wear it, but his fingers were too stiff and cold for him to do even that. Nearby, the company shuffled along.

"Don't surprise me," Toki commented as he passed Miles. "He never was good for anything." He spit in Miles's direction.

Miles put his head down. Somebody came over and grabbed his shoulder. "Come on, Miles." It was Leofric.

"I can't go any further," Miles said.

"I'll help you."

Miles shrugged him off. "No. Leave me alone."

"Miles—"

"Leave me alone, I said." His head dropped, then he looked up again. "Tell Alice and Garth that I—"

"What's going on here?" It was the earl. He looked down at Miles. "What are you doing, English? Get up!"

"I can't. I'm done."

"Get up, I said."

"I can't!"

"Get up, damn you. You're letting me down. You're letting these men down. You're letting yourself down."

"I don't care! Don't you see that. I just want to die."

The earl's voice was cruelly mocking. "Is this the best that English nobility can do? No wonder we beat you so easily."

"I—"

The earl kicked him in the side. Hard. "Never give up while there's still a chance. Do you hear me?" He kicked him again. "Never!"

Another kick.

Miles got tired of being kicked and dragged himself to his feet. He stood, swaying, and looked the earl in the eye. "God damn you," he said.

"Get in line," the earl told him. And he turned away.

Miles rejoined the column and stumbled on.

The rest of day passed in a haze of fatigue and alternating cold and sweat. Miles placed his block-like feet one ahead of the other, then repeated the process. He stumbled going up hills, he stumbled going down. He fell, but he got up. He would show that Frenchman. A man named Wenstan put his foot wrong on the rocky ground and broke an ankle. Oslac, the carpenter, fashioned a crude splint for the ankle. Miles took Wenstan's arm over his shoulder and helped him walk, not because he wanted to, but because the earl had shamed him into it. He'd show that French bastard. He regained his place at the head of the English line. He was barely aware of time, had no idea how long they'd been marching, no idea when, or if, they'd ever stop. Intermittent shafts of sunshine slanted through the clouds, turning spots on the hills and valleys golden against the unremitting grey.

The track they were following split. One path, more traveled, turned north toward a distant mountain pass. The other, barely discernible, continued east. Without comment, the earl took the eastern path. Miles followed. Gradually he became aware that there was no one behind him.

The earl realized this at the same time and turned.

The rest of the company had halted, Toki at their head.

The earl came back to them. “What are you men doing? Why have you stopped?”

Toki said, “Northop’s that way.” He inclined his head toward the mountain pass.

“So? I told you, we are going east,” the earl said.

The men didn’t move.

The earl went on. “We must stay together. That is the only way we will survive. We’re going east.”

Toki said, “You don’t get it, do you, Frenchy? We’re done with you.”

The men growled approval. Save for Miles and Leofric, they were all with Toki now, even Merleswegen. Wenstan detached himself from Miles and hobbled over to his friends. Some of the Flemish footmen left the earl’s side and crossed over to Toki’s group, as well.

“Be seein’ you,” Toki told the earl with a smile.

“We just goin’ to leave him?” asked Burgred.

Toki thought about that, and his smile widened. “Reckon we’ll have to kill him. Can’t have him maybe turning up later, saying what we done.”

At that moment there was a distant shout. “My lord!”

Everyone turned. It was the scout, Wat o’ Riseby, hurrying back, unaware of what was happening with the company.

Wat grew closer. “My lord, there’s a village ahead.”

29

Trentshire, 1106 A.D.

MILES made his way through Dunham Wood, taking the back way to Badford Castle. Chieftain had whined and strained at his leash to come with him, but he couldn't take Chieftain where he was going. He didn't want his old friend getting hurt.

He needed to speak to Aelred, though he had no idea how he was going to do it, since Aelred was being held prisoner at the castle. He had no idea how he was going to find the earl's killer, either, but he had to start with Aelred. It didn't help that the lodge bailiffs were still looking for Miles—Stigand would be looking for him, too, now that Aelred had been taken.

Miles's injured eye throbbed, a blood-stained bandage circled his aching head where Grim had hit him with the stool. He was filthy and smelled of smoke. Everything he possessed had been lost in the fire, so Lord Geoffrey had found him an old linen shirt and hose to replace his torn, blood-covered ones. The woolen overshirt that Geoffrey had given him was of faded green.

He and his family had made it to the manor house, where they had been taken in by Geoffrey and Lady Matilda, with Pierre Courtenay and his wife assisting. Matilda had been her usual efficient self, seeing that everyone was fed and given a place to sleep. Pierre and a couple of beadles had accompanied Garth to the fields this morning, to ensure there were no further incidents with the villagers. Mary, Aethelwynn, and the children had remained at the manor house. Father John and Peter had returned to the village, where Peter had promised to look after Miles's animals. The villagers wouldn't have killed Miles's oxen, sheep, or pigs because they were too valuable. And they wouldn't have stolen them because they could be too easily identified. Most of Miles's chickens had probably ended up in village cookpots, though.

Geoffrey had taken Miles aside last night. "I was afraid of this," Geoffrey fumed. "You've pushed your ideas too far and turned the village against you—the hundred, as well. Not only were you nearly killed, but the manor is in disarray—with harvest coming on."

Miles nodded ruefully. "The jurors are removing me from the post of hundred pledge, but it's not official yet. I still have two days to produce your father's killer."

Geoffrey stared. "You just don't give up, do you?"

"I learned that from your father," Miles told him.

Geoffrey let that sink in. "You're either insane, or . . ." His voice tailed off, as though he were too angry or he couldn't find the right words.

"Or I'm right," Miles said.

Geoffrey shook his head. "There's nothing more I can say, Miles. I'm done with you. Destroy yourself and your family if that's what you wish, and may God have mercy on you."

* * *

Miles reflected on Geoffrey's words as he walked along. *"Destroy yourself and your family . . ."*

But what choice did he have? God had tasked him with finding the truth. Father John had told him so, and that was what he intended to do. It was what he *had* to do. If he didn't, his son would die and the real killer would go free.

The day was warm. Cuckoo and thrush called; the soft air pulsed with the whirr of insects. Miles was enveloped by the scents of wild strawberry and honeysuckle. Last autumn's leaves crackled underfoot. Above him, the clouds built fleecy towers in the sky, while the sun pursued its age-old course around the earth.

No matter how bad things were, Miles thought, no matter how desperate the situation, life always returned to the unchanging rhythm of the seasons and the land. Brutality and injustice might seem to rule the world, but they were fleeting. The land was eternal. Man's soul, given to him by almighty God, could never be broken. There was always hope, and hope was what sustained man in his hour of need.

He began to imagine what his house would look like when he rebuilt it. This time he planned to add a separate stable for the oxen, though the children, who thought of the oxen as pets, might not like that. He would add a sleeping chamber where the present stable had been.

If Grim and the other villagers let him rebuild.

That thought brought him back to reality. The villagers—his "friends" and neighbors—might burn him out again, or kill him. They had nearly killed him and the rest of his family last night, and he could imagine that the attempts would continue until one succeeded. The truth was, he and his family might never be able to return to Ravenswell. And then what? That was a future he did not want to contemplate. Not yet.

Near the River Eal, Miles came upon a meandering brook. He knelt to drink, and as he did, he saw his reflection in the slow-moving water. He shuddered. Sweet Christ, it seemed only yesterday that the image staring back at him had been that of a smiling, beardless lad in the bloom of youth. Now there was a battered old man. Life went by so quickly.

He rose and glanced around for the old elm tree. He found it and traced the worn, crude letters dug into its trunk. He had carved his name on this tree twenty years ago. Everyone had told him it was madness for him to learn how to write his name. No ploughman could do that—why should they, there was no need. Few knights could do it, either. Some lords could, but even then the number was small. Writing was what priests and clerics were for. Miles was stubborn, though, and ambitious; he had wanted that skill for when he became a lord, for when the revolt he had planned brought his family back to the prominence—beyond the prominence—it had once enjoyed. But that had been a long time and many dreams ago. Miles's name was carved on trees throughout Dunham and St. Mary's Woods. Future generations would see those carvings and wonder who he had been. That was something, he supposed, a small form of immortality.

The path led to a ford of the river. A huge willow overhung the river at that spot. As Miles approached the ford, he heard a horse snort. He emerged onto the riverbank and stopped.

A tall woman in a belted blue kirtle was watering a white horse. The lady was alone, with no bodyguard or handmaiden in attendance. As Miles left the trees, she looked up.

It was Blanche, the earl's wife. Her headdress was folded back, revealing braids of lustrous black hair that reached halfway to her waist.

Miles stopped. He had no choice but to go by her in order to cross the ford. The next ford was far downstream, and he didn't have time to go around. Removing his shoes—also a gift from Geoffrey—and hose, he started across, the water cool on his feet and lower legs, the willow tree looming. He drew close to Blanche and spoke without looking her in the eye, as was appropriate for one of his station. He didn't want trouble with her today. "Good day, my lady."

It took Blanche a moment to recognize him, and when she did, she laughed aloud. "It's the hundred pledge, isn't it? My God, every time I see you, you have new wounds and bruises. Are you clumsy, or do people hereabouts just enjoy beating you up?"

Miles kept his head down and continued crossing the stream. As he passed Blanche, she stepped back from from him. "And you *reek*! Mary Mother of God, have you *ever* taken a bath?"

Miles stiffened and kept going.

"Have you?" she demanded.

It was a direct question from a noble; he had to answer. He turned to her, eyes down. "Once, my lady. On my wedding day. During the warm months, however, I bathe in the—"

Blanche threw her head back with laughter. "Once? In your entire life? Why, our latrine shafts are cleaned more than you are. You're no more than an animal, and that wife of yours—by St. Margaret's bones, it must be a rare pleasure to lie with her, for I don't imagine she—"

"Do not speak of my wife," Miles snapped, looking directly into her eyes. "You don't have that right."

Arrogantly, she said, "I have—"

"I won't take such talk from a whore," he continued, "no matter how high bred she may be."

Blanche was livid, dark eyes blazing. She lashed Miles across the face with her riding crop. Miles did not blink.

She hit him harder, with the same lack of effect. She swung the whip once more, and Miles caught her wrist in his powerful grip.

Blanche breathed heavily, her pointed breasts heaving beneath the kirtle.

Miles dropped her wrist roughly and walked past her. As he emerged from the stream, Blanche cried, "I'm not a whore!"

30

MILES turned.

Blanche glared at him, nostrils flaring. "I hate people talking about me that way. Now even you peasants are doing it. I won't have it, I tell you. Those stories aren't true."

Miles remembered Blanche in Abbot Joscelin's arms at the hunting lodge. He remembered what Lady Matilda and Morys Gretch had said about her. He kept his tone noncommittal. "If you say so, my lady, but why are you telling me this? I'm a lowly ploughman. What is my opinion to you?"

"I—I don't know, really. I just . . . I don't know. I'm just tired of it. Go away."

Miles wasn't sure how to react. "In that case, I beg you, accept my apologies. I should not have called you by that name. I spoke in anger." He couldn't resist adding, "Being lashed across the face has that effect."

She looked down. "I'm sorry for putting those welts on your face."

"They can be my new bruises for the day," he said, throwing her earlier taunt back at her.

"The day's not over yet," she reminded him pertly. She went on. "About those stories. I don't know how they get started. But start they do, and they grow, and now I'm apparently sleeping with half the nobles in the kingdom. With my eyes set on the other half." She wrinkled her nose and looked at him curiously. "You smell like smoke."

"That's because my neighbors burned down my house last night."

"Oh." The arrogant edge dropped from her voice, replaced by curiosity. "Why?"

"They don't like me."

"Your family . . . are they . . .?"

"They're safe. They took refuge at the manor house."

She said, "I shouldn't have spoken about your wife that way, either. It wasn't right. I'm sure she's a fine woman."

"She was," Miles agreed.

"Was?"

"She's been dead these sixteen years."

"Oh." Blanche frowned. "And you never remarried?"

"Never had the desire to." Miles grew serious. "You shouldn't be out here by yourself, my lady. There's outlaws in these woods, and they'll slit a noble throat as quick as they will a common one."

"I'm not worried." Blanche stroked the white palfrey's muzzle with her long, graceful fingers. "I often ride by myself. The Monteaux are not overly fond of me, and it's the only chance I get for some time away from them."

"Still, you should be careful." Miles cleared his throat awkwardly. "Well . . . I'll take my leave."

As he started to turn, she blurted, "If it makes you feel any better, I still don't think your son killed my husband."

Miles stopped. "Even after the arrow was identified as his? Even after he was captured?"

Blanche let go of the horse's reins. The animal wandered off, grazing contentedly on the lush grass by the river. "It's too much of a coincidence that Thibault was killed by a poacher. It's too convenient. The killer was someone from the lodge, it had to be, and I don't want him to get away with his crime."

Miles was unsure how to reply. Blanche continued, "The funny thing is, Thibault was sick. He probably wouldn't have lived much longer."

Miles nodded agreement at that. "Etienne said much the same thing."

"The doctors bled him and made him drink urine and hot oil, and there were endless prayers, but nothing worked. It was sad to watch. It was almost as if the killer did him a favor."

"I doubt that was the killer's intent," Miles said.

"No." She paused. "What are you doing about finding the guilty man? You don't seem the type to give up and let your boy hang."

"I'm not, but it's difficult to find proof, and there's not much time."

"And proof would be . . .?"

"A witness to the killing, or Aelred's second arrow."

"If the killer has any sense, he's destroyed that arrow by now."

"He or she," Miles corrected.

"By 'she,' you mean me, don't you?" She raised a hand. "Don't answer that. I know you mean me, and I'll spare you the embarrassment of having to say it to my face."

Miles appreciated that. "Do you have an opinion on who the killer might have been? Assuming it wasn't you, of course."

"Do *you* have an opinion?"

"Lord Galon," he said. "That makes the most sense."

Blanche smiled. "I admit, Galon and his pet, Stigand, are a good choice for just about any kind of evil doing that comes along."

"You don't think it was him?"

"He's not my first choice. Though he's on the list."

"Who is your first choice?"

"Ranulf."

"Ranulf? Why?"

"Because he's a vicious swine. Because at home he occasionally resorts to highway robbery to obtain money, being careful to leave no witnesses alive who could identify him. And because he threatened to kill Thibault the day before the hunt."

31

MILES wasn't surprised. He could believe it of a hothead like Ranulf. "Why?" he repeated.

Blanche shrugged. "Money, what else? Money and a title. Ranulf has neither. He needs the money to support his way of life and the title for his pride, and I'm not sure which he wants the most. The moneylenders pursue him like wolves chase a wounded deer. He has a few small estates in France and England, but he's mortgaged them to the hilt with his gambling and spending. And his wife's just as bad."

"I noticed her jewels and expensive clothes," Miles said.

Blanche said. "Ranulf went on the crusade, on borrowed funds. He fought bravely, they say, but came back with nothing to pay his debts. He was constantly begging Thibault for money—that's why he followed him to England. Two days ago, at dinner, he asked for money yet again, only this time he demanded it. 'I'm done begging,' he said. Thibault asked him what he would do if money were not forthcoming, and Ranulf said, 'I'll see you dead, that's what I'll do.' Those were his exact words."

"And how did the earl respond?" Miles said.

"He laughed. 'God knows how my first wife gave birth to such as you,' he said, and with that, Ranulf threw his cup at him. He missed, of course—he was drunk—and he stalked out of the hall, Mathilde behind him." Blanche's lips curled upward. "Meals with the Monteaux family can be 'interesting.' "

Miles thought. "So if Thibault had no money . . ."

"He didn't, trust me."

"Then Ranulf killed him for what? Spite?"

"Spite. Revenge. The two of them have never gotten along. Ranulf was supposed to go into the Church, but he was dismissed for raping a nun, and Thibault had to make him a knight and give him land. He didn't give him enough, at least in Ranulf's judgment. Nor was there a title, which Ranulf took as an insult."

"Hmmm. Would Ranulf be likely to get money or a title from Galon, if Galon was made earl?"

Blanche snorted derisively. "Galon would give him five *sous* and show him the highway, belike. It will cost a fortune for Galon to buy the post of sheriff, plus there's the aid to the king if he assumes the earldom. I can't think where he will get the funds, but I'm sure he'll find a way. Geoffrey wouldn't even Ranulf the five *sous*—and, yes, I do know about the new will. Thibault told me."

Miles made a face. "Is there anyone in your family who's not in debt?"

"I doubt it. Debt is a way of life for the nobility. It's our little secret."

Blanche turned an eye on her horse, making sure the animal did not wander away. Miles rubbed his chin thoughtfully, feeling his singed beard. "Did Earl Thibault ever mention Wulfhere's Treasure to you?"

She turned back. "Oh, yes. *Ad infinitum.* He came to England to find it. Apparently someone sent him word that they knew its location."

"Any idea who that was?"

She shook her head. "No."

"Would it surprise you if I told you there is no treasure?"

"What!" she said.

"It's true. I'm not sure there was even a Wulfhere. I told that to Earl Thibault years ago, but I guess he didn't believe me. Funny, isn't it? He might have been killed for something that never existed."

"My God," Blanche said. She looked down and dug at the ground with the toe of her shoe, as though contemplating something. At last she raised her head again. "Master hundred pledge . . ."

"Miles, my lady."

"Miles, then. I know this is going to sound ridiculous, and I can't believe I'm even saying it, but . . ."

"But?" Miles said.

"When I heard you were tasked with finding Thibault's killer, I thought it was a joke. I'm still not sure it isn't a joke, but I have nowhere else to turn, not if I wish to see justice done." She paused. "Is there anything I can do to assist you?"

Miles grinned at her obvious discomfort in suggesting such a thing. "You mean you want to work with me?"

"Good God, no. I mean, that's not the way I would word it, but I suppose that's what it amounts to. If nothing else, I can accuse the killer before the assizes if he, or *she*—" she shot him a look— "is a noble."

Miles thought about Lord Geoffrey's promise to do the same thing, and about how he had backed away from it. He raised his brows. "I don't suppose you'd take part in the trial by combat?"

She smiled. “No, I’d hire a champion for that.” She fingered the jewels on her rings. “These would buy a credible champion, I believe.”

“Those jewels are worth a lot of money, my lady. Money that a widow like you may need.”

“It will be worth it. Look, I won’t pretend I loved Thibault. He was too old. But I was faithful to him. He was a good man. He was kind to me, and he raised me from a . . .” Her voice trailed off, as though she’d said too much.

Miles didn’t press her on it. He was thinking. “Are you serious about helping me?”

“I don’t say things I don’t mean,” she told him.

“Even to peasants?”

“Especially to peasants.”

“Then there *is* something you can do.”

Miles told her what he wanted, and she suggested a way that might be accomplished, and they came up with a plan.

“Good,” she said. “Now let us make you ready. After that, I must prepare for my husband’s funeral.”

32

"FIRST you'll need to get clean," Blanche told Miles. "Wash off all that dirt and the smell of smoke."

"You mean bathe?" Miles said, looking around. "Here?"

"Yes. Go into the deeper water over there."

"But . . . I feel uncomfortable bathing with a woman present. Especially a noblewoman."

"I won't look, if that's what you're worried about. I'll go behind the willow."

Miles was uncertain.

"I'll make sure the horse doesn't look, either," she said.

"But—"

"Just get in the water, will you? We're not on peasant time. We don't have all day."

Miles turned and lumbered off.

"Don't forget to wash behind your ears," she cried after him.

Miles cleaned himself as best he could, dried himself hurriedly in the sun. After that, he and Blanche went to the lodge, Miles waiting in the woods while Blanche found him a priest's robe. The robe smelled of damp from storage, but there was no helping that. Next, Blanche unwrapped the bloody bandage from Miles's head wound, her fingers cool and smooth as they parted his hair and layered salve on the cut. "This should be sewn, but I don't have time to shave your head."

Miles said, "Should you be—?"

"You're my confessor," she said. "You can't be seen with that filthy bandage around your head."

"But shouldn't a doctor—?"

"I've survived two lengthy sieges, I know more than most doctors about patching wounds."

Miles said, "But . . . but you're a woman."

"So I've been told. Now hold still."

They parted outside Badford Town, Miles once again waiting while Blanche attended High Mass at the cathedral in honor of her husband. Afterwards, Thibault's body would be placed in a lead-lined casket and taken to Montreux, in Normandy, where it would rest in the family vault. Blanche slipped away after the service and rejoined Miles outside town.

The two of them approached Badford Castle. The day had clouded over, with the prospect of rain. Blanche rode sidesaddle on her white palfrey, head high. Miles walked at her side, wearing a brown priest's robe with a rope cincture, and a cowl with a deep hood pulled well over his head to hide his face. He was glad of the clouds because it was hot wearing the hood.

Miles hobbled on his bad ankle. The ankle had turned purple-black and was so swollen that the ankle bone was barely visible. His shoulder hurt; his left eye had stopped throbbing but was half closed. His neck still burned from Stigand's noose, and his ribs were sore.

Blanche was bubbly; she seemed to be having fun. "How do you feel, Father Damien?"

"Like a man half my age, your ladyship," Miles replied.

"Indeed?"

"A man half my age who's been trampled by a horse."

She tisked. "You must learn to be more careful."

"Good advice, my lady. I'll keep it in mind."

A town was growing haphazardly around the castle. The smells of new-cut wood mingled with those of baking bread and meat pies, with animals and latrines. Blanche halted. She left her horse with Miles and visited vendors to purchase items that she needed.

The castle itself was a wooden tower built on an artificial mound. At the foot of the mound was a courtyard, or bailey as the French called it, surrounded by a wooden palisade and a noisome ditch. Blocks of cut stone were piled in orderly heaps north of the castle. The earl had planned to rebuild the tower and palisade in stone, as was the fashion. The artificial hill would have to be reduced first, because it would not bear the weight of the stone. All this meant a lot of labor and expense, and it had been put on hold for lack of funds.

Blanche returned, interrupting his thoughts. "Ready," she said. She had two leather scrips stuffed with bread and fruit. Miles held them and her reins as she stepped on the wooden block and mounted. He handed up one of the scrips, slinging the other over his shoulder, and they continued on.

They crossed the bridge into the bailey. Inside were a church, a hall for the castellan—or the earl, if he was in attendance—quarters for troops and servants, a well, storehouses, stables, mews, and kennels. When the castellan—Miles didn't know his name—saw Blanche, he rushed up with a groom, bowing profusely. "Welcome, my lady. You do us a great honor."

"Yes," Blanche agreed. She dismounted and left the horse with the groom, while she and Miles, carrying the scrips, headed for the wooden steps that led up the artificial mound.

There was a cry from the bridge, followed by shouts as people scrambled out of the way. Miles and Blanche turned as more horses thundered into the bailey. It was Galon and Ranulf and their squires. They pulled up in a cloud of dust. Like Blanche, they were fresh from the funeral Mass, Ranulf wearing a cloth-of-gold tunic, while Galon wore the same old-fashioned style of clothes as he had before, though these were cleaner and made of better material.

The harried castellan left Blanche and made his way to the newcomers. They dismounted and gave over their horses. "Bring something to quench our thirst," Galon ordered.

"Make it wine, too," Ranulf said, "not that piss the English call ale."

The castellan bustled off, shouting orders. Galon and Ranulf saw Blanche.

"Mother!" Galon cried gaily as he came over. "I didn't expect to see you here."

Blanche kept walking, Miles at her side. Miles tried to burrow his head deeper into the hood. "I've come to distribute alms to the prisoners," Blanche said, "in honor of my late husband."

"Why?" said Ranulf. "They're *prisoners*. Most of them are probably English."

"It's called Christian charity," Blanche said, "a concept with which you seem to have little familiarity."

Galon indicated Miles. "Who's the shave-poll?"

"My confessor."

"That isn't Hainault," Galon said.

"Hainault was my husband's confessor. I have taken a new one, Damien."

Galon frowned. "Big fellow. Seems familiar somehow."

Miles held his breath, but Blanche said, "He should be, he's been with us for years. If you'd been paying attention, you'd have seen him in our retinue."

"How'd he come by the limp?"

Blanche answered smoothly. "He suffers from piles."

"Piles?" Ranulf roared with laughter.

Miles gritted his teeth. *Piles!*

"Acquired from a lifetime of sitting," Blanche went on, and Miles knew she was enjoying this. "They're excruciatingly painful, I take it. Make it impossible for the poor man to walk with a normal gait."

Ranulf turned up his nose. "He smells, too."

Miles resented that. He had bathed for that very reason. *Must be this damned robe.*

Again Blanche replied without missing a beat. "He has taken a vow not to bathe or change his robe until . . ."

"Until what?" Galon said.

"Until the Eastern Church reconciles with the West, of course."

"He's got a wait for that," Ranulf snorted. "Those Greek priests in the Holy Land hate us. Half of 'em would rather have stayed conquered by the towel heads."

"You slaughtered a fair number of Greeks over there, as I understand," Blanche said. "So perhaps they had reason."

"They got in our way," Ranulf said.

Galon stepped in front of Blanche, forcing her to stop. Miles lowered his head still further. He was gauging his chances if he had to get out of the castle fast, and his chances didn't look good.

"You should be moving on, Mother," Galon said, "not giving alms. There's no place for you here, now that my father's dead."

Ranulf was surprised. "Moving on?" he asked Galon. "She's not to be your ward?"

"The wife of an earl?" Galon said. "No, more's the pity. She belongs to the king." He looked over Blanche coldly, as though he were examining a farm animal that was for sale. "I'm just glad she didn't whelp. If she'd had a child by the old bastard, we'd have had to kill it to keep it out of the line of succession."

There was a sharp intake of breath from Blanche. "Kill a babe? That's a bit much, even for you."

"Just being practical," Galon said.

"Speaking of practical," Ranulf added with a leer. He crowded close to her. Miles stepped away; he couldn't let Ranulf see his face.

Ranulf got so close to Blanche that he almost rubbed against her. "Come, Blanche," he said "why so coy? We all know what you are."

Cooly, Blanche replied, "And as you are penniless, that makes me unavailable to you."

"Good one, Mother," Galon laughed.

Ranulf didn't give up. "Everyone else has had you, it's my turn."

Blanche said nothing.

Ranulf had an idea. "Maybe I'll abduct you and hold you for ransom."

"Good luck getting anyone to pay," Blanche said.

Ranulf smiled wolfishly. "That's the idea. No one will pay. You'll be my prisoner, to do with as I wish, for as long as I wish. And when I'm finished with you, I'll give you to Mathilde. She's a witch, you know."

"Yes, I've heard. You must be very proud."

"She likes to . . . experiment."

"I'm happy for her."

"Save it for later," Galon told his brother. He stepped aside and motioned Blanche forward. "Be about your business, lady, and don't take long."

Blanche started up the steps to the mound, Miles trailing. He knew Galon and Ranulf were watching them, and he saw that, despite her outward self-control, Blanche's legs were unsteady and she put her hand on the railing for balance. "Do you think Ranulf means it?" he asked in a low voice. "About kidnapping you?"

"Oh, he means it, all right."

"Your husband's been dead all of two days, and already they're—"

"Yes. The life of a noblewoman isn't what it's made out to be."

"Maybe if Ranulf killed the earl, he did it not for money, but as a way to get at you," Miles mused. "Though that's the same thing they say about . . ."

She stopped and glared at him. "About who?"

Miles swallowed. "The abbot of Huntley."

She turned away again, grumbling, and continued up the stairs. “The abbot. That oaf has more hands than a gaggle of beggars. You no sooner get one off you than another appears. He’s been after me since first we met.”

They reached the top of the mound, where they passed the guard and went into the wooden tower.

“Piles,” Miles muttered.

“I thought you’d like that,” she said.

33

MILES had never been in the tower. The stench from the gaol took his breath away as he entered. In front of him, Lady Blanche flinched, as well, though she did her best not to show it. The castle gaol was a hole in the tower's ground floor. The prisoners were kept down there, regardless of their crime or station in life. A rope fence guarded the hole.

Miles looked around, curious. The rest of the ground floor was stacked with supplies and weapons for use in case of an attack. The tower's first floor contained the guards' quarters, while the second floor held emergency living quarters for the castellan. The tower's flat top would be used by archers, and as a place for a last stand. Stairs led to each floor.

Miles turned back. "I have come to give alms to the prisoners," Blanche was telling the gaoler.

The gaoler considered. He was English, a grizzled, lantern-jawed fellow, missing most of his teeth, probably an ex-soldier or bailiff. "Just toss 'em down, my lady. That's what them who brings alms and such usually does. Causes no end of a riot down there. Gets right funny to watch."

"I wish to distribute them personally," Blanche said. She indicated Miles, still with the priest's hood pulled over his head. "My confessor and I."

The gaoler rubbed his dirty mouth with an equally dirty hand. " 'T'aint safe down there, especially for a lady like yourself. One o' the gaolers, not long back, he got drunk of a night and fell over the rope. Landed down there, and the prisoners, beat 'im to death."

Blanche peered over the rope into the hole, studying what she could see of its occupants. "Where do you put female prisoners? I assume you get some from time to time?"

"Oh, they go in the hole with everyone else, but 'tween one thing and t'other, they don't last very long."

Blanche grimaced. "Well, I'm going down. Father Damien will protect me, I'm sure." She smiled benignly at Miles, who bowed.

The gaoler shrugged. "Can't say I didn't warn you, my lady." He hauled over the long ladder and lowered it. Miles climbed down first and held the ladder for Blanche. She climbed down gracefully, missing a beat only as she neared the bottom and the full force of the smell hit.

Some two dozen prisoners were crowded into the hole. They lay on blackened straw, groaning with sickness and thirst. The latrine was wherever one found an open space, save for the seriously ill, who fouled themselves. Water and food were lowered once a day by rope, to be fought over, with the strongest men getting the most. No blankets or spare clothes were provided.

When the prisoners saw people coming down the ladder, they roused themselves, some of them standing. When they saw that one of those people was a woman, they eagerly crowded in on her. Most of these men would be hanged at the assize; they had nothing to lose. Blanche showed not the least bit of fear, though Miles could only imagine what she must be feeling. These men could rape her or tear her to pieces before any help could come. That old gaoler up there couldn't stop them, and Miles knew he wouldn't try. Miles braced himself for a fight.

"Get back!" Blanche told the men icily.

They stopped.

Head high as ever, she said, "I am Blanche, widow of Thibault, earl of Trent, and I have come to distribute alms in honor of my late husband."

"The earl's dead?" somebody said.

"We never heard that," said another.

"Well, he is," Blanche said.

"What if we takes you, 'stead o' the alms?" grinned a black-bearded fellow with a festering sore on his neck.

"Then long before my bailiffs finish with you, you'll plead with them to hang you," Blanche told him. "Now stop acting like sheep and form a line. There's enough for everyone."

Reluctantly, the tattered men got in a line, even the black-bearded fellow, though he continued leering at Blanche. Calmly, Blanche took her scrip and opened it. "I charge each of you men to say a prayer for my husband's soul. Do you understand?"

"Yes'm," they said.

"Yes, my lady."

She gave each man a round loaf of bread and some fruit, along with a few pennies to buy additional supplies from the gaolers. "Thank you, my lady," they mumbled. One even kissed the hem of her blue robe. "Stop that," she told him. "You'll get it dirty."

While the prisoners crowded around Blanche, Miles distributed alms to the men who were too sick to rise, looking for Aelred as he did. He found Aelred in a corner, curled on his side in the filthy straw, his head on the lap of a fellow prisoner, who seemed to be protecting him. Aelred's nose was broken, clotted blood covered his chin and fouled his long, wispy beard. One eye was purple; his mouth and jaw were swollen. His green leather cap was gone; his hair was matted with mud and straw and bits of leaf.

Miles knelt, and Aelred's blue eyes flickered at him uncomprehendingly. "Father?" He spoke as though he'd found himself in a dream.

"Shhh," Miles said.

"Are you his father?" whispered Aelred's wide-eyed companion, a pock-marked giant of about Aelred's own age. "Miles, the hundred pledge?"

Miles nodded, looking around to see if anyone had heard.

"I'm Wada. It's good you come. Aelred, he's hurt bad."

Wada helped Miles raise Aelred to a sitting position. "How are you?" Miles asked his son.

"All right." Aelred sucked the fetid air through his mouth because of the broken nose.

Miles felt his eyes moisten. "They did a fair job of beating you."

"You look worse," Aelred countered with a flash of his old humor.

"Why didn't you run, like I told you?"

"Why should I?" Aelred said. "This is my home. I shouldn't have to leave it for something I didn't do."

"Your stubbornness may well get you hung," Miles told him. "I've brought food and a bit of money."

He gave Aelred and Wada bread and fruit. They ate, shivering in the damp cold. Aelred inclined his head close to Miles and, in a low voice, he said, "I believe I know the earl's killer."

Miles stiffened. "Who?"

"David, the Welsh hermit who lives in Rock Glen. He took my arrows, I'm certain of it. He visited my camp the day they went missing. He'd always seemed harmless, so I said naught about it. Reckoned the old coot needed them for hunting. Then the earl was killed, and . . ."

"Why would this David kill the earl?"

"I don't know. The old fellow's crazy. Who knows why crazy people do things?"

"Why didn't you tell me this before?" Miles said.

"I was glad a Frenchman was dead, for one thing, and I didn't want to see David get in trouble. Now, though . . ." He looked around him, and his voice tailed off, and there was a tear in his eye.

Something brushed against Miles's ankle and he glanced down. A big, sleek rat stood on its hind legs, sniffing Miles's scrip. Miles backhanded the rat across the room.

"Father Damien?" Blanche called from across the room. "Are you ready?"

"Almost, my lady."

Aelred's friend Wada appeared in better condition than most of the prisoners. His straw-colored hair and beard were filthy, and his flesh hung, but there was still a spark in his eyes. His tunic must have been inherited from his father or an older brother, because his brawny arms stuck well out of the sleeves, and his chest looked ready to burst through the grimy wool.

"How long have you been here?" Miles asked him.

"Two months, as I reckon. See that lad there?" He motioned at a heap of rags in the corner. Miles hadn't been able to rouse the fellow to give him alms. " 'E's been here over a year, waitin' on his trial."

"What'd you do?"

"Neighbor says I was ploughin' his land. 'Twasn't true—'twas him what moved the boundary stones. Anyways, there was an argument, and I broke the bastard's head. Don't know my own strength, I reckon. So now I waits on the assize."

"Father Damien?" Blanche repeated, an edge to her voice.

"One more moment, my lady." Miles rested his big hand on Aelred's shoulder. "I'll get you out of here, son."

"Father!" Blanche's voice was insistent.

"Coming, my lady." To Aelred he said, "Take care."

"I'll look after him," Wada said.

"Thanks," Miles said, handing him a few coins. "You're a good man."

Miles rose and crossed the room. Blanche's alms were long given out. Led by the black-bearded fellow, the men were still crowded around her, grateful and admiring, not threatening.

Not yet.

"Stop dawdling," she told Miles in a low voice, "we can't stay here. Did you learn anything?"

"Yes," Miles said. "I'll tell you when we get out of here."

Miles put his foot on the ladder. He would go first and hand Blanche up. He started climbing, then stopped.

34

VOICES sounded above him. "D'ye think young Geoffrey will rebuild this castle?" Ranulf asked. "Assuming Father's will goes through, that is?"

Blanche pushed Miles from behind, urging him up the ladder. He turned, put a finger to his lips, got a dirty look from her.

"If he wants to keep it, he will," Galon answered. "Geoffrey's not fond of war, like a good knight should be, though, so who knows what he'll do." A thump of fist against wood. "Not many of these wooden castles left in Normandy. This place is a relic—I could take it in a day. Doesn't say much for the English that they haven't. Haven't they ever heard of fire?"

I have, Miles thought.

Blanche nudged Miles again, harder, and he motioned with his hand for her to wait.

Ranulf chuckled. "Castle did what it was supposed to—kept the English down. Lucky they never had a proper rebellion here."

They could have had a proper rebellion, Miles thought. Would have, if he hadn't changed his mind. Burn the Frenchmen's wooden strongholds, kill the lot of them.

Blanche recognized the voices now, and she stood still.

"You returning to Normandy?" Galon asked Ranulf.

"In a bit," Ranulf said. "I have something to do here first. What about you?"

"I'll stay here and join the king's army. I expect to be well rewarded when Duke Robert is overthrown."

"You mean when you betray him? I know Robert well from the crusade. He's a good man, a good knight. It's sad to see him brought so low. He's the oldest son, after all. He should have inherited."

"Fortune's Wheel, brother. Fortune's Wheel. Who knows, I may be brought low one day myself." Galon laughed. "Though I doubt it."

Ranulf said, "I pray we do not meet on the field of battle."

"That's wise of you, because I shan't take you prisoner if we do, unless of course you have something to ransom."

"I have my estates, but they're mortgaged to the Jews."

"Then there's no problem," Galon said jovially. "I'll kill the Jews and take the estates."

More muffled words, and suddenly Galon's feet were on the ladder. Miles ducked back down and got out of the way, motioning Blanche to do the same. Galon half-climbed, half-slid down, followed by Stigand, the perpetual smirk on his face. Miles was surprised to see Stigand; he had figured Stigand would be out looking for him. Miles averted his head, lest Galon or Stigand recognize him.

Galon looked surprised to see Blanche. "Still here, Mother?"

"Just leaving," Blanche said. "Don't tell me you've come to give alms."

"Hardly," Galon said. "I've come for a look at my father's killer." To Stigand he said, "Which one is he?"

Stigand pointed at Aelred. “There, my lord. In the corner.”

Galon motioned to Wada. “You! Stand him up. Let’s see the beggar.”

Wada rose to his feet. “Beg pardon, my lord, but ‘e’s hurt too bad to stand.”

Galon’s voice went cold. “I said, stand him up.”

“But your lordship, he can’t—”

With one step Galon crossed the room and stunned Wada with a blow to the neck. He punched Wada again, just below the heart. Wada doubled over, and Galon kneed him in the face.

Wada did not resist, nor did any man come to his aid. Miles wanted to help the boy, but couldn’t, lest he be recognized. Galon was wild eyed. He kicked Wada in the groin; he rained blows on the big ploughboy’s head and shoulders. Wada bent. He backed against the wall, crying, but refused to go down. His face was pulp; blood splattered Galon’s brown shirt.

Suddenly Galon’s fist was grabbed in mid-air. “That’s enough!” Blanche cried.

Galon whirled on her, red faced. “How dare you!”

“You’ll kill him,” Blanche said.

“What if I do?”

“Then you’ll be thwarting the king’s justice, you fool. Killing a villein with your bare hands is against the laws of this kingdom.” She paused. “It is also against the laws of knighthood. And of God.”

Galon’s chest heaved. Miles thought he was going to hit Blanche. At last he calmed. “If you were not a woman . . .”

"Don't let that stop you," she said.

Galon drew back his fist.

Quickly Stigand moved between them. "My lord."

Galon hesitated, then stepped back, lowering his arm. He pointed. "Look to your safety, Lady Blanche. You no longer enjoy my father's protection. You have no one on your side but that sore-assed priest, and he's not likely to be much help."

Galon shouldered past Blanche and mounted the ladder, the prisoners scurrying out of his way. Stigand smirked at Blanche, "My lady," and followed.

"Are you all right?" Miles asked Blanche when they were gone.

Her breathing was quick and shallow. "Yes. Galon was right—you weren't much help."

"I'm wanted, you know that. If Galon found out who I was, he'd string me up right here, without waiting for the assize. I can't find your husband's killer if I'm dead."

"You always have an excuse."

Miles went over to Wada, who had collapsed to his hands and knees, blood dripping to the dirty straw beneath him. Miles gently eased him to a sitting position against the earthen wall. "I'm sorry, boy. I wish this hadn't happened."

"So . . . so do I," joked Wada through a blood-filled mouth. "Wanted to look pretty when they hang me."

Miles had nothing to say to that. Blanche came up behind him. She handed Wada a silver coin. "Buy whatever you need from the gaolers," she told him. "If you need more, have the gaolers send to me for it at St. Mary's Lodge."

“Th-thank you, my lady,” Wada said.

Miles cast Aelred a furious glance. “Are you happy? Because of your stupidity, this boy’s been beaten half to death.”

Aelred hung his head.

Blanche took Miles’s arm. “Be quiet for once, English, and let’s leave this place while we still can.”

35

"WHY did you call me that?" Miles asked Lady Blanche as they left the tower.

"Call you what?"

" 'English.' "

"What was I supposed to call you? 'Spanish?' "

"Miles is my name."

"We're not on a name-to-name basis. You call me 'my lady,' and I call you whatever comes to mind."

" 'English' is what your husband used to call me, when we were in Wales."

"Maybe you never shut up for him, either. Merciful God in Heaven, I thought you were going to stay in that hole talking forever."

They went down the steps of the artificial mound and reached the bailey, where Blanche retrieved her white palfrey. She mounted, Miles again holding the reins, and they left the castle through the nascent town.

"Were you scared back there, my lady?" Miles said.

"Of course I was scared. I was scared out of my wits. I still am. I thought they'd—I'm not sure what I thought they'd do, but I didn't think it would be pleasant. That black-bearded rogue with the sore on his neck terrified me. I get a chill down my back when I think about the way he looked at me."

"You backed him off with that talk of your bailiffs," Miles said. "You don't have any bailiffs, do you?"

"No, but he didn't know that. Then Galon showed up, to make everything perfect. And all the while, you babbled away. Now what was it you learned? It had better be worth it."

Miles told her what Aelred had said about the hermit, David.

Blanche reined in the palfrey. "A hermit? What nonsense is this? Do you seriously believe some hermit killed my husband?"

"No, but Aelred does. Either way, I'll have to talk to the fellow."

"You mean, 'we.' I'm coming, too."

"My lady, I—"

"You think I trust you to do this on your own? You haven't made a smashing success of things so far."

"My lady—"

"Why do you keep interrupting me? You're not going to change my mind. I—"

"Because there's something we need to do first," Miles told her.

Blanche sighed. "Does it involve nearly getting me killed?"

"I don't think so."

"If you don't think it, it's probably a dead certainty that it does. Let's go before I change my mind."

36

MILES and Lady Blanche reached St. Mary's Lodge in late afternoon. More rain clouds gathered in the west; the temperature had fallen. Miles was still disguised as a priest, and he pulled the hood of his cowl up as they neared the gate, so he wouldn't be recognized—he had escaped from the lodge gaol but a day before. His hands were still sore from the splinters that had gotten stuck in them as he went over the lodge wall.

"Last time I passed through this gate, I was tied to a horse like a sack of grain," Miles said.

"An appropriate disguise," Blanche said, "you'd make an excellent sack of grain. I wish I'd thought of that."

"Not many people about," Miles observed.

Blanche halted the palfrey and jumped gracefully from the sidesaddle. "Today's hunt started late because of my husband's funeral Mass. They'll be back soon, though. Is it really necessary that we stop here?"

"Yes," Miles said. "Something Morys Gretch said got me thinking."

"Ah, Morys Gretch. How did your talk with Morys go?"

"He's an interesting fellow, if 'interesting' is the right word for a man like that."

"What do you mean, 'a man like that'?"

"For one thing, he left me in no doubt that I was fortunate to depart Badford alive."

"Why? Wait, let me guess. Like a sack of grain, you came right out and asked him if he was the killer?"

"I didn't have to. He figured out that's why I'd come to see him."

"It was probably easy for him to do. You're not terribly subtle."

Miles spread his arms helplessly. "I'm a peasant, my lady. I'm not supposed to be subtle."

"I take it you don't think Morys did it then. Otherwise, we wouldn't be here."

"Morys is capable of it, but the reasons he gave for not doing it were pretty convincing. To me, anyway."

"Who did he think did it then? Wait again—me. Right?"

"He, ah, did allude to that possibility." Miles didn't repeat Morys's boast about being able to bed her. He was still unsure which Blanche was the real one—the faithful wife, eager to find her husband's killer, or the wanton that everyone described.

She sighed. "And here I barely know the fellow. Why does he think I did it?"

Miles reddened, and before he could answer, she said, "Never mind. 'My Satanic lust' or something like that, right?"

"Something like that, my lady."

She shook her head. "So what did he say that makes you want to come back here?"

"He—"

At that moment, a large alaunt charged across the yard and leaped on Blanche, putting its paws on her shoulders and licking her face. She pushed the dog down, stunned at first, then laughing.

"Brutus, stop!"

It was Abbot Joscelin. The handsome abbot hurried over, the knotted cords of his cincture swaying as he jogged, and he took the dog by its thick collar. "Sorry about that, my lady."

Blanche brushed dirt from her blue kirtle. "That's all right." She petted the dog. "Good boy."

Despite the clouds, the heavy gold and silver crucifix Joscelin wore on his chest seemed to shine. "I've been looking for you," he told Blanche. "You disappeared after the funeral."

"I stayed in Badford to distribute alms," Blanche explained. " 'Looking for me'—is that why you're not with the hunt?"

"Yes. Much as I enjoy the hunt, I was hoping to spend some time with you, instead." With a meaningful look toward Miles, he added, "Alone."

A squirrel caught the dog's eye, and it whimpered. Joscelin let the dog go, and it chased the squirrel into the garden. Joscelin indicated Miles. "Who is this?"

"Father Damien, my new confessor."

"Big fellow," Joscelin remarked. He talked about Miles like Miles wasn't there. "Why does he limp?"

"He used to be a knight," Blanche replied blandly. "Injured himself in the Holy Land." She was enjoying herself again at Miles's expense. "Fell from his horse, or fell from a whore—I couldn't quite understand him when he told me about it—and after that, he decided to devote his life to Christ."

Well, it was better than saying that he had piles.

Blanche turned and gave Miles a knowing look that went unseen by the abbot. "Father, would you give us a moment? Perhaps say a few prayers in the chapel?"

Miles bowed and moved off. He didn't say anything for fear that the abbot would recognize his voice. Blanche and the abbot were next to one of the storehouses. Miles entered the storehouse from the rear. It was nearly empty this close to the harvest. The air was thick with dust; it smelled of straw and grain and moldy canvas. A battle-scarred cat ignored Miles while patrolling for mice. From outside, Miles heard voices. He went to the front and peered through the crack between the doors.

Joscelin was speaking. ". . . think you've learned where that treasure is, and you don't want to share it with me."

"Are you interested in me or the treasure?" Blanche said.

"You, of course, but I also—"

"That's what I thought."

"You make it seem as though you don't wish to see me anymore."

"My," Blanche said, "aren't you astute? Next you'll be telling me you can count to five."

"You've never indicated that my attentions toward you were unwanted before."

"Yes, but now I weary of them. I'm not naïve, Joscelin. I know your intent. Your reputation as a womanizer is legendary."

"Perhaps, but I've never felt about any of those women the way I feel about you." He took her hand. "I'm in love with you."

This seemingly heartfelt declaration seemed to have no effect on Blanche. She raised her eyebrows airily. "Aren't you supposed to be in love with Christ?"

"You're a cold woman, Blanche. I'm a man of the cloth because I have to be, not out of any calling, you know that. I'm a second son, I was put into the Church to advance my family's interests. It was never my desire to live a life of chastity, and it still isn't."

Blanche was unimpressed. "But now that you're part of the Church, don't you—?"

"No, I don't." He took hold of her shoulders. "I'm a man. I have needs. And what I need is you. I need you beside me, or at least near me. Always."

"And when I bear your children as a result of this arrangement? As I most assuredly would."

"They will be looked after by my family in Normandy. Raised as nobles. A word from me can get you into the priory of Mt. Carmel. Mt. Carmel isn't far from Huntley, and they are discreet there—"

Blanche held up a hand. "Don't bother. I've found your company amusing, Joscelin, but I'm never going to share your bed."

Joscelin stepped toward her. "You vixen. You led me on."

"No, you led yourself on. You believe you're irresistible to women." She paused, suspicious. "Did you kill my husband? Is that how you hoped to get the treasure?"

"What!" he said. "Of course not. You were with me when I found the body, how could I have—?"

"You could have paid someone to do it."

"What kind of man do you take me for?"

"I don't know. It occurs to me that I really don't know you at all. It also occurs to me that you had little to lose by committing such a crime. Were you to be charged with my husband's death, you could only be tried in Ecclesiastical court, and Ecclesiastical courts never reach a guilty verdict on someone referred to them by the civil authorities."

That was a good point; Miles hadn't thought of that.

"I did not have your husband killed," Joscelin told her.

"Then who did it?"

"That boy, of course. The one they're to hang the day after tomorrow."

"You can't really believe that. Thibault's death was too convenient for too many people for it to have been done by some peasant boy."

"You sound like that hundred pledge."

"You mean Miles?"

Joscelin's eyes narrowed. "How do you know his name?"

Blanche didn't miss a beat. "I was there when Galon tried to hang him, remember? He's a bumptious oaf, but I believe he means well."

"Not for long," Joscelin said smugly. "I had my steward knock down some more of his fence posts. The village cattle will get through his fence and into the crops."

Miles clenched his jaw. He hoped Garth discovered the break before any damage was done.

"How chivalrous of you," Blanche told the abbot.

"Why do you care? He's only a peasant. Since when have you shown any sympathy for peasants?"

"Since never. Still, it seems unfair."

"Maybe it is, but they'll remove him from being hundred pledge for that, so there's a thorn out of my side when the suit for Morton Chase is heard in court. His grandfather was a witness to the English earl's charter, and he might have been called to give evidence."

"I heard they already removed Miles from office for lying," she said. "He's in disgrace, so your good deeds weren't needed."

"You seem to know a lot about this peasant," Joscelin said.

"I know a lot about a lot of things."

"Where did you hear that he'd been removed?"

She had heard it from Miles, but she recovered and replied glibly. "Someone mentioned it at the service this morning. It was Geoffrey, I—"

Without warning, the abbot took her arm, pinned it behind her back, and pulled her to him. He kissed her. She struggled. He put his hand on her breast, fondling it, moaning with desire. She pushed away from him and slapped his face, hard.

They glared at each other, then the abbot spun on his heels and started across the yard, followed by the dog, which had emerged from the garden, tail wagging.

When Joscelin was gone, Miles exited the storehouse. Blanche was shaking. "Are you all right, my lady?"

"I'm fine," she snapped. "Did I question him to your satisfaction?"

"You did, my lady, thank you. It was luck, you running into him."

"Yes, I feel very lucky," she said, wiping his taste from her lips.

Miles went on. "He'd never have allowed me to ask him those things. I forgot the part about Ecclesiastical court." He added, "You missed your calling, you know. You should have been an inquisitor."

She didn't appreciate the joke. "Don't overstep your bounds, master ploughman. I'm only here because I wish to find my husband's killer."

"Yes, my lady. Sorry."

"Now go and do what you came here for. The hunt will return soon."

"Does Stigand sleep in the servants' quarters or the hall?"

"The servants' quarters, thank God. He hasn't risen high enough yet for Galon to let him sleep with us in the hall."

They approached the building where servants were quartered when the lodge was occupied for hunting. Miles's heavy-set acquaintance Eanred stood guard by the building, armed with a spear, to prevent anyone stealing what little the servants might possess. Miles followed Blanche, head down.

"Fetch me some wine," Blanche ordered Eanred as they drew near.

Eanred looked unsure. In his high, gravelly voice, he said, "My lady, I'm not supposed to leave . . ."

He stopped when he saw the look on her face. "Yes, my lady," he said hurriedly, and he started for the hall.

"Quickly," Blanche told Miles.

Miles ducked into the building. There were some old tables inside, along with piles of dirty straw bedding for the lucky few. Everyone else would sleep wrapped in their cloak. Miles looked at the scarred chests scattered about, wondering how he would find Stigand's; he didn't have time to go through them all. Then he saw one with the swan of Trent carved into it—a gift from Galon, probably.

Fortunately, there was no lock on the chest; Stigand's rank did not merit the expense of a lock. Miles rummaged through the chest, sweating lest Eanred return and he be discovered. The chest was filled mainly with clothes—spare linen and heavy clothing for the cold months. At the bottom, he found an ornamental dagger, loot no doubt, and something else, something with a sharp point, wrapped in a linen shirt. He pulled it out.

It was Aelred's second arrow.

Carefully, he arranged everything else in the trunk the way it had been. He closed the trunk and stepped back outside.

Blanche saw the arrow in Miles's hand and her eyes widened. "Is that it?"

"Aye. It was in Stigand's trunk."

"Why didn't the fool get rid of it?"

"That's why I wanted to come here. Morys said that Stigand thinks he's cleverer than he really is. I wondered if he might have kept the second arrow as some kind of souvenir."

"Or maybe as something to hold over Galon's head later, if the two of them fell out?" Blanche suggested.

"My lady!" It was Eanred, carefully walking with his spear in one hand and a full goblet in the other, balancing the goblet so that what was inside wouldn't spill. "Your wine!"

Miles lowered his head and slipped the arrow into his voluminous sleeve.

"I've changed my mind," Blanche told Eanred.

"But . . ."

"Drink it yourself. I won't tell."

"Thank you, my lady," said Eanred. He was puzzled, but not so puzzled that he didn't gulp down the wine before someone saw him doing it.

"Well, that's it," Blanche said as she and Miles walked away. "Stigand killed my husband."

"At Galon's behest, no doubt," Miles said.

"He does everything at Galon's behest. I doubt he takes a piss unless Galon tells him to. I would have sworn Ranulf was Thibault's killer, but the truth is what it is."

"But how did Stigand come by Aelred's arrows?" Miles mused. "How did he know where to find Aelred's camp?"

Blanche didn't seem interested. "The court will drag that out of him, never fear."

A horn sounded in the distance. Another. The hunt was returning.

Miles said, "I still need to talk to that hermit."

Blanche's brows knit. "Why? What use can he be to us now? We know who the killer is."

"There's a few things I don't understand. Like why your husband's body was moved from the place where he was killed."

"Very well, then," Blanche sighed. "It's too late to get there now. We'll go in the morning."

"You're going, too?"

"Of course I'm going. I can't leave it to you. Besides, I'm having fun."

"Where will I—?"

"Stay in that storehouse tonight. It's not being used. Use the loft. After the hunt leaves tomorrow, I'll bring you a horse. It will be quicker if you ride. If you walk, it may be dark ere we leave the forest, and I have no wish to spend the night out there."

Miles cleared his throat. "I—I've never ridden a horse before."

Blanche waved a hand dismissively. "There's nothing to it."

37

Wales, 1086 A.D.

THE company exploded into the village. Urged on by Toki, they had hurried forward on hearing the news from Wat. They had devolved into a straggly line, with Toki and Burgred in front, and that was how they went into action. The earl followed the main body, along with Miles and Leofric, Etienne, and Waleran of St. Just. Wenstan and the other walking wounded brought up the rear.

Some of the villagers saw the English soldiers coming and fled, but most were caught unaware. The English burst upon them in a frenzy of killing. Men and teenaged boys were slaughtered without mercy. They were chased through the village street and into the hills, and there they were killed, their bodies left in the gorse and bracken. A few tried to defend themselves, but were quickly dispatched with axes and swords. Women and children hid under beds or in outbuildings or attempted to escape into the hills.

The village houses were small, most built of rock with thatched roofs; some of the roofs had weeds and grass growing from them. Meager crops grew on the flat land along the stream. Sheep dotted the hills, along with a few cows. Pigs and geese ran or flew away from the killing.

Miles and the earl reached the village. Miles knew—and the earl knew as well—that there was no stopping the violence. It was the way soldiers had behaved from time immemorial. The Flemish footmen joined in the killing. They had seen many of their comrades die and, like their English comrades, they wanted revenge. The two washerwomen cowered next to the earl and Waleran and tried to make themselves look small. They knew that this could get out of hand, and that they could be its next victims.

Just killing the Welsh was not enough. The dead were hacked to pieces, the English soldiers' rage and frustration with the campaign boiling over. At last the killing subsided, the men's blood lust sated. Bodies and pieces of bodies lay everywhere; the men were covered with blood and other things.

"Casualties?" Toki cried. There was no doubt he was in charge now, a Viking warlord at last.

The vintenar Merleswegen took stock. "A few cuts. Nothing serious."

The survivors—women and children, old men—were brought from where they had been hiding and herded onto the village common. The looting of the buildings commenced, starting with the church. Anything of value that could be carried was taken, but there was little of value in this village. Purses were cut off the belts of living and dead. The priest's house was ransacked—he had been one of the first to die. While the men looted, they ate anything they could find, mostly bread and goat's cheese. A lucky few found ale and guzzled it down.

Miles and Leofric had taken no part in the killing, and they took no part in the looting. While the other men dismantled the village, Leofric nudged Miles and pointed toward the hills. There stood a white horse, its color brilliant against the drab, brownish-green of autumn. Other men saw it, as well. "That horse is probably worth as much as this whole village," Burgred said.

"You could get a small fortune for it in Chester," added Merleswegen.

"Forget it," Toki told them. "We don't have the time to chase it down."

Guthric, the pedlar, ducked his head as he emerged from one of the stone houses. "Look at this!"

He showed Toki what he'd found. It was a purse. Inside the purse were coins, more coins than anyone in this village could be expected to possess. The coins, and bits of coins, bore pictures of the English king, William. English coins were discovered in other houses, as well, along with a jeweled clasp and tin badges bearing the earl of Chester's three wheat sheaves.

"They was in on it!" Guthric told Toki. "They was part of the bunch what jumped our army."

Other men had gathered around, and they shouted angrily. Toki's brow darkened. He gestured toward the prisoners. "Kill them all."

The men fell upon the village survivors with renewed fury. Even crippled Wenstan and the wounded joined in, killing in a kind of mad fit, as if they were only vaguely aware of what they were doing. The villagers tried to run, but the English soldiers had them encircled, and only a few were lucky enough to break through the line. Axes were used to kill them at first, aimed at cleaving skulls, but because the villagers attempted to dodge the blows, most of the strikes cut through shoulders or took off parts of arms, or missed entirely, and it took several tries to kill the intended victims. They found it more efficient for two men to hold a villager while another rammed a scramasax or dagger into him or her. There were cries for mercy in the strange Welsh tongue, cries of pain.

"Hey! Look what we got!"

The killing stopped. Everyone turned.

Two men, one of them Oslac, came down a nearby hill, dragging a red-haired young woman between them. The woman resisted fiercely, snarling with the effort, interspersed with what Miles assumed were curses aimed at the two men.

"That's nice," a blood-splashed Burgred observed, watching them. "A beauty, that 'un is."

The men dragged the young woman onto the common. Burgred was right—she was beautiful, her fiery hair bright against her pale skin. Her dress and cloak were made of finer material than that of the other villagers. She was scared but defiant, and as she struggled, she glared at Toki.

Toki returned her stare with a cold smile. "This one's mine," he said. "The rest of you can have her when I'm done with her. We'll see how many of us she can take before it kills her."

He yanked down the front of the woman's dress, exposing high, firm breasts.

"No!" cried the earl. He grabbed Toki's arm, but Toki threw him off.

The earl grabbed him again.

Toki whirled but before he could do anything, Burgred hit the earl in the back of the head with his axe handle.

The earl fell to the ground. Toki stood over him and hefted his own axe. "Should have done this a long time ago."

He raised the axe with both hands, but before he could bring it down, Miles stepped in front of him and plunged his scramasax into his chest, just below the breastbone.

Toki's eyes widened with surprise. Miles twisted the blade, feeling things rip apart inside Toki's body, and he watched the life sliding out of Toki's eyes.

He pulled the scramasax from Toki's chest. Toki let go of the axe, dropped to his knees, and fell on his face.

Miles was aware of a commotion behind him. Waleran and Etienne had restrained Burgred from attacking Miles and had pinioned his arms. On the ground, the earl moaned.

Miles turned on Burgred, on fire with rage, and he jammed the bloody point of his scramasax into Burgred's bearded throat. "Do you want the same? Because I'm happy to oblige, if you do."

"No, no," Burgred choked, drawing his head back as far as he could.

Miles turned on the rest of the company. "What about you? Who's next?"

The men stepped back; no one wanted to face Miles. "Oslac?" Miles said. "Merleswegen?"

"No," they mumbled.

"Look at you," Miles went on, addressing the men, and it no longer seemed to be him talking. "Most of you know who my grandfather was. Do you think he would approve of what you're doing? No. He would be ashamed of you, just as I'm ashamed of you, just as your wives and mothers would be, just as you should be ashamed of yourselves." He paused, went on. "You're supposed to be soldiers, not rabble. We killed the men of an age to make war on us, honor is satisfied. We don't kill the old, and we don't kill women or children. My grandfather wouldn't stand for this, and I won't, either." Another pause. "Now take your loot—that's a soldier's right—but leave these people alone. Then form up. We have to get out of here."

The men hesitated.

Miles flourished the bloody scramasax, ready to use it, wanting to use it. "Now!"

The men hastily began gathering what loot they could and falling into line. "What about Toki?" Burgred asked sullenly.

"Leave him," Miles said. He braced one foot on Toki's back and cleaned his scramasax blade on the dead man's cloak. "These villagers can feed him to their pigs. If the pigs will have him."

Waleran and Etienne had helped the earl to his feet. "Thank you," Thibault told Miles in an unsteady voice.

"Are you all right, my lord?" Miles asked him.

The earl shook his head, as though trying to clear it. "A bit dizzy."

Miles shouted at the men. "Hurry up!" He could have killed any of them and not thought twice about doing it.

Then, for some reason he was never after able to explain, Miles approached the red-haired woman. She stood watching, covering her breasts with the torn remains of her dress. Two older women had taken position beside her, like attendants, one at each side.

Miles halted in front of the woman and bowed deeply to her. “I’m sorry,” he said. He knew she didn’t understand him, but hoped she would guess what he was saying from the tone of his voice.

Her green eyes met his. They looked deep into him, as though she were reading his mind, as though she were reading his soul, and Miles knew that had circumstances been different, he could have fallen in love with her. She gave him the slightest nod of acknowledgment.

He turned and cried. “All right, let’s go. Tie up a couple of these sheep and take them with us. We’ll chance a fire before dark and eat them.” He turned again. “With Earl Thibault’s permission, or course.”

The earl nodded in return. “Granted.”

Merleswegen said, “Which direction, Miles?”

“Which way do you think? East. Now move.”

38

Trentshire, 1106 A.D.

MILES landed on his back in the dirt. He shook his head, trying to clear it.

The horse twisted its head and looked down at him, seemingly amused.

Blanche sighed. "And here I thought you might get through a day without being bruised, bloodied, or beaten. I got you the tamest animal I could find. If he was any tamer, he'd be dead."

Miles hauled himself to his feet, wincing. "Lucky I didn't break my back."

"Stop complaining and get back on," Blanche told him. "At this rate, it will be Christmas ere we lay eyes on this hermit of yours."

Eventually, Miles got the hang of riding. They made their way through the forest, Blanche in the lead. "How do we find the hermit?" she asked over her shoulder.

"I'm not sure," Miles admitted. "Lord Geoffrey said he saw sign of one, but he didn't say what the sign was."

Blanche rolled her eyes. She glanced up through the leaves at the leaden sky, from which raindrops were starting to fall.

"Rethinking your decision to come along, my lady?" Miles asked her.

She didn't answer, but after a moment, she said, "Do you get the impression we're being followed?"

Miles turned as best he could in the saddle without falling off. He didn't see or hear anything. The forest animals had taken shelter because of the rain, so their behavior told him nothing. "Why do you say that?"

"Just a feeling."

They took the same path the hunt had taken on the day of Earl Thibault's death. Blanche had brought Miles some food—quite a bit of it, actually—and he ate as he rode, famished because he'd had nothing since early yesterday. They reached the ford that had been blocked by the overturned cart and continued on, as the earl had done. The path was less well traveled here. After a while it split, one part continuing upstream, the other bearing off to the right, leading deeper into the forest. They took that trail. From time to time, Miles looked back to see if anyone was behind them, but nothing caught his eye.

The rain became steady. They lost the faint trail twice and had to work their way back to it. Blanche wore a sleeveless green bliaut over her blue kirtle, and she wrapped her white cloak around herself and pulled up the hood. Miles had changed from his priest's garb into the clothes given him by Lord Geoffrey after the fire. He had kept the priest's clothing, though, and he put on the brown cowl and hood. Rain pattered on tree leaves and in the undergrowth. The horses' hoofs clopped monotonously. The terrain grew rugged. Trees blocked the view in all directions. The path twisted down one hill and up another.

"Look," said Blanche.

Ahead, by the side of the path, was a shrine. Beneath a narrow timber roof was a box with an image carved inside. The image depicted a man with his hands folded in prayer, a cross haloed behind his head. At the foot of the shrine was a riser on which one could kneel and pray. Next to the shrine was an alms box. The shrine was well kept up, despite the desolate surroundings.

"Lord Geoffrey said he saw sign of a hermit," Miles said. "This must be it."

"The hermit tends the shrine?" Blanche guessed.

"Aye. It must be David, the man we're looking for."

"I wonder why it's out here? Not many tavellers come this way."

"Maybe they did at one time," Miles said.

They rode on. As the path took yet another turn, Blanche said, "See here, English, the assize is tomorrow. We know who the killer is. Riding around in the rain is getting us no— "

She stopped.

Two men blocked their way.

The men wore mail hauberks and conical helmets. They carried long, triangular shields and drawn swords. One was Ranulf. The other was younger and must be his squire. Rain splashed off their helmets in a spray.

Ranulf smiled, the kind of broad smile a predator gives its prey. "Greetings, Lady Blanche. I told you we'd meet again."

Blanche stiffened in the saddle.

Ranulf indicated Miles. "Is this your latest conquest?" he asked Blanche. "A peasant? Scraping the bottom of the barrel, aren't we? But maybe a slut like you likes to—"

"Shut up, Ranulf," Blanche said. "You're disgusting."

"You haven't begun to know disgust, lady. But you will."

Ranulf's squire couldn't have been more than sixteen. He looked both mean and nervous—a bad combination. Miles had only his belt knife. If he tried to draw it, Ranulf and the squire would hack him to pieces.

"What do you want?" Blanche asked Ranulf.

"You, of course. I told you I'd kidnap you. There's a boat waiting for us in Bishop's Lynn. We'll be back in Normandy before anyone even knows you're gone. They're so wrapped up in tomorrow's assize, they've quite forgotten the grieving widow. When you disappear, everyone will think you were killed by some Englishman and your body hidden. They'll think there's a revolt under way. After my father's death, they'll be ready to kill every—"

"Did you have anything to do with Thibault's death?"

"Alas, no. Trust me, if I had, he'd have suffered more."

"What about your money problems?" Blanche said. "You'll not solve them by abducting me. And for certain no one will give you a title for it."

"I've made a deal with my older brother. If I'm able to be of service to his side during the coming hostilities—"

"You mean, if you can betray Duke Robert as he has?"

"If you choose to use such terms. Anyway, if I do, Galon and King Henry will reward me. It's not much, but it's a start."

Blanche waved a hand. "How did you know where . . .?"

"Where to find you? It's well known that you like to ride by yourself. Purcell and I followed you from the lodge. I remember this forest from my youth, and it was a simple matter to get ahead of you."

Blanche looked around, as if for succor, but Ranulf laughed. "No one is coming to rescue you. Before long, you'll be forgotten as though you never existed. And by the time Mathilde and I get through with you, you'll wish you never *had* existed. Now, let us go."

The squire indicated Miles. "What about this one, my lord?"

Ranulf grinned at Miles. "Not so smart-mouthed today, are we, peasant? I hope you don't think I'm going to let you live. I never forget an insult, especially one from a half-human tiller of the soil. My only regret is that I have to kill you quickly. Still, I'll chop you in so many pieces, they'll never be able to recognize your body."

Ranulf raised his sword and spurred his horse forward.

There was a *thunk* as an arrow struck him in the back.

39

RANULF'S eyes widened; he pulled on his reins and swayed in his saddle, trying to keep his seat.

Even as Miles was aware of the squire coming at him—the damned boy had kept his head, Miles gave him that—Miles kicked his own horse forward. He threw himself on Ranulf and dragged him to the ground. He took Ranulf's sword and rose to face the squire.

He was not going to be in time. He saw the eager look in the squire's eyes as the boy started to bring his sword down on Miles's head. Then something hit the mail coif on the side of the squire's head—a knife. It didn't penetrate the mail, but it stunned the squire and threw him off for a beat. Miles dodged the squire's blow, and the horse rumbled past him, and when the squire wheeled the horse and raised his sword again, Miles was ready. It was like twenty years had fallen away. As the squire prepared his blow, Miles stepped into a two-handed strike, pivoting at the hip, and slashed his sword across the boy's belly, opening it from side to side. The squire rode a few yards down the path, then toppled into the mud.

Miles turned. It was Blanche who had thrown the knife. "Thank you, my lady. You saved my life."

"It's a skill I developed to fend off my husband's relatives," Blanche said, "but it seems I must practice more. I meant to hit that fellow in the eye."

Blanche dismounted and the two of them went over to Ranulf, Miles tossing away the bloody sword. The arrow had penetrated Ranulf's mail and gambeson. Ranulf had fallen on the arrow when Miles pulled him from the horse, and the arrow's shaft had snapped, slewing the point around inside his body and causing more damage. Ranulf was coughing blood; more blood ran from his nose. The blood was diluted by the rain.

"There's nothing we can do for him," Miles said.

"There's nothing I *want* to do for him," Blanche said.

There was a rustling behind them and a man emerged from the trees, walking cautiously, bow drawn, a nocked arrow pointed at Miles. He was a wizened, bandy-legged fellow, with wispy grey hair. "What do you want here?" he demanded.

Miles recovered and greeted him pleasantly. "You must be the hermit, David."

40

THE bandy-legged man frowned and kept the bow aimed at Miles's chest. The man's clothes were made of roughly woven cloth. He wore no tonsure; only a small cross around his neck marked him as a man of faith. "How do you know my name?" he said, revealing what remained of his teeth. He spoke with a soft, singsong accent.

" 'Twas you we came here to see," Miles told him.

The man's look of puzzlement deepened.

"I am Miles, Aelred's father."

"Ah, Aelred." The hermit David lowered the bow, relaxing the tension on the string. "Good lad, Aelred." He took the arrow from the bow and stuck it in his quiver.

"He's been charged with the earl of Trent's death," Miles said.

"Aelred? That's hard to believe. Did he do it?"

"No. This lady and I are trying to find the real killer before Aelred hangs tomorrow."

"God send you luck," David said, "but—"

"We're hoping you can help us."

"Me? Don't know what help I can be. Didn't even know the earl was dead till you told me just now. Don't get much in the way of news out here, you know. Got what he deserved, no doubt—high rank and sin go hand in hand. I'll pray for his soul, though. What was his name?"

"His name was Thibault," Blanche said. "He was my husband."

"Oh." David stammered, "I—I'm sorry, my lady. I—I didn't—"

"No doubt," Blanche said.

"When was he killed?" David asked.

Miles said, "Three days past."

"We should get out of the rain," David said. "There'll be no game about on a day like this."

Blanche indicated Ranulf and his squire. "What about them?"

David sighed. "We'll have to dispose of them. If they're found here, I'll be the one the authorities come to see."

"That, or they'll start this damned *murdrum* business again," Miles said.

The hermit had never heard of the *murdrum* law, and Miles explained it to him. "The French are more clever than I gave them credit for," David said when Miles was done.

"Yes, and they're using that law to hang my son. Lady Blanche and I believe the real killer was another Frenchman."

"Or French *woman*," Blanche said brightly. "Don't forget, I'm a suspect, too."

"I hadn't forgotten, my lady," Miles told her.

"Is she really a suspect?" David asked Miles. He clearly wondered why the two of them were together if that was the case.

Blanche answered for Miles. "I'm the main suspect, according to many."

The hermit scratched his head and got on with the business at hand. The squire, Purcell, was dead, chopped almost in half, his entrails spilled across the ground. As David approached Ranulf, Miles stood between the two of them and Blanche, blocking her view. "Don't look, my lady."

"I told you, I've survived two sieges," she said. "I know what happens to wounded men who have no chance of surviving."

Ranulf looked up at David. "Please . . ."

"You've suffered a death wound, son," David told him. "I'm a holy man. Do you wish me to hear your Confession?"

Ranulf nodded.

David leaned in close as Ranulf whispered in his ear. David grimaced at what he heard. When Ranulf was done, David used his thumb to make a sign of the cross on Ranulf's forehead. "*Ego te absolvo a peccati tuis,*" he told Ranulf, even though he lacked authority to do this because he was not a priest. Then, with a practiced move, he drove his dagger into Ranulf's left eye and up into his brain. Ranulf's legs jerked spasmodically. He kicked a few times and was still.

"Looks like you've done that before," Blanche observed.

"That I have," David said. "Done it to many a pirate in my day, and the French are no better than pirates to my way of thinking." Hurriedly, he added, "Present company excepted, my lady."

"That's quite all right," Blanche said. " 'Pirate' is much more flattering than what I'm usually called."

"We need to get rid of the bodies," David said. "Help me strip them of their armor."

There were no shovels, so they couldn't dig a grave. They would have had to cut away the undergrowth in any case, and there was no time for that. Miles and David removed the dead men's hauberks, pulling them over the corpse's heads. Then they dragged the bodies to a heavily wooded ravine some distance away. They pulled the bodies down the ravine and hid them in the undergrowth. They did the same with the dead men's arms and armor, and their blood-stained saddles. Blanche helped, carrying swords, helmets, shields, and bridles.

All this took considerable time, and Miles was glad of the rain to wash the dirt and sweat from his clothes and body.

"With luck, it'll be years before their bones are found," David said when they were finished. "If ever. Will there be a search party, d'ye think?"

Miles said, "Aye, but if we're lucky, they won't come out here. This is off the beaten path. No reason for these two to be here."

The horses, they let go. David said, "The animals will eventually find their way back home, but no one will have the slightest idea where their riders got to, and this rain will wash out their tracks fairly fast, just as it's already washing away the blood."

Using the rain, Miles scrubbed the blood from his hands and arms as best he could. "Tell me, why did you help us just now?" he asked David. "It was none of your affair."

"I'm a man of the cloth, and it's my duty to help those in need. I didn't like the looks of your friends."

Blanche said, "Believe me, they weren't our friends."

"We passed a shrine earlier," Miles told the hermit. "Do you tend it?"

"I do," David said. "St. Egidius, the hermit, it's to, though why 'twas built, or when, is beyond my ken. From the looks of it, it's been there a long time, as has my cell." He cleared his throat and looked from Miles to Blanche expectantly.

Blanche handed the hermit a penny from her purse. "For the saint's alms box."

"Thank you, my lady." David put the coin in his own purse.

David led Miles and Blanche through the forest, on a path only he could see. Miles and Blanche had to walk their horses; the undergrowth was too heavy for riding. "How long have you been here?" Miles asked David.

"Don't know, rightly. Years. I was a ship's captain in another life. A merchant. Had a family, traveled the world. Had a lot of money, a lot of material things. Then one day I saw the light. Gave it all away and came here to worship."

"Why did you come to England?" Blanche asked him. "Why not stay in Wales?"

"Because you damned English are always invading my country," he said. "It's safer here. My village in Wales was destroyed must have been twenty years back, while I was on a voyage to Jutland."

Miles remembered the village his company had attacked during the retreat. Was it possible . . .? *No*, he thought.

The rain was still coming down. Miles and Blanche were soaked to the skin and cold. The bottoms of Blanche's white cloak and green bliaut were muddy from walking. The path brought them to a dell at the foot of a craggy cliff. Boulders were strewn about the cliff, and a waterfall tumbled down its face, feeding a brook. The dell was wild with larch and elm and thickets of blackthorn.

"Rock Glen," David announced.

There was no sign of habitation. The hermit must only come here to meditate, Miles thought. Where was his—?

Then something caught his eye—a recessed opening, like a door, in the cliff bottom. As the hermit led them closer, Miles saw that it *was* a door, cut into the rock. Above the door was a tiny window.

"This cell had been abandoned for a long time when I found it," David told them. "Took a bit of fixing up."

They passed a rubbish pile. Cords of firewood were stacked against the cliff side, protected from the wet by an awning made of pine branches.

Miles and Blanche tethered their horses, and David pushed open the heavy plank door. They ducked and entered, and Blanche wrapped her arms tightly about herself in the damp of the hermit's chamber.

The hermit swung aside a thick wooden arm from which hung a three-shilling cook pot, and he put tinder and wood on the smoldering ashes in the fire pit. The room's soot-blackened walls showed decades, if not centuries, of use. One end of the room had been fashioned into an apse, with a crude altar. Near the altar was a table with bread, tools, and a tallow candle. Against one wall was an oven. Against the other was a sturdy bed and, at its foot was a pair of wooden clogs. Miles couldn't imagine how long it must have taken the original inhabitant, or inhabitants, to carve this cell. He marveled at the religious fervor that had driven those older generations.

As the fire took hold, Blanche held her hands over it, rubbing them briskly. David cut slices of bread and handed them out. A slab of smoked gammon hung from a hook in the wall. David sliced them some gammon, as well, and they crammed it in with the bread. Eating made them feel warmer.

"Sorry, but there's no wine, my lady," David said. "Will ale do?"

"I was raised on ale," Blanche said. "It will do nicely."

The ale was surprisingly good. As they ate and drank, David held out his hand. "An offering for the food, perhaps?"

Blanche took a penny from her purse and put it in David's hand.

"Thank you, my lady."

Miles spoke through a mouthful of bread and gammon. "Now, three days past. Did you see anything?"

David hesitated.

Blanche handed him yet another penny. "Are you sure you're a hermit, and not a highwayman?"

David put the pennies in a clay jar. "Three days, eh? I was hunting that day, but nothing extraordinary happened. Sorry." He raised a finger. "Though I do remember seeing a man on white horse in the distance."

"Thibault," Blanche told Miles.

To David, Blanche said, "This man, did anything strike you about him? Anything odd?"

David thought. "Well, it seemed like he was looking for someone—or something."

"Did you see anyone else?" Miles asked.

David shook his head. "No. Funny you should ask, though, because I got the impression there was someone else out there. Just a feeling, it was, didn't see anyone. Mind you, I wasn't looking too hard. I didn't want to get myself arrested for poaching."

Miles said, "This man on the white horse, where was he going?"

"It's strange, you know, because it looked to me like he was headed for Thor's Seat."

Blanche raised her brows. "Thor's Seat?"

"It's supposed to be a huge chair carved out of an oak tree," Miles told her. "The Old Ones used it as a throne, 'tis said."

David added, " 'Twas on that spot blessed King Wulfhere was converted to Christianity." He crossed himself.

"Wulfhere?" Miles said.

Forgetting his station, Miles grabbed Blanche's arm.

"What—!" she exclaimed in surprise.

"Let's go!"

41

THEY left David's cell but David did not follow. Miles ducked back inside. "We need you to take us to Thor's Seat," he told the hermit. "I don't know the way."

David said nothing.

"He wants another penny," Blanche surmised.

"Two," said David.

Blanche stared at him.

"The rain, my lady. And the lateness of the day."

With a sigh, Blanche gave him two pennies. "At this rate, I'll be selling off my inheritance. Maybe I should become a hermit. It seems to be more profitable than being a noblewoman."

David smiled. "This way, my lady."

He led them off, looking every inch the old sailor with his bandy-legged gait. Miles and Blanche followed, walking their horses. The rain had eased, but daylight was fading.

"We need to get home, English," Blanche said. "It will be dark soon."

"I have to see something," Miles told her, "and it can't wait. The assize is tomorrow."

"It had better be worth it," she said.

They walked on, threading their way through the wet undergrowth. Miles said, "I apologize for touching you back there, my lady."

"It's all right," Blanche replied. "I'll have the bailiffs cut off your hand when we get back."

Miles raised a brow. "Only my hand?"

"I'm feeling generous. Though if I have to spend the night in the woods, I may change my mind."

Miles shared her feelings about that; every sane person did. No one wanted to be in the forest after dark. The darkness was Satan's time. Evil spirits were abroad at night, and evil men. If it was at all possible, people remained indoors till the coming of the morrow's light.

The woods ended and they came to a narrow valley, bisected by a stream. At the valley's head was a tall, weathered pillar of blue stone. A series of white rocks, spaced evenly apart, circled the pillar's base.

"A hoar stone," David explained. "The Old Ones erected it to commemorate some event that took place here. Each Hollow's Eve, at midnight, those rocks become men and dance around the stone."

"Dancing rocks?" Blanche scoffed. "Surely you don't believe that pagan nonsense? You're a man of the cloth."

David crossed himself. "I'll not go against the Old Ones, my lady."

They continued up the valley, giving the hoar stone a wide berth. At the valley's far end, at the edge of the forest, was a dark object, set off by itself.

David stood aside and extended a hand toward the object. "Thor's Seat."

Miles and Blanche approached slowly. Miles had heard about this place, but he had never been here and he had always doubted its existence. At some time in the past, a massive oak had been felled, and the base of its trunk had been carved into a chair—or throne, for that was what it resembled. The throne looked like it had been built for a giant; it would take a large man—larger than Miles—to sit there and not appear dwarfed by his surroundings. Not for the first time, Miles wondered who the Old Ones had been, and what had happened to them. Two half-logs of different heights were placed at the throne's right hand, as steps for a person to mount and sit. The throne's armrests featured a carved head at each end, worn by time and use but still recognizable—on the right side, the head of a man; on the left, the head of a woman. On the throne's back was a shield-like device with strange writing on it. Miles had never seen that kind of writing, even in Wales. The figures reminded him of chicken tracks. At the throne's foot was another shield with more of the strange writing. Flecks of color showed that the throne had once been painted. Disc-shaped fungi grew in cracks in the tree's roots and on other parts of the throne.

"I've never seen anything like it," Blanche marveled. She turned to David. "How old—?" She stopped. "Where did he go?"

David was nowhere in sight. While Miles and Blanche had been examining Thor's Seat, the hermit had slipped away.

"Why, that . . ." Blanche stopped, because in her anger she couldn't come up with the proper word.

"Guess he didn't want to be out after dark," Miles said.

"Neither do I," Blanche snapped. "I mean this whatever-it-is is nice, but why did we have to come all this way to see it?"

Miles had stopped looking at the throne. He squatted nearby, holding his horse's reins with one hand, running his fingers through the muddy soil with the other. “See this?” He held up some of the dirt. “It’s loam. This is the soil that was on your husband’s clothes when he was killed.”

Blanche moved closer, peering at the dirt in Miles’s hand. “So you’re saying . . .?”

“I’m saying Earl Thibault was killed here. Or near here.” He got up and inspected the ground, walking the wet grass in a widening circular pattern. “The rain has washed away any tracks. I’d like to have known how many horses were present. It’s washed away the blood, too, so we won’t know the exact spot where the crime was committed.”

Blanche shook her head. “I don’t understand. Why kill Thibault here?”

“Wulfhere, the legendary king of Mercia,” Miles told her. “David said this is the place where Wulfhere converted to Christianity. If that’s so, it stands to reason that this spot would also have some link to . . .”

Blanche understood. “To that treasure,” she said.

Miles nodded. “Wulfhere’s Treasure. Your husband was lured to this spot by someone who knew about the treasure and your husband’s infatuation with it.”

Miles rubbed a hand across his bearded face, and of a sudden everything became clear to him. He knew why the earl’s body had been moved. He also knew who the killer was.

42

NIGHT was closing in. The rain had picked up again.

"Sorry, my lady," Miles told Blanche. "I was hoping we could get back before dark."

Blanche was clearly unhappy about having to spend the night in the forest. "Was coming out here worth it?" she demanded.

"It was," he said.

She waited, but he did not say more.

"Would you care to elaborate?" she asked.

"I'd prefer to wait, my lady."

"Mary's milk, you still don't trust me, do you?"

"It's not that, my lady, but I could be wrong, and I don't want to accuse an innocent person. We'll know the truth soon enough."

"You have a plan, then?"

"I do, my lady."

"And I suppose you won't tell me that, either?"

"Not just yet."

"My God, I—"

"I'm still thinking it through," Miles said.

"Of course, all this assumes that we live through the night."

"We should be all right," he assured her, hoping he sounded more confident than he felt. "Demons won't be out in this weather." He changed the subject. "We'd best look for shelter while there's still light."

They left Thor's Seat, moved out of the valley and into the higher—and hopefully drier—ground of the woods. They spread out, walking their horses, seeking a place to spend the night.

"English!" Blanche called.

Miles joined her; it was already so dark among the trees that he had to follow the sound of her voice. "Look here," she said.

She stood on a spot of more or less level ground, amid the ruins of an old stone building. The stones were ancient and badly dressed, piled upon one another. Only the base of two walls remained, along with bits of the other walls. Large trees grew in what had been the building's center. The point where the two walls intersected was out of the rain, though just barely.

"Some kind of temple, belike," Miles said, "made of stone the way it is. No idea who built it. Well, it's as good as we're like to find."

He and Blanche unsaddled and hobbled their horses. The animals stood patiently with their heads down in the rain, Blanche's white mare standing out in the deepening gloom. Miles spread armloads of old leaves and topped them with layers of branches for a seat. He drew the priest's robe from his saddlebag and donned it for warmth in place of his sodden regular clothes. Blanche looked away out of modesty as he changed. He and Blanche sat against the ancient wall, the stone rough and grating against their backs. The dry area provided by the walls was small, and they were forced to sit uncomfortably close to one another. Blanche had a bit of bread in her scrip, which she shared.

"Thank you, my lady," Miles said. He shivered as he ate. "Wish I had my old rabbit fur cloak."

"It burned with your home?" she said.

He nodded. "Everything did."

"Will you rebuild?"

"That's the plan."

"And the neighbors who burned you out? What will they say to that?"

"That's the problem. We might get burned out again. *Will* get burned out, if some of my neighbors have their way. Still, I don't see what else we can do. Ravenswell is our home. We have nowhere else to go." He paused. "What about you, my lady? Where will you go when this is over? Galon said you'll be a ward of the king?"

"Galon was wrong," Blanche said. "I'll not be married off to the highest bidder like some brood mare."

"But you must remarry."

"You didn't," she shot back.

"That was different. I'm just a—"

"Just a peasant; yes, I know. I won't remarry, and I won't enter a nunnery. Thibault gifted me with two manors in the west of this shire, as part of our marriage settlement. I shall retire there and live a life of peace and solitude. Raise horses, perhaps."

"King Henry will never permit you to go out of his gift," Miles said.

"Oh, yes, he will. He'll grant me that favor if I have to sleep with him to get it."

Blanche's voice was filled with such vehemence that Miles believed she might just succeed. It was full dark now, the rain coming down. Miles huddled, trying to keep warm. His arm accidentally brushed Blanche's, and he edged away from her in apology.

Blanche said, "What was your relationship with my husband? He mentioned you once or twice, you know, though I didn't know who you were then. When he was talking about Wales. 'Miles and those English rogues,' he'd say. 'Stout fellows, wish I still had them with me.' "

Miles thought about how to describe it. "We were close, my lady. Close in the way that only men who have fought together in war can understand. He saved my life. I saved his. Earl Thibault was like the father I never knew. I learned a lot from him, a lot about life. I could have stayed in his service when the war was over, perhaps I should have."

"Why didn't you?"

"I wanted to return to my village and my family." He laughed ruefully. "You see how that's worked out."

They sat in the darkness, listening to the rain beat on the old walls, on the leaves of the trees, on the grass.

Blanche said, "Miles . . . I have an idea."

"My lady?"

"I've told you of my intent to live on my manors. I shall have need of a steward for them. Would you be interested in the post?"

Miles was flummoxed. "I—I don't know what to say. That's most unexpected."

"I'm being practical. I think you'd do a good job. You're honest, if nothing else. You're also pig headed and insolent, but those can be useful traits for a steward. There would be a timber house for your use and a share in the year's profits. Your sons can farm your lands here, or you can rent them out."

"I'm flattered, my lady, truly, but you don't want me. I'm an old man."

"Nonsense, you have the constitution of an ox. You're constantly being beaten, or hung, and you just shrug it off and keep going."

It might actually be a good arrangement, Miles realized. The villagers of Ravenswell were angry at *him*, not at Garth and Mary. It might do him—and his family—good for him to get away from the village, make a fresh start. His relationship with his neighbors had been poisoned, and he didn't know if it could ever be fixed. They had always resented him somewhat, even as they had also looked up to him, because of what his family had been, and now a clean break might be for the best.

Still . . .

"I don't know," he said. "A great lady like yourself. I'd feel strange . . ."

She hesitated. "Would it help if I told you that I was not always a great lady?"

He stared at her, her face and hooded white cloak pale blurs in the darkness and rain.

"My father was born a villein," she said.

Miles's eyes widened.

Blanche went on. "He left the manor and became a soldier, worked his way up, and eventually got himself knighted. He married me to a castellan in the Vexin. The castle was made of wood and surrounded by bog, but for our family it was a good match. Auteuil, my husband, did not love me, but he did not beat me, either. Then Auteuil took the cross. He marched off for the Holy Land and left his bones bleaching in Anatolia. His brother made himself regent of our estate—he stole it, actually—and I became a ward of the duke of Normandy."

"You never had children?"

"Auteil's brother killed them."

There was a long pause, then Miles said, "I'm sorry."

She gave a little shrug, and Miles couldn't see it in the dark, but he knew her eyes were misting, just as he knew it was a subject she didn't want to talk about. He said, "How did you come to marry Earl Thibault?"

She sniffed and there was a hitch in her voice as she went on. "Two years past, Thibault was a guest at Duke Robert's Christmas court in Rouen. He met me and became infatuated. He asked the duke for my hand. His family was against the union because of my peasant background, but Thibault was adamant. He gave the duke a small fortune for me, though I brought nothing in return."

Miles digested that, and she said, "You remind me of my father in a way. You have that same stubborn pride."

"I'll take that as a compliment," Miles said. "May I think on your offer?"

"Yes," she said, and he could hear the smile in her voice, "but don't take too long. We women are notoriously fickle, you know."

After that, they sat in silence, the rain falling.

Time passed, and Miles felt Blanche's head against his shoulder. She had fallen asleep. Her touching him was an immense breach of etiquette. Even though he hadn't initiated the contact, he could be whipped for it—worse, maybe. He didn't know what to do, but he decided to let her remain that way. If he woke her, he was liable to incur her wrath. It was an uncomfortable position. Her head dug into his left shoulder, making his lower arm and hand go tingly, then numb. Plus, her head could loll off him at any time, and that might wake her.

Slowly, he moved his left arm. He brought the arm up and put it around Blanche's left shoulder, guiding her head to his chest. He wrapped his right arm around her waist to keep her steady. It had been a long time since he had held a woman. She was warm and soft against him. Her low breathing contrasted with his own rapid heartbeat. She murmured and dug her head into his chest, twisting in her sleep to make herself more comfortable. He arranged her muddy cloak around her, drawing the hood further over her head, smoothing the wrinkles.

This position grew awkward, as well. Because of the angle at which she lay against him, he had to brace his right arm to keep her weight from dragging her down. Carefully, he lowered her to his lap, on her side, cradling her against him in the "v" formed by his bent knees, terrified that she would wake and discover what he'd done. Once again, she shifted and made herself comfortable. She felt somehow natural like this, and it was only with difficulty that he resisted the urge to draw her even closer to him.

His eyes closed . . .

He came awake with a start. Alert.

The rain had stopped.

It was cold. Blanche was still in his arms, breathing peacefully.

Above him the clouds had blown away. The moon cast a silver glow over the valley below, reflecting off the stream, off the woods, off the bottoms of the few remaining clouds. The stars sparkled like uncounted gemstones.

He heard a *snap*.

He tensed, ready to . . .

To do what? Run? What about Blanche?

More noises. All around him. Movement.

Demons? Evil spirits?

Miles was terrified. He and Blanche were far from help. What was out in those woods? He said that he didn't believe in demons, that he didn't believe in the Old Ones, but deep inside, with feelings inherited from generations long past, he really did, no matter what the Church told him. There were forces even the Church could not control, and this was their ground.

His heart pounded. He was unsure of time. The moon set, leaving only the stars and the noises of the forest. He sat and he prayed, and after what seemed like an eternity, had the stars grown paler? Was that grey light behind the hills across the valley? Could he make out the woods on the far side?

Yes.

They had survived.

He put his head against the rough wall, watching the shadows around him take on substance, thanking God for his and Blanche's deliverance.

In his lap, Blanche stirred. She wrapped the cloak more tightly around her in the dawn chill. She opened her eyes and took in the grey light. "Are we alive?" she asked.

Miles said, "I believe we are, my lady."

"I'm shocked."

She said nothing about the sleeping arrangements, about finding herself in what would be regarded as a compromising position with a peasant. She sat up, straightening herself. She had used him as she might have used a piece of furniture and probably felt about him the same way.

"Now will you tell me your plan?" she asked. "As the earl's widow, I must attend the assize today."

Miles stood, his voice formal. "Good, because the first part of my plan is that I attend the assize, as well."

43

Wales, 1086 A.D.

THE company was camped in a small wood. At what he guessed was about midnight, Miles led the four relief guards to their posts. The last man was Leofric, and his post was just inside the tree line. "We'll reach Northop tomorrow," Miles told him. "So don't fall asleep out here."

"No chance of that," Leofric joked. "Too cold."

It had been two days since they had destroyed the village, two days since Miles had killed Toki. Two days of marching with little rest, two days of looking over their shoulders for an enemy who had yet to appear.

The earl was still unsteady from the blow to his head, and Miles had taken over the company. Even the nobles Waleran of St. Just and Etienne followed his lead. He willed the exhausted men along, chivvying them, berating them, kicking them, anything to keep them moving.

Not all of the men had been able to keep up. Two more had died, their bodies left where they fell. More sick and wounded had been left behind, with unspoken instructions to kill themselves. The same with one of the Flemish washerwomen, the stocky one, Jehanne, who was the same age as Miles. Miles felt sorry for Jehanne, but there was nothing for it; she was too ill to continue. He hoped she used the dagger he left with her, because she faced a harsh fate at the hands of the Welsh if she didn't. At best, they would sell her as a slave. At worst they would do to her what Toki had planned to do to the red-haired woman in the village. Wenstan had hobbled at the rear of the company on his broken ankle, using a makeshift crutch, but the constant stress of walking up and down hills, on uneven ground, had taken its toll. He had fallen farther and farther behind the little column, until eventually they lost sight of him.

One of Miles's shoes had fallen apart; many of the men were completely barefoot. Their bodies crawled with lice. Hair and beards were filthy and untrimmed. Clothes were in tatters; leather jacks were torn. The helmets that remained were dented and rusty; shields were hacked up. The roasted sheep from the village were long gone. Everyone was hungry, but at least water was plentiful.

And tomorrow they would be safe.

Miles sank down wearily and propped his back against an oak tree. Earl Thibault and Etienne were making the rounds of the little camp, Thibault doing it more for show than anything else, letting the men know he was still there, moving slowly because of his injury. When they were done, the earl sat beside Miles, Etienne with him. This gesture was unusual; the earl usually kept to himself at night, with only Etienne and Waleran of St. Just to join him.

The earl said nothing, so Miles made an attempt at conversation. "Almost there, my lord. One more day."

The earl rubbed his cold hands together and looked over. "I've never properly thanked you for saving me back in that village."

Miles shrugged. "I've never properly thanked you for saving me beside the road, when I wanted to give up."

"I had faith in you," the earl said. He paused. "How old are you, Miles?" It was the first time he'd called him "Miles" and not "English."

"Twenty," Miles said, surprised by the question. "I know because I was born the year of the great battle."

"Old enough to be my son," the earl said. Then he sighed. "I wish you were my son. I'd feel a lot better about the future."

"Why . . . thank you, my lord, that's a very kind thing for you to say."

The earl fiddled with a stick, digging the tip absently into the wet ground. "I haven't had much luck with sons. The oldest, Galon, is fifteen. He's a squire now, but the reports I get about him aren't good. He's brave enough and smart, but he has a vicious streak. When he was little, he liked to torture animals. Now he tortures men—for the fun of it. He beats serving women who won't sleep with him. I don't look forward to him being my heir. My second boy, Ranulf, is no better. He's eleven and supposedly bound for the Church. But he's abysmal at his studies and doesn't even pretend to show interest in Church doctrine. He seems more intent on becoming a wastrel."

Miles wasn't sure how he should respond. "Are those your only sons, my lord?"

"There's Geoffrey. He's four, lively little fellow. Clever, too." The earl smiled. "Already charming the ladies. He's the one I set my hopes on, but we'll see. Have you any boys?"

"One, my lord. Garth, he's two."

"Mmmm. You know, in one respect you commoners are lucky. You get to keep your children with you as they grow. You don't have to give them up early, like we do. I left home to be a page at eight—what about you, Etienne?"

"The same, my lord," young Etienne said.

"I rarely saw my parents after that. After I was a page, I was a squire. I didn't return home for good until I'd been knighted, when I was full grown. I barely knew my father by then. My mother died while I was away." His voice grew distant. "I can hardly picture what she looked like anymore."

They sat in silence for a while, then the earl lowered his voice and Miles got the idea he was getting to the real reason for his visit. Etienne inched closer, and Miles could almost see his ears prick up as the earl said, "Tell me, Miles, what do you know about Wulfhere's Treasure?"

Miles was startled to hear this subject brought up in these circumstances. "I know it doesn't exist, my lord. It's just a story."

Etienne seemed put off by that news, but the earl wasn't. "You're wrong," he told Miles. "It does exist, and I'll find it one day."

Miles couldn't argue with an earl, so he said, "If you say so, my lord. How did you learn about the treasure, anyway?"

"I had the story from my father, who got it from his brother Bogo. Bogo captured the English earl of Trent at Senlac Hill. The earl begged for his freedom, promised Bogo he'd tell him where the treasure was if Bogo would let him go. The earl had been wounded, though. The wound mortified, and the earl died before he could reveal the treasure's whereabouts."

"Why are you so determined to find it?"

It was the earl's turn to look taken aback. "Money, why else? Money is power, Miles, and if that fortune's as large as my father said it is, I can be the most powerful man in the kingdom. Maybe the most powerful man in France. In all of Europe, even." His eyes gleamed at the thought, and he went on. "You have *no* idea where I can find it? Or even where to start looking?"

Miles grinned. "Trust me, my lord, if I had any idea where it was, Leofric and I would have dug it up years ago and gotten out of here."

The earl wasn't happy. "This is not what I was hoping to hear from—"

There was a startled shout from the camp's perimeter, where the guards were. Another.

Miles jumped to his feet. "That sounds like Leofric."

Another cry. A clash of steel. Then silence.

Everyone was on their feet now. Those who still had helmets put them on. Weapons were drawn. Waleran of St. Just came over, pale faced and sweaty, the bandage on his arm wet.

"Form a square," Miles whispered to Merleswegen. "Quietly."

Merleswegen hustled the men into a square. Its sides were uneven because of the trees. The remaining washerwoman huddled in the square's center, terrified.

To the earl, Miles said, "I'm going to bring in the guards."

"No, I'll do it," the earl said.

"But—"

"You're needed here. Etienne, come with me."

Swords drawn, the two men started into the darkness. They returned with three guards. Leofric was not one of them.

Miles said, "Where is Leofric, my lord?"

The earl shook his head. "His post was empty."

Miles's heart seemed to rise into his throat. The three remaining guards took places in the square. "The Welsh aren't going to surprise us," Thibault explained to Miles. "Not now. No sense leaving those men out there by themselves."

Miles nodded in agreement.

The men stood in the dark silence, not talking, no longer feeling the cold, many of them sweating with fear.

A piercing scream came out of the night, a drawn-out note of agony.

Another.

The Flemish washerwoman fell to her knees crying.

"Shut her up," Oslac hissed, "she'll give us away."

Merleswegen dropped to his knees beside the woman and put a hand over her mouth. "Shhh. It's all right, miss. I won't let them hurt you, I promise." He held her to his chest, muffling her sobs.

"Help!" It was Leofric's voice. "Miles! Help me!"

Miles gathered himself.

"No," the earl told him. "That's what they want you to do."

Another scream, the most gut-wrenching yet. "Miles!"

This time, Miles started forward, but the earl grabbed his arm and held him back. "Stay here, son."

The earl held Miles's arm in an iron grip as the screams continued. Hot tears cut channels down Miles's cheeks. Men shuffled nervously, trying not to listen. The washerwoman sobbed into Merleswegen's shoulder. The earl stood tall, staring into the darkness, eyes unreadable.

Waleran whispered, "Should we move out?"

"Too dark," the earl said. "They know the ground, we don't. We'll march at first light."

At some point, the screaming stopped. The men rested in place, every second one sitting and getting what rest he could while the others remained on alert, half-expecting to see the Welsh come pouring out of the darkness.

Miles felt hollowed out. He felt as though a part of him was missing. He couldn't remember a time when Leofric hadn't been beside him. They had been like brothers, but closer than brothers. They were like pieces of the same whole.

The earl had let go of Miles's arm, but Miles didn't remember when. Now the earl shook Miles's shoulder. "Are you all right?"

Miles snapped out of his reverie and nodded glumly.

The earl pointed to the east, where a faint grey light diffused the cold edge of darkness. He made a beckoning motion with his hand.

Miles tapped Merleswegen. They got the company into line and started them forward.

48

Wales

THE column hurried, strung out, no longer in any kind of order. Some of the men were almost running in their haste to reach safety, and some stumbled along, barely able to stay on their feet.

The Welsh were behind them, but how many and how far? Wat o' Riseby, the company's best runner, had been left as a rearguard to watch for them.

The earl was feeling a little better. He was in the center of the column, with Etienne and Waleran of St. Just. Miles stayed back to urge on the rearmost. "Faster!" he cried, waving a hand. "Faster! Keep going, there. Northop's just ahead."

Once, the only thing that had kept Miles going was the thought of Alice and Garth and the unborn babe. Now there was something else—duty. He felt what his father and grandfather must have felt. He was responsible for these men. It was his job to get them home to their families. It was his job to keep them safe.

"That's it, lads! Keep going."

The base at Northop had been hastily constructed—Miles and the English soldiers had been detailed to help with the building. It consisted of a wooden stockade and a central tower. It wasn't big, but it, and its garrison, would protect them until help could be summoned from Hawarden or Chester.

The ground was more level than it had been in a long time. More and more, the dense forest gave way to cultivated fields, almost looking like English fields, except they were empty. A bad sign—as though the people who worked these fields knew what was coming. The River Dee was visible to their left, grey under the lowering sky.

"Keep going. Almost there."

Merleswegen had the exhausted Flemish washerwoman's arm around his shoulder. "Hurry, miss. That's it. Watch your step now."

The men burst through the last belt of trees and stopped.

Ahead lay the village of Northop. It was deserted.

Behind the village, the stockade and tower had been burned to the ground.

45

Trentshire, 1106 A.D.

THE assize was held on the open ground between Badford Castle and Badford Town. With the growth of the town, the distance between it and the castle seemed to shrink a bit every year, until Miles could envisage a time in the future when the two would merge. Justice had been given in this meadow since before anyone could remember—before the castle, before the town, even. A gallows had been erected in the meadow, near the Great Oak of Trentshire, which was the traditional venue for hanging criminals. They must be expecting a lot of trade today, Miles thought. Aelred would be the featured victim, of course, but there would be more. Miles thought of Aelred's young friend Wada, and the other men from the castle gaol.

From a distance it looked more like a fair than a judicial event. Gaily colored tents dotted the green fields around Justice Meadow. Miles heard music and the swell of voices. He smelled food cooking.

Miles was in his priest's robe with the hood pulled up, walking once more at Lady Blanche's side. He had left his horse at the lodge.

Blanche hadn't had time to clean up or change clothing. Her cloak, bliaut, and linen headdress were rumpled and mud spotted, as was her white horse. "I wish you'd tell me what you intend to do," she said to Miles.

"I would, but I'm not all that sure myself," Miles said.

"That's what worries me." She added, "You never replied to my offer, either."

"Probably best to wait and see if I'm going to be hung before I do that, my lady."

"True," Blanche admitted. "I can't imagine your corpse would be of much use to me. Scare away crows and small children, perhaps, but that's about it."

They came to the outskirts of the crowd, and Miles said, "I'll leave you here, my lady. The assize hasn't started yet, and I have a few things to do."

"I'll see you later?" she asked.

He grinned. "Oh, you'll see me, all right."

She leaned down and placed a hand on his shoulder. "Please tell me I won't see you dangling from that tree."

Her touch, so unexpected, almost made him forget why he was here. "I hope you won't, my lady. Not if my plan works."

She squeezed his shoulder softly and gave him a knowing smile. "Good luck."

Surprised again, he returned the smile as best he could. "Thank you, my lady." He bowed to her and started off, trying to regain his sense of purpose. This was not the time to be distracted.

He made his way through the throng. There were men, women, and children from all over the shire, nobles and clergy and peasants, many of whom had camped in the meadow overnight. There were musicians and jugglers, vendors of pasties and ale. Whores plied their trade next to clerics selling relics and indulgences. Off to one side was a bear-baiting pit, though what bear-baiting had to do with the king's justice Miles couldn't say. Grim and his wife, Diote, were watching the spectacle, along with Ralf, howling with laughter each time one of the dogs was slashed by the scarred old bear's claws and hurled yelping across the pit.

Miles passed a fish griller's stand, his mouth watering, wishing he had money to buy something. He'd had a quick drink of water and a bite of black bread at the lodge, and he was hungry. A band played on a stage nearby, people dancing to the music, and next to that was a puppet show. In a short while, the children watching the puppet show would watch men hang, and they would laugh and cheer at that spectacle the same way they laughed and cheered at these puppets.

In the crowd by the puppet show, Miles saw Garth. Mary was with him, watching the painted puppets with delight. Nearby were Aethelwynn and Peter, holding hands. Father John and Agnes were there, as well.

Miles moved up beside Garth and rested a hand on his shoulder.

Startled, Garth turned. "Father!"

"Shhh!" Miles said.

Mary looked over in surprise. Peter and Aethelwynn dropped one another's hands in startled embarrassment. Agnes put her hand to her mouth, while Father John grinned at Miles.

"Where have you been?" Garth asked Miles in a low voice.

"Finding the earl's killer," Miles said.

Mary looked less happy to see Miles than the others did. Maybe she hoped he'd run away. "Were you successful?" she said.

"Yes," Miles told her. "I just have to convince the court." To Garth he said, "Why are you here?"

"To give support to Aelred. We wanted him to see some friendly faces when . . ." His voice tailed off.

"Let's hope it doesn't come to that," Miles said. "Where are the children? At the manor?"

"Cecily and Alfstan are playing with Pierre's youngest," Garth said. "Chieftain's watching over them. Alfred's in the fields, hoeing."

"Were our animals recovered?"

"Yes, save for the chickens. There was an argument about the rest. Grim and that bastard Martin wanted to distribute the animals around the village, but Pierre put a stop to that."

Father John bent over, coughing. Agnes assisted him as he straightened. "I'm keeping them in my croft for the moment," he rasped, "until the new house is built."

"New house?" Miles said.

Garth said, "Aye. 'Twas Osbert's idea. He came to me in the fields yesterday and said people felt bad about what happened. They were angry at you, and things got out of hand, what with the drinking and all. We've started cutting and shaping wood for the frame. Everyone is helping—save for Grim and his lot and a few others like Martin and Four-Fingered Hugh."

"That's great news. When is the house to be built?"

"Two weeks from Saturday, if all goes well. Shouldn't take long with everybody lending a hand. There will be a separate barn for the oxen, like you wanted, but that will come later. Mary's brewing ale for the occasion."

"Gunhild's letting me use her pots," Mary said. She added, "It's only because you're gone that we're getting the house rebuilt, you know."

"Mary!" Garth admonished.

"It's all right," Miles told him. "I know it's true."

To Garth, Miles said, "Keep an eye on our fence posts opposite the cattle pasture. The abbot of Huntley's been knocking them down."

"So that's who it is," Garth said. "I've had to fix them every morning. What's he up to?"

"Long story. It's got to do with that suit over Morton Chase. My grandfather's name is on the charter, and the abbot wants to discredit me so I can't testify."

Miles turned to Peter, who took a step back, expecting to be admonished for holding hands with Aethelwynn. "Peter, I want to thank you for all you've done for us. Your father would be proud. And I . . ." He glanced at his daughter. "I'd be proud to have you as Aethlwynn's husband."

Aethelwynn gasped with surprise and delight. People around them looked, and she lowered her voice. "When did you change your mind?"

"It's more like I grew up," Miles told her. "I realized that love is too rare to put aside because of something like one's station in life." He clasped Peter's hand. "I hope you two will be very happy. Now, I need to see Lord Geoffrey."

Miles made his way through the crowd and found Lord Geoffrey, Matilda, and Pierre Courtenay chatting with some other nobles, knights of the shire, mostly. Miles caught Pierre's eye. Pierre did a double take and said something under his breath to Geoffrey.

Geoffrey and Lady Matilda drifted away from the other nobles and approached the hooded priest. "What are you doing here?" Geoffrey hissed. "I thought you must have run for it. You're a wanted man, they'll hang you."

Miles said, "I've found proof of Aelred's innocence."

Geoffrey gave him a skeptical frown. "What proof?"

"You'll see when the assize starts, my lord. I have a witness to when and where I found it, as well. A noble."

Matilda rubbed her swelling belly protectively. "Will this noble swear that what you say is true?"

"Aye, my lady." Miles was careful to say nothing that would give away the witness's sex.

Geoffrey was quiet for a long moment. Then he said, "I'm sorry, Miles, I should have believed you. I told you I'd help you, and I let you down."

"Worked out all right in the end, my lord. Just thought you should know before the trial starts."

"Thank you for keeping me informed. What do you need me to do?"

"Nothing, my lord. Least for right now. We'll see how things go."

"Good luck to you."

"Thank you, my lord."

A horn blew, signaling that the assize was about to begin.

Pierre took Miles's arm. "I'm glad you're all right, *mon vieux.*"

"Tell me that if I'm still alive at vespers," Miles said.

46

ON the far side of the clearing, plank tables had been lined up for the high-ranking nobles. In times past, the assemblage had met under the Great Oak, but the crowds had gotten too large for that. The tables were set with wine and cheese and honey cakes. In their center was a gilded chair that Lord Tutbury carried with him on his official duties. To the right of that was an ancient carved chair traditionally reserved for the sheriff of Trentshire. The rest of the nobles would sit on benches. The twelve jurors of Guildford Hundred occupied benches to one side of the tables, Duncan Brown at their head. Most of the jurors, including Duncan, looked uneasy. Morys Gretch and some of his men were nearby, as well. So was one-legged William the Beardman.

Miles pushed through the sweating, jostling crowd, needing to get to the front. The crowd grew thicker the farther forward he went, and people started pushing back, cursing, some of them, even though he was supposed to be a priest.

"Watch where yer goin', ye daft shave head."

"Piss off, Father. This is my spot."

Miles kept his head down, so he wouldn't be recognized, and mumbled. "I'm Lady Blanche's chaplain. I've got her medicine in case she gets sick."

At the front of the crowd, guards held people back, spears lowered to prevent anyone from approaching the justice's table. By the time Miles fought his way there, most of the nobles were in place, standing by their benches. The bishop of Badford was present, along with Etienne, Lord Geoffrey and Lady Matilda. So were the abbot of Huntley, Galon and his pregnant wife, Rosamunde, and Ranulf's wife Mathilde, who looked worried. The chief nobles of the shire were there, as well. Galon had appropriated the chair reserved for the sheriff. He stood with his hands on the chair's low back, looking around.

"Where's Ranulf?" he asked irritably. "We're ready to begin, and that lout is nowhere in sight."

Lord Geoffrey seemed unsurprised. "You know Ranulf, he's never on time."

Mathilde said, "He didn't come back to the lodge last night."

"Not unusual, from what I hear," Rosamunde sniffed.

"His squire Purcell is missing, as well," Mathilde went on.

"It's a wonder Ranulf made it to the crusade on time," Galon muttered. Then his eye was caught by someone approaching. "Mother!" he cried. "The grieving widow come to see justice done."

Lady Blanche said nothing as she made her way to her place at the bench. The sun was out, and she had removed her cloak. Her braided hair had not been brushed, and there were bits of leaves in it which she had missed picking out. Her clothes looked like she had slept in them, which she had. Dried mud caked the lower part of her bliaut.

Galon went on, grinning. "You look a bit the worse for wear, Mother."

"She looks a *lot* the worse for wear," Rosamunde observed gleefully.

The abbot of Huntley's brow darkened. "*You* weren't around last night, either," he said to Blanche.

"Oh, ho!" Galon said. "Mother and Ranulf, perhaps?"

Rosamunde snorted. "What, a stable boy wasn't available?"

Miles felt sorry that Blanche had to put up with this. He noticed that Geoffrey and Matilda felt the same way; Geoffrey seemed embarrassed by his family's behavior.

Mathilde blocked Blanche's path. "Where is my husband?"

"I've no idea where your husband is," Blanche lied coolly. "Nor do I care."

Mathilde's eyes widened in anger and she took a deep breath. "You peasant whore, don't you dare—"

Abbot Joscelin interrupted her. "Where were you last night?" he asked Blanche.

Blanche arched her brows. "I went for a ride yesterday, as I am wont to do. I got lost and was forced to spend a rather uncomfortable night in the forest."

"By yourself?" the abbot said.

"Of course by myself."

"A likely story," Galon chortled. "Are you sure you weren't with that new priest of yours? Big strapping fellow like that? Bet he could—"

"Galon!" snapped Geoffrey. "Enough!"

Galon whirled on Geoffrey. People stepped back.

The horn blew again.

Heads turned as Lord Tutbury exited his gold-and-black-striped tent. Before the tent flap closed, Miles glimpsed a young woman inside, clad in only a shift. Tutbury smoothed his robe. Accompanied by a herald with the horn, the king's justice moved at a stately pace toward the gathering. Two squires followed in his wake. Galon threw Geoffrey another savage glance, but didn't say anything. Blanche looked relieved at no longer being the center of attention.

Galon had called Tutbury a "pompous toad," and while Tutbury didn't look like he missed many meals, he didn't look like a fool, either, not to Miles. There was steel in his eyes, ruthlessness even, as he approached the assemblage. He wore an embroidered yellow robe and brown hose. His hair was neither fashionably long, nor cut short like Galon's, but mid-length, curled at the bottom, probably with an iron.

Tutbury reached his chair, which was pulled back for him by one of the squires. There was an invocation from the bishop of Badford, then Tutbury sat, followed by Galon and the rest of the nobles, Galon casting another dark look at Geoffrey.

The two squires stood behind Tutbury's chair, along with the herald, with the horn tucked under his arm. "In the name of Henry, king of England . . . et cetera, et cetera . . . I pronounce this court in session," Tutbury said. He looked around the tables and cleared his throat. "We have a busy schedule, my lords, so let's get to it. The first case we must hear, of course, is that of the killing of Thibault of Monteaux, earl of Trent. Said killing taking place in the hundred of Guildford." He added, "Later today, or perhaps tomorrow, whenever the criminal cases have been decided, we will read the earl's will and adjudicate it." He turned to Galon on his right. "Are you assuming the role of acting sheriff, Lord Galon?"

Galon rose from his chair, bowing. "I am, my lord. Soon to be made permanent sheriff, I trust."

"Yes, well. We'll see. Now, as I understand it, the earl's killer has been apprehended?"

"He has been, my lord," Galon said.

"Good, that saves us a lot of problems."

Galon went on. "The killer is English, of course. A poacher. Aelred, called With-the-Beard." He beckoned a finger at Stigand, who stood in front of the guards, with the day's other witnesses.

Stigand stepped forward, holding an arrow in both hands, presenting it to Lord Tutbury. "This is the arrow that killed the earl, my lord. It has been identified by a number of witnesses as belonging to Aelred."

Tutbury examined the arrow, fingered its blood-stained tip, handed it back. "And why did this poacher kill Earl Thibault?" he asked Stigand.

Stigand spread his hands. "We've questioned him, my lord, but he won't say. Hatred of his betters, perhaps?"

Tutbury looked toward the jurors' bench. "Is the pledge for Guildford Hundred prepared to swear to this individual's guilt?"

Duncan Brown stood. "The pledge for Guildford Hundred is Aelred's father, my lord, and he has been dismissed from his post for attempting to hinder the investigation."

A buzz swept through the crowd.

“Criminal charges coming there, eh, Galon?” Tutbury said over his shoulder.

“Of a surety, my lord,” Galon replied. “The former pledge has fled, but we’ll catch him.”

Tutbury sipped his wine thoughtfully. “I remember that fellow from other assizes—Miles, I think his name was. Didn’t seem the type to shirk his duty, but you never know.”

Galon shrugged. “English, my lord. Can’t be trusted.”

“Mmmm.” Tutbury indicated Stigand. “You seem to trust this fellow,” he told Galon, “and he’s English.”

Galon took the rebuke more gracefully than he would have had it come from a man of lower rank. “Point taken, my lord.”

Tutbury turned to Duncan Brown again. “You’re acting in the missing hundred pledge’s stead?

“I am, my lord. I am Duncan Brown, president of the jurors.”

Tutbury gestured for him to begin.

Duncan stood straighter and cleared his throat. In a formal voice, he said, “The jurors of Guildford Hundred hereby declare that on the twenty-eighth day of June, in this, the One Thousand, One Hundred and Sixth Year of Our Lord, Aelred, surnamed With-the-Beard, of Ravenswell Manor, did shoot an arrow into Thibault of Monteaux, earl of Trent, causing said Thibault to expire. The jurors are sworn to this, each of them.”

Tutbury nodded approval. “Is the prisoner at hand?”

Galon motioned to Stigand. Stigand waved, and two guards brought Aelred forward. They had to hold him up so he wouldn't fall. There was a gasp from the crowd when they saw Aelred's condition, bruised and beaten, one eye closed, his clothing torn and his long, wispy beard stiff with dirt and dried blood.

"This is the man, my lord," Stigand said.

Tutbury looked Aelred over, his distaste obvious. "Have you anything to say?"

Aelred shrugged off the guards. He stared Tutbury in the eye and held his head up. "Not to a Frenchman."

Tutbury was unimpressed. "Very well, take him to the Great Oak and—"

Miles pushed aside a guard's spear. He threw back his hood and stepped before Lord Tutbury's table. "My lord, Aelred did not kill Earl Thibault."

47

AELRED stared dumbly at Miles. Aelred had been beaten so badly, he seemed barely aware of what was happening.

Standing behind her table, Blanche smiled with anticipation.

Galon leaped to his feet. "That's no priest!" he cried in astonishment. "It's that Englishman, Miles." He turned. "Stigand! Arrest that man."

Stigand started toward Miles, who quickly stepped closer to Lord Tutbury, bowing as he did. "I am Miles Edwulfson, my lord, pledge for Guildford Hundred. It is my duty to name Earl Thibault's killer, and I tell you, that killer is not Aelred."

Duncan Brown raised his voice. "You have been removed as pledge, Miles. You have no standing here. Leave this place while you may still salvage your—"

Duncan was drowned out by the crowd yelling around them. Half were yelling in surprise; half wanted Miles's head. Stigand grabbed Miles's arm, but Lord Tutbury raised his hand, staying him. "Wait a minute. Let us hear what the fellow has to say before we hang him. Go on," he told Miles.

Miles waited for the tumult to subside, then said, "It's true I've been removed as hundred pledge, my lord, but before that, I conducted the official investigation into Earl Thibault's death. I have continued that investigation since, and I believe that gives me the right to address this court."

Galon realized the import of the priest's garb, and he tugged his drooping moustache. "By God, that was you in the gaol with Blanche the other day. You've been posing as her confessor all this while. You're a bold rogue, I'll give you that."

The bishop of Badford addressed Tutbury. "There are penalties for impersonating a priest, your lordship. Severe penalties. In this world and the next. This man must be—"

"I said, continue," Tutbury told Miles.

Miles drew himself up. "It is my belief that the earl's killer was not my son. Indeed, the killer was not an Englishman at all, but a member of the earl's hunting party."

More shocked uproar, followed by laughter and catcalls from the English in the audience, aimed at the French nobles. "My lord, must we listen to this?" said Galon's wife, Rosamunde, cradling her swollen belly.

Abbot Joscelin joined in. "An Englishman can't be allowed to speak before the assize, my lord. Think of the precedent it would set. There'd be no end to it. We'd have to let them—"

Tutbury held up a hand. To Miles, he said, "Aren't you forgetting something? The *murdrum* law has been invoked, and it stipulates that an Englishman is the killer."

"Just because the law stipulates something doesn't make it so," Miles told him. "Wouldn't the court rather know the truth?"

"*I* certainly would," Blanche said, standing. She'd been waiting for this moment. "Thibault was my husband. I want to see his real killer punished, not some poacher who's been set up for the crime."

"You say that because you've been cavorting with this Englishman," said the abbot, flicking a dismissive hand toward Miles. "For all we know, you—"

"Leave her alone," Lord Geoffrey told him. "I want to know who the real killer is, as well."

"As do I, your lordship," Etienne said to Tutbury. "I served the earl for many years. I don't want his killer to go unpunished, no matter what his rank, and neither should any member of this court."

"Save, perhaps, the one who killed him," Blanche said, and she stared at Galon as she spoke.

Etienne stared at Galon, as well, but Galon seemed unperturbed. He indicated Miles. "The matter is moot, Lord Tutbury. By law, this fellow may not accuse a Norman in court."

"But I can," Blanche told him. "And I'll be more than happy to do it."

"Whore," Rosamunde sneered.

"And I'll second the charge, if need be," Geoffrey said.

"As will I," said Etienne.

Miles noticed Morys Gretch watching with interest nearby. The men around him were not trying to hide the fact that they were armed, though bearing arms was in violation of the terms of the assize.

"We're getting ahead of ourselves," Tutbury said. He gestured to Miles. "I'm letting you speak, Miles Edwulfson, only because I remember you as an honest man. Don't give me reason to change my mind."

"No, my lord."

"So, who are you saying killed Earl Thibault?"

Blanche leaned forward expectantly.

Miles replied, "I don't know . . ."

This set off the loudest outcry yet.

Blanche's eyes opened wide in surprise.

Miles held up his hands for quiet. "Wait, wait! Hear me out!"

The herald had to sound his horn to silence the crowd. Tutbury rose with his fists on the table, and his brow clouded. "I warn you, Englishman. This had better be good. If you're wasting my time . . ."

Miles said, "I was in St. Mary's Wood yesterday, my lord, and I spoke with a hermit named David. This David said he'd seen a man on a white horse on the day of the hunt, a man I believe to have been Earl Thibault."

Galon said, "My lord—"

Tutbury cut him off with an upturned hand. "And?" he asked Miles.

"David said the man seemed to have been heading for Thor's Seat."

Tutbury looked at the nobles around him. "What the Devil is Thor's Seat?" But the nobles seemed equally perplexed.

"It's a spot sacred to the Old Ones," Miles told them. "The spot where King Wulfhere is said to have been converted to Christianity."

"Wulfhere?" said Tutbury. "Who is Wulfhere, and what does he have to do with anything?"

Miles explained. "That means the spot is also connected to Wulfhere's Treasure, a treasure that Earl Thibault had been seeking for the last twenty years."

Miles could tell from the look on Tutbury's face that he hadn't heard of the treasure, either, but the mention of it started a low buzz among some of the nobles and a much louder one in the audience.

Miles went on. "It grew dark ere I was able to go to Thor's Seat, and there wasn't time to do it this morning." Blanche was staring at him as though he were mad.

"Were you with Lady Blanche?" Abbot Joscelin demanded. "She said she was in the forest last night."

Before the abbot could say any more, Lord Tutbury cut him off. "Stop prattling about Lady Blanche, will you? What are you telling us, Miles? Make it quick."

"I'm asking for one more day, my lord."

"What nonsense is this?" Galon cried.

"Absurd," said the bishop of Badford. "We have a schedule to keep."

Miles went on, his voice growing stronger, more commanding. "We know that the earl's body was moved after he was killed."

Tutbury turned. "Is this true, Galon?"

Galon was taken aback. "Well . . . yes."

Miles explained. "There was little blood at the scene, and the earl's clothes were covered with a soil not found there."

"Why wasn't this mentioned before?" Tutbury asked Galon.

Galon said, "It didn't seem significant, my lord."

"Not significant? Of course it's significant, you fool. Why would a poacher go to the trouble of moving his victim's body? That makes no sense, and the fact that it makes no sense makes it significant."

Miles went on. "My lord, it is my belief that Lord Thibault was killed at Thor's Seat. His death had something to do with Wulfhere's Treasure. The body was moved so that no one would make that connection. My son's arrow was stolen to use in the killing so that the *murdrum* law would be invoked. The killer wanted an Englishman to be suspect. He didn't want suspicion falling on members of the hunting party, and thus on himself."

"That's a considerable leap of the imagination," Tutbury observed.

"It's the only explanation that accounts for the earl's body being moved. I believe we will find soil at Thor's Seat matching that on the earl's clothes. I also believe that the killer left something at the site that will enable us to identify him."

"God's sandals," Galon said, "now it's evidence in the trees. My lord Tutbury, stop coddling this peasant and—"

Miles said, "I'm only asking for one more day, my lord. You have a reputation as a just man. Is one day too much to see justice done?"

Blanche gave Miles a puzzled look. Why hadn't he mentioned the arrow he'd found hidden in Stigand's belongings? She went along with him, though. "I agree, my lord."

Tutbury considered. "And if we find nothing at this Thor's Seat?"

Miles swallowed. "Then I will bow to the will of the court."

"You'll bow to a noose is what you'll do," Galon growled.

Tutbury stroked his jaw. He looked back at the gold and black tent, possibly thinking about now getting to spend an extra night with the young woman inside. "This is most unusual."

"It is also most ridiculous," Abbot Joscelin said. "I must protest, my lord. This fellow's obviously playing for time to free his son. Like as not, he has some kind of escape planned for the boy."

"You have nothing to lose, my lord," Blanche told Tutbury.

"I agree with Lady Blanche," Etienne said.

"As do I," said Geoffrey. "What's another day, if we find out who the real killer is?"

Tutbury said, "Technically, there's no reason for the court to comply. As the bishop says, we have a schedule to keep. Still . . ." His voice tailed off and there was another glance back at the tent. He sipped more wine and said, "Very well. I will hold court tomorrow at this Thor's whatever-it-is. We will go there directly after breakfast. Does anyone know the way?"

"I do," Blanche said.

"I knew it," Abbot Joscelin swore. "You *were* with Miles last night. You're sleeping with a peasant!"

More uproar from the crowd. Ranulf's wife, Mathilde, pointed a bony finger at Blanche. "It was her, Lord Tutbury.

She killed the earl. And she killed my husband. She's trying to keep that treasure for herself."

Tutbury frowned. "Your husband has been killed?"

"He hasn't come home. His squire's horse is back at the stable, without its saddle, but there's no sign of Ranulf or Purcell. *She* killed them, and she killed her husband—her and this English cur, Miles."

Blanche gave Ranulf's wife a withering look, maybe to hide how close she was to the truth. "If I had killed my husband and I wanted to hide my guilt, I would just let them hang this poacher, you beetle-brained buffoon. As for your husband, 'tis well known he engages in highway robbery from time to time to obtain money. Perhaps one of his escapades went awry. Or perhaps he's simply gone back to Normandy."

"Why would he go back without me?" Mathilde said.

Blanche smiled. "You're probably the reason he left."

There was laughter from the audience. Mathilde swelled with rage.

Blanche baited her. "What are you going to do? Turn me into a newt?"

Mathilde moved forward, to be restrained by Rosamunde and Abbot Joscelin.

Tutbury ignored them, addressing Miles. "If we do not find proof that one of the hunting party killed the earl of Trent, we will return here and hang your son forthwith."

"And you after," Galon added.

"Aye, my lord," Miles said. It was as much as he could ask for.

"Take him back to the gaol," Tutbury told the men guarding Aelred.

As they led Aelred away, Tutbury said to Miles, "And you, stay here, where we can keep an eye on you."

"I will, my lord."

Miles had no intention of doing that. Blanche was still giving him that questioning look. He met her eyes and inclined his head, trying to assure her that he knew what he was doing. He faded into the crowd, intending to slip away while the rest of the day's cases were being heard. He saw Morys Gretch whisper something to his scarred companion, Cerdic, who bobbed his head in reply. Cerdic beckoned a couple of his men, and they started after Miles.

Miles moved faster, trying to lose himself in the crowd.

Cerdic and his men spread out, pushing through the crowd after Miles, trying to keep him in sight.

Miles turned and made his way down the lane of the food sellers. As he did, he pulled the priest's robe over his head, revealing his own clothing beneath. He had worn his clothes beneath the robe for just such an eventuality.

He chanced a look over his shoulder. Cerdic's men had turned onto the foodsellers' lane, as well, with daggers drawn. But they were searching for a man in a priest's robe, and they didn't see one, so they moved slower, heads turning.

Miles dodged down another lane and came to the puppet show, whose owners were packing up. Miles tucked the priest's garb under his arm. "Here, let me help you," he told the head puppeteer. The man smiled and said something in a foreign language. Miles helped the puppeteers pack puppets and props into their boxes, then loaded the boxes onto their cart. Cerdic's men passed the puppeteers' tent with barely a glance inside.

Miles waited. Cerdic's men reached the edge of the crowd, looking around, puzzled, still watching for the brown robe. Cerdic angrily motioned them to spread out and go back the way they had come. When they did that and passed the puppeteers' tent, Miles lowered his head and left the first the tent, then the busy castle grounds, a faceless peasant going about his business.

He had a stop to make later, then he would head for the forest. If his plan succeeded, the killer would be at Thor's Seat at dawn tomorrow.

Miles intended to be there first.

48

Wales, 1086 A.D.

THE village of Northop lay in the angle where two roads merged and went on to Hawarden. The base had been constructed opposite the village. As the company approached, they were hit by an overpowering stench. Outside the burned fort, they found broken wagons, dead horses and mules.

Weapons drawn, the men entered the fort. Most crossed themselves at what they saw. The courtyard was littered with naked bodies, hacked to pieces—mostly men, but a few women. They were well into the process of decomposition. Crows pecked at a few of the corpses, and they reluctantly flapped away at the soldiers' entrance. The village pigs were at the bodies, as well, but they ignored the newcomers. The tall Flemish washerwoman, whose name was Fleur, looked like she was going to scream, but Merleswegen steadied her.

When the fort had been built, there had been no time to construct a mound for the wooden tower. It had been placed on level ground and was now fallen over, a heap of blackened wood, as was the palisade. The supplies stored in the burned sheds were all gone, save for some empty sacks and smashed crates. Miles touched the tower's burned wood. "Cold," he told the earl. "They took it a while back."

Earl Thibault nodded. “About the time we were being ambushed, I’d guess.”

There was a noise behind them, and Wat o’ Riseby jogged through the remains of the fort’s gate. “They’re coming,” he breathed. “About three miles back.”

“There is no protection here,” the earl said. He was steadier on his feet and seemed to have regained much of his strength. “We must go on.”

“My lord,” ventured the squire Etienne, “Maybe we should go to Chester instead of Hawarden. Chester’s a bit farther off, but it’s big and well defended. The Welsh likely wouldn’t attack us there.”

Miles didn’t like that idea. “Hawarden’s only a couple of miles down the road.”

The castle at Hawarden hadn’t been big enough to handle supplies and reinforcements for the Welsh campaign, so this base had been built at Northop. The thinking was that the two forts would be mutually supportive, meaning an attack on one would prompt a response from the other.

Etienne said, “Hawarden must have fallen, as well, Miles. Why else didn’t they march to stop this attack?”

“Maybe Northop fell so quickly that there wasn’t time to send a relief force,” said Waleran of St. Just. Waleran’s black and swollen arm would have to be drained of pus and blood, but there was no time to do it now.

Miles said, “If we go to Chester, we’ll have to cross the river and the Welsh can trap us there. Hawarden has a proper castle and it’s close.”

Etienne said, “But—”

The earl cut him off. "Miles is right. Even if Hawarden *has* fallen, the castle mound will give us a place to make a stand."

"Unless the Welsh just decide to stand back and shoot us full of arrows," Waleran pointed out.

The earl managed a weak smile. "In that case, *mon ami*, I hope you are without Mortal Sin, for you shall surely be facing God's Judgment by day's end." He turned to Miles. "Form the men, and let us go."

Miles and Merleswegen got the men into line, and the company started off. They kept together this time. They couldn't afford to become strung out, because now the Welsh were right behind them and they might have to fight at any moment.

The road was a rutted track, muddy from the rain. The cold, thick mud caked the men's feet and slowed them down. Where they could, they walked on the verge.

Wat o' Riseby was optimistic. "We got a three-mile lead," he told Oslac and Guthric. "We should get to the castle before they catch us. Or maybe the garrison'll see us coming from the tower and come out to relieve us."

"If the garrison's still alive," Guthric muttered. "Told you, this expedition's marked."

"Cheery sort, ain't you?" Oslac said.

The countryside around them was relatively level, the road bordered by fields and woods and hedges. "Keep going, men," Miles said, standing by the road and waving them on. "Keep going." He watched the rear for signs of pursuit. The mud would prevent a dust cloud from forming, so there was no telling how close the Welsh were.

The road took a sharp bend. The company rounded it and stopped.

A line of armed men blocked their way. The men, maybe a hundred and fifty, were spread out, so there was no easy way to go around them. There was no time to fight through them, either, because if they tried that, they'd be overtaken from the rear.

The first arrows began to fall. One arrow transfixed a man's bare, mud-caked foot, and the man cried out.

Miles looked to the rear again and saw a distant horseman. He said, "My lord—"

"I see him, too," the earl said. "I'm looking for a place to make a stand."

"Where's one o' them damned hills when you need it?" Oslac cracked to Wat. "Flatter'n your wife's chest around here."

To their right, a copse of woods lay in a field dotted with sheep. Miles pointed. "That wood. The trees will keep them from killing us with arrows. They'll have to come at us man to man."

"Very well," said the earl. He raised his voice. "Make for that wood to our right."

The men left the road in a ragged rush as more arrows fell among them. They blundered through the thick brush beside the road, across a small brook, through more brush, and then they were in the field, going as fast as they could. Sheep bleated and lumbered out of their way.

"Hurry!" Miles cried. He, the earl, and Etienne, covered the rear, weapons drawn. Waleran joined them, though he had the use of but one arm.

The Welsh in the road started after them, shooting arrows. Guthric turned to look at them and fell with a shaft through his face. Wat and Oslac picked him up by the arms and dragged him along. The earl's white horse was hit and went down hard, trapping the sick man who'd been tied to its saddle. Two men headed back to cut the man loose. "There's no time!" Miles yelled at them. "Go!" An arrow stuck in Miles's shield. He pulled it out and tossed it away.

The Welsh horseman came into view, a big man with iron-grey hair and beard, wearing a mail shirt and a helmet and riding a chestnut horse. His men hurried up the road behind him and began forming a battle line.

The earl's men were in the trees now. The earl, Miles, Etienne, and Waleran joined them. "Form your square," the earl told Miles calmly.

"No, a circle," Miles countered. "A square's vulnerable at the angles, and they can't form a line against a circle."

The earl stared at Miles. "Very well, a circle."

"Form a circle!" Miles cried. "Quickly!"

The men got into a rough circle. Miles wished he hadn't thrown away his helmet earlier. The washerwoman Fleur was by a tree in the circle's center, tending Guthric and the man with the arrow in his foot, who was yelling with pain. Guthric couldn't do anything but cry, because of the arrow through his face.

Outside the trees, the Welsh from Northop had linked up with the party in the road. The grey-haired chieftain issued orders. The Welsh spread out and advanced into the field to surround the small wood. One stopped to kill the man trapped beneath the earl's horse.

The chieftain rode his horse into the woods alone. When he was close enough, he flung something toward the circle of English soldiers.

It was Wenstan's head. He had been beaten, and his eyes were gouged out.

The chieftain rejoined his men.

There were five crossbowmen left among the Flemish mercenaries. Miles said, "Crossbowmen, be ready. Make every shot count. Get that fellow on the horse if you can."

The Welsh began beating swords and spears and axes on their shields, chanting in their singsong tongue. They came forward behind a flurry of arrows, most of which stuck in the trees or bounced off them.

The men in the circle locked shields. Those without shields stood behind the first rank, ready to thrust weapons over the shoulders of the men in front of them. The circle was pitifully small, seventy-four English soldiers and nine Flemings, cold, wet, and hungry, many of them sick, all weak from dysentery.

It started raining again, raindrops dripping through the trees. The low sky was black with cloud. "Welcome to beautiful Wales," Oslac muttered.

Closer and closer the Welsh came. They entered the trees. A horn blew and they broke into a run.

Miles cried, "Crossbows—now!"

Five iron bolts flew. All struck home—all but one. The one aimed at the man on horseback hit his shield at an angle and bounced away. The chieftain didn't bat an eye. He rode among the trees, waving his sword and yelling encouragement to his men. The mercenaries, who were in the second line, threw their now useless crossbows in front of the circle, hoping to trip some of the attackers, and drew their swords, holding their small shields before them.

The Welsh slammed into the circle. There were grunts and screams. Clash of steel on steel, bang and thunk of steel on wood, softer thunk of steel on flesh. The earl was to Miles's right, and Wat o' Riseby was to Miles's left. That was all Miles could see of the fight, all he knew of its progress. He was yelling obscenities at the top of his lungs. He stabbed a painted man in the face, felt bone shatter, took a heavy blow on his shield from the left, was splashed with blood from somewhere. Beside him, the earl was yelling in frenzied French. A spear thrust slid off the earl's shield and was deflected across Miles's arm, gouging the sleeve of his leather jack.

They were being pushed back by the sheer number of men opposite them. They fought to maintain the circle, knowing that if the Welsh broke the circle, the battle was lost and they were all dead.

Conscious of protecting his uncovered head, Miles kept low behind his battered shield. He reached around the shield and stabbed a man in the thigh. The man fell, his leg squirting blood. The man behind him stepped impatiently over the first man. He slipped in the blood and rain and fell onto Miles's outstretched sword blade, impaling himself. His momentum nearly jerked the sword out of Miles's hand, and as Miles stepped back to pull the sword out, an axe flashed past the spot where his head had been a moment earlier. He punched the axe man in the face with his sword hilt. Beside Miles, Wat o' Riseby grunted and dropped to one knee.

There was a lull to Miles's front. Miles dragged Wat from the line and the circle contracted. He took Wat's helmet and put it on. Wat crawled away on his hands and knees, speared in the gut. Miles glimpsed Fleur with the wounded in the circle's center. Her near hysteria of before had been replaced by a fatalistic calm, as she gave the men water and tended wounds as best she could.

The Welsh came on again, yelling, swinging swords and axes, thrusting spears over the English shields. Burgred was to Miles's left now, wielding a long axe, his face lit by the battle madness of his Viking forebearers. Miles stumbled over a tree root and lost his footing for a moment. As he regained it, an axe swung down and smashed his shield in half. He was left with half a shield and a dangling buckler. He hit his opponent with the metal buckler, threw the rest of the shield at him as well.

He saw a man with a raised club. Saw the club coming down.

Miles's skull seemed to explode and everything went black.

* * *

His eyes opened. He was being pulled to his feet. By the earl and Etienne. His head was spinning. He seemed to see two of everything. He lost his footing and staggered. Blood ran from his nose and ears. He didn't know how much time had passed. It was still raining.

The earl handed him his scramasax and a new shield. His helmet lay nearby where someone had taken it off of him. The top was caved in and the helmet was cracked almost in half.

The circle was down to a handful of men, maybe fifteen or twenty—Miles couldn't count in his condition. It wasn't even a circle anymore, just a group of men standing back to back, brandishing weapons defiantly. Etienne was covered with blood, crying and trying to pretend that he wasn't. Only one of the Flemings remained. Waleran of St. Just was gone. Oslac lay dead nearby; so did Burgred, entwined with the bodies of their enemies. Merleswegen's helmet and shield were battered almost beyond recognition. He had a protective arm around Fleur, a scramasax in his other hand to prevent her from being captured.

"They pulled back," the earl told Miles.

"Why?" Miles said. The inside of his head pounded like a blacksmith was beating on his skull.

"Who knows?" said the earl. "They could have ended it. I don't know why they stopped."

"They done it sudden like," Merleswegen added.

Miles staggered again. He managed a weak grip on the scramasax's hilt, a grip that would not survive the first blow he tried to strike with it. He readied the shield, knew he would never see Alice and Garth and the new baby again, and felt bad about that.

The Welsh were drawn up just outside the trees, quiet, not howling to finish the English off, as Miles would have expected. Then the Welsh line parted, and two riders entered the trees.

The first rider was the chieftain with iron-grey hair, proud and erect. The second rode a white horse, the same white horse Miles and Leofric had seen on the hillside when the company had destroyed the village. It was lathered and muddy, as though it had been ridden hard. Its rider was a woman. She let down the hood of her cloak, revealing pale skin and a mass of fiery red hair.

She rode forward alone and stopped before Miles.

She bowed her head to Miles. As she lifted her head again, her green eyes met his, those green eyes he could have fallen in love with. Then she wheeled the white horse and rode away, followed by the chieftain.

Outside the trees, the Welsh turned and left the field.

49

Hawarden, 1086 A.D.

MILES came to.

His head was wrapped in bandages. It hurt.

He was lying on a straw bed. In a smallish building with a thatched roof. Around him were other beds, most with men in them, some of them moaning. Someone was sobbing. The building smelled of waste and vomit and festering wounds.

"You're awake," said a voice in French.

It was Fleur, the tall Flemish washerwoman. He almost didn't recognize her. Cleaned up, in new clothes, she was attractive.

Miles was surprised to see her. "Where are we?" he asked, and his throat cracked painfully from thirst.

"Hawarden," Fleur said. In halting English, she added, "Drink water."

She held a wooden cup of water to his lips, and he drank. The cool liquid felt good. More than good. He started to gulp it.

"Not too much," Fleur cautioned in French. She pulled the cup back. "You fell unconscious right after the Hawarden garrison came to rescue us. We're safe now."

"I don't remember any of that," Miles admitted.

She held the cup to his lips again. "Drink more."

"You're speaking English," Miles said.

She blushed and went back to French. “Merle’s been teaching me.”

“Merle?” Then he realized. “You mean Merleswegen?”

She blushed again. “Yes. We are to be married.”

“That’s wonderful,” Miles said with a smile that made his head hurt again. “I’m happy for you. How long have I been here?”

“Two days. You suffered a bad head injury, you’re lucky to be alive. Now I must leave for a moment.”

She hurried from the building, which Miles guessed must be the castle infirmary.

He lay back. He was going home. He was going to see Alice again. He was going to see Garth. He was going to see his newborn child. Then he remembered Leofric, and the others who weren’t going home, and he felt a stab of sorrow. And guilt.

His becoming a soldier had all been for nothing. He was never going to lead a revolt. What would be the point? To kill good men like the earl and Etienne and Waleran of St. Just, just to replace them with other men who spoke English? Would it be worth the blood and fortune, the homes destroyed and families broken? What a fool he had been.

Fleur returned. Earl Thibault and Etienne were with her.

Miles struggled to a sitting position as Fleur went to tend other patients. The earl regarded Miles. “How are you?”

“I’m alive,” Miles said. “I think.”

The earl laughed. “We didn’t think you were going to make it for a while. Is there anything I can get you?”

“Something for this headache.”

"Mmmm. There's a physician at the abbey nearby, one of the brothers. I've heard he's good with herbs and such. I'll have him sent to you."

"Thank you, my lord. How are you feeling?"

"Good. Fully recovered. I'm leaving Hawarden today; I wanted to wait until you were awake before I departed. I must go to Badford first and consult with the cartulary clerks. King William is making a written record of every estate in England—what's on it now, its value, and the taxes owed, and what was on it at the time of English rule."

Miles frowned. "A large undertaking."

"A lot of damned work," the earl complained. "After I attend to that, I'm off to Normandy."

He turned to Etienne. "See to the horses, would you, Etienne?"

"Yes, my lord," Etienne said. He shook Miles's hand. "Goodbye, Miles. I can't say it's been fun, but it *has* been a pleasure." He grinned and pointed at Miles. "Be honest, you know where that treasure is, don't you?"

The earl said, "Away with you, you scamp."

Etienne laughed, waved to Miles, and left.

The earl sat on a stool beside Miles's bed. "I waited for you to come to, because I want to make you an offer."

Miles wondered what this was about. "Yes, my lord?"

"I want you to come into my service, as a man-at-arms. You'd be in charge of footmen first, but we'll teach you to ride and wield a sword and spear, and when you're good enough, I'll make you a knight. Take you into my household, give you land."

Miles forgot the pain in his head. He'd never expected anything like this. "You're serious, my lord?"

"Serious as I can be. You're a good man, Miles. I like you, and I want you with me. I think you can do great things—I think *we* can do great things. You'd be a noble again, a baron, as you were born to be, and from there, who knows?"

Miles's head was spinning, but this time not from his injury. This was everything he'd ever dreamed of.

The earl smiled. "What do you say?"

"I . . . thank you, my lord, but I can't accept."

The earl's eyes widened in surprise.

Miles said, "I don't want to be a knight. I don't want to be a soldier of any kind. I've had enough of war. I just want to be with my family and raise crops."

"Are you sure that wound didn't addle your brains? This is a great opportunity, Miles. For you *and* your family."

"I know," Miles said, "but . . ." How to explain? Alice would never leave Ravenswell. She would never leave her friends and neighbors. She wouldn't want to be a baron's wife, associating with Frenchwomen who would put on airs and act superior to her. "But I can't do it." *Sometimes dreams are best left as dreams.*

"You're certain?"

"I'm certain, my lord."

Disappointment tinged the earl's face as he stood. "Let me know should you ever change your mind."

"I will, my lord."

Thibault stuck out his hand and Miles took it. Thibault said, "Goodbye, son. And I mean that—you've become like a son to me."

“And you’ve become like a father to me,” Miles said. “It’s been a great experience.”

“That it has,” said the earl. “Well, goodbye for now.”

The earl turned and left the building. Miles never saw him again.

Alive.

50

Trentshire, 1106 A.D.

MILES made his way into St. John's Wood. He carried a thick wooden staff that he'd taken from the hunting lodge while he was there.

The sun was sinking as he passed the shrine to St. Egidius. He hurried on, bypassing Rock Glen and the hermit's cell; he needed to be in place by dark. By the time the assize was over for the day, it would have been too late for the killer to ride from Badford Castle to Thor's Seat and back again. The killer would have to go there early tomorrow morning. Depending on how much time they spent at breakfast—and how much they'd had to drink the night before—Tutbury's party would not arrive at Thor's Seat much before terce at the very earliest. That would give the killer time to dispose of any evidence he might have left there and to blend in with Tutbury's group, hopefully with no one the wiser.

The valley looked peaceful in the dying light. Miles passed the hoar stone and came to Thor's Seat. The ancient chair, or throne, seemed to be almost alive in the purpling dusk. Miles could have sworn that the eyes of the faces beneath the armrests were following him, but he knew that this was pagan superstition, and he said a brief prayer to Our Savior to forgive him for indulging in it.

He didn't go up the hill to camp this time. He needed to be near the Seat in case the killer came earlier than expected tomorrow, and the ruined building on the hill was too far off. It was too risky to build a fire, because demons might see it. Miles found a spot in the crook of a downed tree. He drew the priest's robe and cowl over his clothes, pulled up the hood, and nestled in as the last bit of light disappeared from the sky.

Around him, frogs croaked. A cricket began to chirp, slowly at first, then with confidence. The forest darkness was absolute; Miles couldn't see five feet in front of him. He missed Blanche. He hadn't felt so alone and vulnerable when she had kept him company, no matter how arrogant she was. Maybe the demons were scared of her.

The west wind grew stronger, and just as it had done the night before, it started raining, a steady downpour. For long hours, Miles huddled, cold and miserable, shivering and sniffling. Rain seeped through his hood and down his back. His feet were wet and cold. At least the rain kept away the ants and other insects.

Again, just as it had the night before, the rain stopped and a breeze shredded the clouds. Moonlight flooded the valley, bathing Thor's Seat in silver so that it almost seemed like a real throne, made of precious metal, and Miles was glad the two faces were looking away from him.

But they weren't looking away.

They had detached themselves from the Seat and floated in the air, coated in silver light, staring at Miles, their red eyes boring into him.

Miles heard music.

Where was it coming from? The other end of the valley. He strained to see.

By the hoar stone, ghosts were dancing . . .

And those red eyes were staring.

Miles cringed and pressed himself against the tree.

He jerked his head around. What was that?

He swallowed and peered into the dark woods around him.

There it was again, a booming cry echoing through the trees.

Miles fought back the urge to get up and run. The cry sounded again. Was it devils, seeking Miles in his hiding place? Would he have to fight them? He prayed for this awful night to pass.

The moon set; the noises ceased. Miles didn't know if he nodded off or not, but when he looked, light filtered through the trees.

He rose stiffly, surprising a rabbit that bounded into the undergrowth. He was soaked through, half frozen even though it was June. A ground mist covered the valley. He walked around, loosening his limbs, trying to warm up. He sneezed and wiped his nose on his wet sleeve.

He drank from the stream that ran down the valley. From his scrip he pulled a honey cake, also taken from the lodge, and ate it. He gathered his wooden staff and chose a hiding place screened by undergrowth, with a good view of the valley and Thor's Seat.

The killer had to come. On the day of the earl's death, the hunting party had a wild ride through the woods. No doubt many of them had lost bits of clothing and harness. The killer could not be certain that one of his missing items had not been left at Thor's Seat. He could not take that chance.

And if no one came? Then perhaps Aelred was the killer, after all. Either way, Aelred would hang for the crime. And Miles would hang, as well.

It grew warmer. The rising sun gave the ground mist a pearl-like luminescence. Insects hummed. Miles took off the hood and priest's robe. The foliage gave off steam, the smell of wet earth was strong. A lark rose, trilling.

There. A noise.

A faint jingle of harness.

The slow clop of hooves, the snuffle of a horse.

Miles did not move. He scarce breathed, lest he give himself away. The jingling grew louder. The hooves moved cautiously past the hoar stone and down the valley. They stopped at Thor's Seat, and the killer dismounted.

Miles took a deep breath and strode from his hiding place. "Good morning, Lord Geoffrey. I've been expecting you."

51

"GOOD morning, Miles!" The young lord flashed his wide grin, for all the world as if the two of them had met in the village lane on this summer's day. In a friendly voice, he added, "Tell me, how did you know?"

"It was your wife, my lord. Lady Matilda is Mercian; her family's been in these parts forever. Only she would have known about Thor's Seat. None of you French knew about this place's existence, much less how to find it, or its connection to Wulfhere's Treasure. She suggested the place, and you did the killing."

Geoffrey inclined his head equably. "And, as you suggested yesterday, I moved the body to prevent someone from drawing just that conclusion. I presume your little act at the assize was put on to draw me out here?"

"It was, my lord."

"What made you so sure I'd come?"

"Your glove, the one you lost on the hunt. You couldn't take the chance that you hadn't lost it here."

"And was it here?"

"No, my lord. I've no idea where it is."

Geoffrey sighed and shook his head. He drew his sword and began absently scything the long grass of the clearing. The razor-sharp blade sent tufts of greenery flying. "What's this business about you pretending to be Lady Blanche's confessor?"

"Lady Blanche offered to help me, my lord. She was like me, she didn't believe Aelred was the killer. She thought it was Ranulf, and I thought it was . . . well, it turns out we were both wrong."

"Mmmm, maybe that's why things didn't work out properly—you going partners with Blanche. You were supposed to find your son's second arrow, you know. I placed it in Stigand's chest at the lodge."

"I did find it, my lord."

Geoffrey stopped swinging his sword at the grass. "Then why didn't you bring it to me? Or at least mention it at the assize yesterday?"

Miles couldn't help but grin. "I believe Lady Blanche wants to know the same thing. Fact is, it just didn't seem right. It seemed too easy somehow."

Geoffrey sighed. "That wasn't the conclusion you were supposed to make, Miles. One of the reasons I wanted the *murdrum* law invoked was because I wanted *you* to investigate the crime. I knew you wouldn't give up, no matter what happened—even when I said I was done with you. I counted on you eventually searching Stigand's belongings. You were supposed to bring me the second arrow, and I was going to accuse Galon of killing my father. I would have challenged him to trial by combat. He's a good knight, but I'm better. I'd have rid the world of that fat fool forever."

"And if I hadn't found the second arrow?" Miles said.

"I would have contrived to find it myself. It would have been trickier that way, of course. Lord Tutbury might have guessed that I planted the evidence. The other way, there was no connection."

"How did you come by Aelred's arrows, if I may ask?"

"Your friend Grim. He's my eyes and ears in the village. Grim told me once that your son was a poacher. He was just up to a bit of nastiness, of course, hoping to get Aelred's hand cut off, but I remembered what he said. On my instruction, Grim followed your boy—who is not as clever as he thinks—discovered his camp in the woods, and stole the arrows."

Miles nodded in appreciation. "It was a good plan, my lord. You'd have got away with it, too, save for that hermit, David. It was your bad luck that Grim took the arrows on the same day that David visited Aelred's camp. Aelred thought the hermit stole his arrows and killed the earl, so I reckoned I'd better talk to him. Hadn't been for that, I'd never have learned that your father was headed for Thor's Seat."

Geoffrey gave a mock bow. "I congratulate you. You've done well."

"Thank you, my lord. I must say, I'm disappointed, though."

"Disappointed?"

"Disappointed in you, my lord. I'd always admired you. You seemed to personify what a lord should be, you and your father, and Lady Matilda seemed a model noblewoman. I always looked forward to those Christmas feasts at your hall . . ."

Miles's voice tailed off with sadness, and Geoffrey said, "You must allow for the failings of mortals, Miles. We're not perfect."

"Did you force Lady Matilda to help you?"

Geoffrey laughed. "God's grace, no. It was her idea. Making me earl is a way of aiding her people. It's also her way of getting revenge against my family for the way they've treated her."

Miles was puzzled. "Making you earl? Is that why you did it? But you were going to be earl anyway, what with your father's new will."

"No, I wasn't." Geoffrey removed his cloak and used it to wipe wet grass from the sword blade. "Primogeniture, Miles—the first born inherits everything. It's a French principle, and King Henry is a firm believer in it. He'd never have let me inherit, no matter what the will says. I had to get rid of Galon. Galon stands in my way, always has. I mean to make my mark in the world, but I'm a younger son, so I have little land of my own. And I married for love, so I acquired no large dowry. Father was ill these past years; it was only a matter of time before he died. If I was to kill him and have Galon take the blame for it, this was the perfect time—when they were both together in England."

"And you arranged for them both to be here," Miles said. " 'Twas you who sent the message to your father about Wulfhere's Treasure."

Geoffey nodded and set the cloak aside. "Grim again. You'll remember, he was gone for a few weeks at the end of the winter. I knew Father would come; he was obsessed with that treasure. I made sure Galon learned about the message, as well."

"But with Galon out of the way, Ranulf is next in line to inherit," Miles pointed out, "not you."

"Ranulf is a fool. He will be dealt with, and his wife sent back to whatever Breton bog she sprang from." Geoffrey placed the sword's point in the ground and stood straight, resting his hands on the quillions. "Look, Miles why don't you join me? It's not too late. We can still work out a plan to accuse Galon. You can't deny I'll make a better earl than he will. I'm the kind of lord England needs. The kind who will stay here in England, not in Normandy. The kind who will work for the people, not oppress them. I'll be at the king's elbow; you can be there as well."

"That all sounds good, my lord, but in reality I was never supposed to make it out here today, was I? You tipped the nod to Morys Gretch, and he sent his men after me."

"Yes, though I did so most reluctantly," Geoffrey said. "You gave them the slip, however, so here we are, and we have a chance to start over."

"Was Morys in on your father's killing?"

"No, but I've given him to understand that with Galon gone, I'll be earl—and presumably sheriff—and that having me on his side can be beneficial to us both. It's worth his forgiving my father's debt to him." Geoffrey smiled. "But that's by the by. There was nothing personal in what I had Morys do, it was business. I like you, Miles. Now that you know the truth, you can join us. What do you say?"

Miles shook his head. "Your father was my friend. It's in the natural order of things that you should pay for killing him."

"Your way gives Galon power," Geoffrey warned. "That won't be good for anyone."

"Maybe, but I can't be party to a lie."

Geoffrey sighed. "Honest Miles, sanctimonious Miles. It will be your undoing. Actually, it already has been."

"My lord?" Miles said.

"You don't think I'm going to let you walk away from here, do you?" Geoffrey raised the sword and slashed it through the air, loosening his wrist and arm.

Miles let out his breath. It was though a weight had been lifted from his shoulders. Everything was simple now.

He crossed himself and hefted his staff. "I always wanted to catch one of you bastards without your armor."

52

GEOFFREY turned the sword idly in his hand. "Sorry to do this, Miles, I mean that."

Miles said, "I'm in the right, my lord. God will not let me lose."

Geoffrey smiled. "The graveyards are full of people who thought that way."

Without warning, Geoffrey slashed backhand, then overhand, driving Miles back, Miles parrying as best he could with his blackthorn staff. Geoffrey was fast, and either of those blows could have killed him.

"Still not too late to change your mind," Geoffrey said, circling.

"Sorry, my lord," said Miles.

"See you at the funeral, then."

Geoffrey aimed another overhand blow. Miles raised his staff to block it, realized too late that it was a feint, and Geoffrey turned it into a sweeping cut that, had it connected, might have sliced Miles in half. Miles propelled himself backward, slipped and landed on his butt in the wet grass. He rolled just in time to dodge another blow aimed at his head, and regained his feet.

Geoffrey grinned, toying with him. Miles was already breathing hard; Geoffrey was as calm as if he'd just gotten up from a nap. "You're out of shape, Miles. You're getting old."

While Geoffrey made fun of him, Miles feinted a blow of his own. He aimed at Geoffrey's head, then lowered the staff and drove the end into Geoffrey's chest, knocking the wind out of him and forcing him back. He rapped Geoffrey on one side of the head, then the other.

Geoffrey fell, stunned. Miles raised his staff to smash the end into Geoffrey's face, but Geoffrey recovered to aim a blow at Miles's legs. Miles barely jumped over the sword blade, landed awkwardly on his bad ankle and cried out. Before he could recover, Geoffrey was on his feet again.

"Nice one," Geoffrey commented.

Geoffrey launched a series of blows, driving Miles across the clearing, cutting him, knocking chips from Miles's staff. Frantically moving backwards, Miles was not helped by his swollen eye. He bumped into Thor's Seat, dodged as Geoffrey unleashed a blow that hacked a slice from one of the armrests, splinters flying.

Slash after slash after slash, then, suddenly, a thrust. Miles wasn't expecting that. He threw himself onto his back desperately, the sword's point passing just over his upturned face. He raised his staff to block the next blow and the blow cut his staff in half.

Miles dropped the useless pieces of his staff. He lay on his back, heaving for breath, wounded in a half-dozen places. He somehow crawled to his knees as Geoffrey readied his sword for the final blow.

Never give up while there's still a chance.

As Geoffrey brought the sword whistling down, Miles threw himself at Geoffrey's legs, wrapped them in his arms, and dropped Geoffrey on his back.

From somewhere, Miles summoned the energy to jump on Geoffrey and hit him in the mouth. Stunned, Geoffrey let go of the sword. He recovered and grabbed Miles's hair. He yanked Miles's head back, aimed a blow with his fist at Miles's throat but before he could deliver it, Miles hammered his own fist down onto Geoffrey's nose, breaking it. Geoffrey relaxed his grip on Miles, and Miles hit him again. Again. He hit Geoffrey until Geoffrey's face was covered with blood, punching him over and over, his anger intensified by a feeling of betrayal. He saw a tooth go flying.

Geoffrey offered no more resistance. The blind hatred drained from Miles, and he dropped his sore, bloodied fist. This was Lord Geoffrey, after all, who had been, if not Miles's friend, then something close to it.

Miles rolled off of Geoffrey and lay on the ground. His heart was pumping so hard, he thought it might explode. He struggled to get air into his lungs. He ached all over, his good eye was blurred by sweat.

He heard laughter and clapping hands, and he turned to see Galon emerging from the trees.

53

"BRAVO, Englishman!" Galon cried, still clapping his hands. "You've done well." He was followed from the trees by Lord Tutbury, Stigand, and a party of bailiffs.

Miles lifted himself painfully onto one elbow. "You were supposed to seize him as soon as he confessed," he told Galon.

"You were having so much fun, I couldn't bear to stop it," Galon said. "Anyway, Tutbury and I decided to bet on the fight. He picked you." He walked over and kicked the fallen Geoffrey in the head. " 'Fat fool,' is it?"

Miles had visited Galon after the assize. He had revealed the killer's identity and urged Galon and Lord Tutbury to be at Thor's Seat early the next morning. He had counted on Galon's dislike of his brother to make him come. He had counted on Lady Blanche to remember the way and lead them here, but there was no sign of Blanche.

Miles stood. No one helped him, and he staggered a bit before getting his legs under him. His blood-covered fist hurt and was starting to swell. He was bleeding from sword cuts, and his ankle throbbed.

At Miles's feet, there was labored breathing. Geoffrey was coming to. His head lolled. One heel dug weakly in the mud.

Galon pulled on his long moustache and looked down. "Anything to say for yourself, brother?"

Geoffrey spit blood from his mouth, and Galon laughed. To Miles he said, "I would have loved to impose that *murdrum* fine, you know. Ah, well, another day. Now you won't have to pay me *merchet* for your daughter's hand, either."

"Sorry to disappoint you," Miles said.

Galon turned to Lord Tutbury, whose yellow surcoat was muddy at the hems. "You heard enough here—right, my lord?"

"Most assuredly, I did," Tutbury said. "We'll take Lord Geoffrey back and ready him for the headsman."

Galon went on. "His wife was in on the scheme. We should cut off her head, as well."

"No," Geoffrey pleaded, "please. Do what you will with me, but leave Matilda alone."

"He's right," Tutbury told Galon. "She's English, we can't risk making a martyr of her. These people will turn her into a saint, and then where will we be? Let her live out her days doing penance at the priory of Mt. Carmel."

"Can I have her for a while first?" Galon asked.

"No!" Tutbury said.

"Pity. Nice piece."

Geoffrey glared at Galon, who laughed again. "That's all right. I know where the priory is." To Miles, he said, "You'll need a new lord for your manor, Englishman." He turned. "Stigand, would that post appeal to you?"

The sallow Stigand appeared surprised. "Aye, my lord," he replied in his North Country accent. " 'Twould appeal to me very much. Thank you, my lord."

"Have to make you a knight, of course," Galon mused. "Oh, well."

Miles groaned inwardly. Stigand was the last person he wanted as his new lord. Galon laughed at Miles's obvious discomfort. "Don't worry, Englishman. Stigand won't be around much. He'll be with me most of the time. He's going to be my seneschal when I'm made earl."

Stigand's eyes lit up; this was a great honor. He'd gone from thug to baron in one morning. "My lord, I—I don't know what to—"

"Then don't say anything. Just do your job. That's what's got you this far."

Tutbury cut in. "Is this wise, Lord Galon?" He indicated Stigand and lowered his voice. "He's English."

"So what?" Galon said. "He does what he's told, and that's what I want." He went on. "The present steward can continue running your new manor. That's acceptable to you, isn't it, Stigand?"

"Aye, my lord."

Lord Tutbury changed the subject. "Who is this Morys Gretch that Geoffrey was talking about?"

Galon replied. "An Englishman. Only met him a few times. Some sort of merchant, I believe."

Miles spoke up. "He's a criminal, my lord. He more or less runs Badford Town."

"Does he?" Galon purred. "Well, not for long."

Tutbury said, "You'll bring the fellow to trial, first, won't you, Lord Galon?"

"Of course, my lord," Galon replied smoothly, but they all knew that he wouldn't.

Galon continued. "That reminds me, Stigand. That miller—Grim, or whatever he's called. Hang him on your way back to the castle, would you? No need for a trial, we've heard enough."

"I'll need a new miller for the manor, then," Stigand said.

Galon turned to Miles. "Your boy, Aelred. Knows he aught of milling?"

Miles was taken aback, but recovered. "He's a quick learner."

"Maybe we'll give him the job. I suppose it's the least we can do after what we put him through."

Galon looked at Stigand, who nodded assent. He wasn't going to say no to Galon.

Miles said, "Thank you, my lord."

"No need for thanks. Hothead like that is bound to botch the job. Stigand will like as not be appointing a new miller within a few years."

Galon untied a purse from his belt and held it out to Miles.

"What's this?" Miles said.

"Fifty marks. The reward for bringing me my father's killer."

"I don't—"

"Take it, you earned it." He tossed the purse to Miles, who caught it. It was hefty, with the clink of metal inside. "Don't worry," Galon said. "I'll get it back from you. I'm sure there's something I can fine you for."

Before Miles could say anything, Galon went on. "This changes nothing between us. I'll see you a villein yet."

Miles smiled and bowed. "I've no doubt you'll *try*, my lord."

"Cheeky bastard, that's what I like about you. I almost wish we were on the same side."

"I cannot thank you for that compliment, my lord, for I would not be on your side."

Galon shrugged. "Your loss."

Miles cleared his throat. "There is one more thing, my lord."

Galon cast a baleful gaze. "Yes?"

"The abbot of Huntley. He's been destroying my property. I can't take him to court . . ."

"I'll speak to him," Galon said. "Huntley is scared to death of me. He'll jump through hoops if I tell him."

"And . . . my lord?"

"Now what?" said Galon impatiently.

"Wada, Aelred's friend in gaol. The one you beat up. If he hasn't been hanged already, could you consider releasing him? He's innocent of any crime."

"Oh, very well," Galon said. "Now is there anything else you'd like—a knighthood, a castle, a partridge in a pear tree?"

"No, my lord."

"Good. Then let's get back to Badford Castle."

"Yes," said Lord Tutbury, "we have much to do. I got precious little sleep last night, and I'm in need of a lie down."

Galon smiled because he knew who Tutbury intended to lie down with. He pointed to Geoffrey, "Get him on his feet and tie his hands."

The bailiffs hauled the bloodied Geoffrey upright and bound his hands with rope. One of the bailiffs took the reins of Geoffrey's horse. Galon booted his brother in the rear. "Move!"

The bailiffs marched Geoffrey off, followed by Galon and Stigand, then bulky Lord Tutbury, negotiating the churned-up ground. They disappeared into the woods and Miles was left alone in the clearing.

Miles stretched his battered body and hobbled down the little valley, carrying the purse. He would go to the manor house and tend his wounds, then he would head for the fields. There was work to be done.

He looked up and halted.

Lady Blanche was there.

Blanche started toward him. Slowly at first, then with a quickening pace. Miles quickened his own pace to meet her. It was almost as though they were going to embrace. And as they came closer, and Blanche returned his smile, Miles wouldn't have been surprised if embrace was exactly what they did.

54

LATER, after Miles and Blanche had left the clearing, a gust of wind blew away some of the trampled earth near Thor's Seat, uncovering rotted wood and, beneath that, a glimmer of gold. Then another gust of wind blew dirt and dried leaves over the gold, burying it once more.

About the Author

Robert Broomall is the author of a number of published novels, including the popular *Death's Head* (Roger of Huntley) trilogy. Besides writing, his chief interests are travel and history, especially military history, the Old West, and the Middle Ages. He also likes to cook, much to the dismay of those who have to eat what he prepares.

Amazon author page:
https://www.amazon.com/author/robertbroomall

Facebook:
https://www.facebook.com/RobertBroomall.author

Connect with Bob:
robertbroomall@gmail.com

Made in United States
Orlando, FL
16 July 2022

19828539R00196